God's Server

Jeff Davis series book 2

Tim Koop

PRAISE FOR TIM KOOP'S WRITING

"Interesting"
>   - almost everyone

"Good writing. Good action and suspense."
>   - Cynthia A. Robison

"Well paced... the technical aspects were accurate... the story was interesting... I want to read the next one."
>   - Thomas Sewell, editor

"It was very interesting and held my attention. You did a nice job of developing the characters and making them believable. The plot developed quite well also."
>   - Jenn Haslam

"It's great!"
>   - 17 year old young man, after staying up till 4:30am to finish the book

"I just finished reading [God's Email Address] and I love it! First, it is a great story that kept me involved from beginning to end. The contemporary themes were totally relatable. The story arch is very well done and the characters were well-developed and recognizable."
>   - Patti Virkler

"This could be the best book I've ever read in my life."
>   - Tim Koop

There's more *free **stuff*** at the end of this book.

(It's true.)

THE JEFF DAVIS TRILOGY

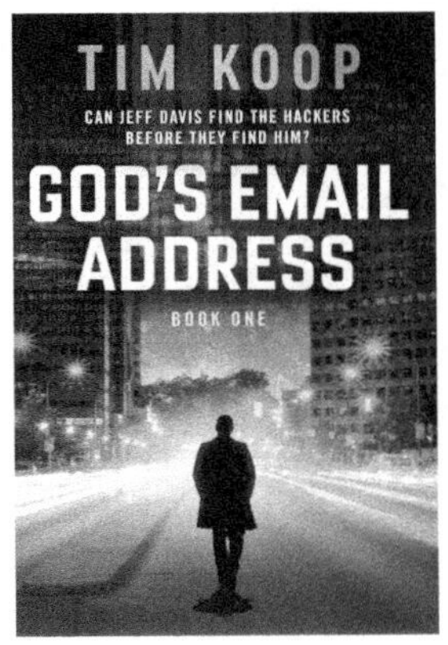

God's Email Address

Corporate email servers are being hacked. Private information is sold to the highest bidder. And they're blaming the software company.

A shy computer programmer tries to stop the corporate espionage before the men with guns stop him, permanently.

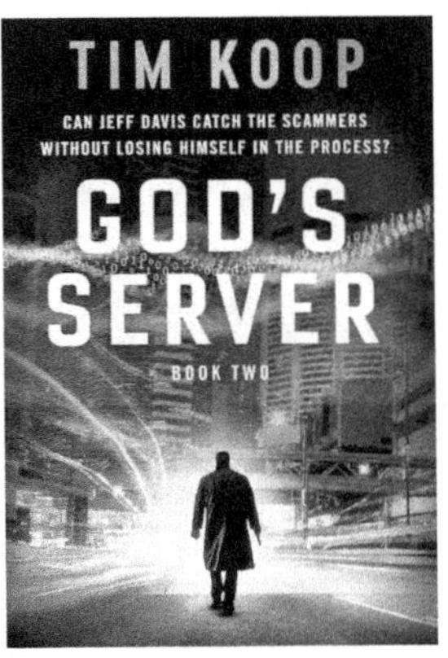

God's Server

Scammers are on the loose and nobody is safe, not even Jeff's mom.

But when this shy computer programmer tries to catch the bad guys, he finds there is more standing in his way than he realizes.

God's Network

Someone is trying to kill Jeff Davis, and succeeds.

This shy software developer has put so many bad guys behind bars, that he has made enemies, and now he is being hunted.

This book is dedicated to

Ray Duerksen,

for creating a culture of confession and repentance.

PROLOGUE

"You have reached Tech Support Services. How can we help you?"

"Hi. This is Julie. I just got a pop up on my screen saying my computer is infected with viruses and my hard drive is going to be erased."

"It's a good thing you called us Julie, alright. We can certainly help you with that. Are you at your computer right now?"

"Yes."

"Then let me guide you through some steps you can take to remove those viruses and ensure your files will not be deleted. Is that alright?"

"Well, I would normally get my son to look at it. He's a computer guy himself."

"That's OK. I can help you right now. These sorts of problems require highly skilled technicians, such as myself, to fix."

"Oh, Jeff is very skilled. He works as a computer programmer."

"They also require specific tools that I can offer you that an ordinary programmer wouldn't have. So let us begin, then OK?"

"Well... maybe I should talk to him first."

"Julie, it sounds like this son of yours must spend a lot of time helping you with your computer. He may not have told you that he gets tired of helping you all the time."

"No, he's never mentioned anything."

"He would probably be proud of you for handling the situation yourself instead of always getting him involved."

"Maybe..."

"I will show you a few steps we can take to fix the situation, then you can brag to your son that you fixed it all by yourself. Shall we begin?"

"Oh, OK."

"The first thing I will have you do is to download and run some software that will let me take a better look at your screen."

"OK."

The man on the phone directed Julie how to download and install the software that would give him full access to her computer. When it was set up, he said, "Do you see now that I am moving the mouse pointer?"

"Yes. I'm not touching it."

"Good. Do not touch the mouse or the keyboard now, ma'am. I will show you where your computer is infected."

The man on the phone opened up the system log, which normally contains a long list of harmless information, warning, or error messages.

"Do you see all those errors? Your computer is infected with hundreds of viruses."

"Oh, no. I didn't know it was that bad."

"Yes, it is bad, ma'am. But we have some anti-virus software that will clean up your computer system entirely. It will remove all the viruses so your files will not be deleted."

"How much does it cost?"

"You are in luck today ma'am, because we are currently running a promotion. In exchange for some user feedback from you, we will not only install it for free, but we will actually pay you five hundred dollars."

"Wow. Really?"

"Yes, ma'am. Does that sound like a good deal to you?"

"It sure does. What's the catch?"

"There is no catch. Your feedback is very valuable to us. So shall I get started?"

"Yes, please."

"Excellent."

"I will start by transferring the five hundred dollars to your bank account. Do you bank online, ma'am?"

"Yes, I do."

"Then please log in to your bank's website right now. Don't worry, you don't have to tell me your password. It is all completely safe and secure."

Julie opened up a web browser and logged in to her bank's website. Of course, the man on the phone was recording every keystroke.

"Excellent, ma'am. Now while I transfer the money and install the anti-virus software, your screen will go blank."

The man on the phone blanked out Julie's screen so she couldn't see what he was doing.

"It went all black."

"Good. Just a minute now while I fix your computer."

He cleared the system log with the click of a button, then back in her browser, he saw that Julie had a full savings account. He shuffled fifty thousand dollars from her savings account to her checking account. Then he turned her screen back on and showed her the system log.

"As you can see, ma'am, all the viruses are gone."

"I see that. That's good. Thank you."

"You are welcome, ma'am. And you can also see that I have transferred the five hundred dollars into your account."

He opened her browser and showed her the large balance in her checking account, saying, "And here is your account balance that now has an extra five hundred dollars in it."

"That's a lot more than five hundred dollars!" Julie said.

The man on the phone said, "Oh! Oh! I made a terrible mistake! I transferred way too much money to you. I don't know what I'm going to do. This is a terrible mistake."

"Yeah," Julie said.

"I'll tell you what. I'm going to go talk to my manager and see what he says."

A few minutes later the man came back and said, "My manager says that because of my mistake of accidentally giving you fifty thousand dollars instead of five hundred, he said that you should be allowed to keep five thousand of it, if you would be willing to give us forty-five thousand dollars back. I'm terribly sorry for all this, ma'am. I have made a terrible mistake. But if you would be willing to send us some of our money back, it would stop me from getting into trouble. I'll probably be fired for that. Would you be willing to help us out, ma'am? You could keep a full five thousand of it."

"Of course I'm willing to help. You've been more than helpful to me."

"Thank you so much for that. I will tell you the details of how to send us the money. You'll have to do it in person at your bank, because you can't send that much money to us with your account type."

"Oh. OK. I can do that."

"Will you do it right now, please? Your computer is all fixed, and I would like this done as soon as possible."

"Yes, of course."

"Thank you very much, ma'am."

The man on the phone opened a text editor on Julie's computer and typed in his banking information. Julie wrote it down and drove to the bank. Then she sent this scammer forty-five thousand dollars of her own money.

CHAPTER 1

Tuesday 7:55 AM

If I hadn't been distracted by the text from my mom saying she got scammed out of forty-five thousand dollars, I would have seen the car driving straight towards me, and I would have been able to avoid it.

So I only noticed the vehicle coming at me when it was too late. Since we were both in a parking lot, the one where I work, not an open road, neither of us was going very fast. It was an intersection of sorts, and we should have been looking, but we weren't.

I was staring at my phone, shocked by what I read, when I saw the car coming at me from my left side. The only thing I had time to do was to lift my hand up to my head in a weak gesture of self-preservation. I heard a horrible crunching sound as their car struck mine. My door came at me and pushed me over. My side window came at my head and smashed it, or rather smashed my hand that was trying to protect my head.

I did not lose consciousness, but I was dazed. The force knocked me over onto the passenger's seat – the top half of me did anyway, because the bottom half was still belted in. When I sat up I noticed the force had pushed my car a few feet sideways. I tried to open my door, but it was stuck, due to the fact it was smashed in. So I unbuckled and crawled out the other side. When I did, I noticed my left hand hurt.

Standing in the parking lot, I took inventory of myself. My head didn't feel good. My left hand hurt. So did my left shoulder and hip. But I could still walk. I could probably still talk too, if I wanted to, I guess.

Two men from the car that hit me came up to me. "Are you OK?" The tall one asked.

I shrugged. "I guess so."

The shorter one said, "Good. It's too bad about this accident, but accidents happen." They seemed to have a slight accent from somewhere. India maybe, I didn't know. That wasn't uncommon for a multicultural city.

It was my turn to ask them. "Are you OK?"

"A little banged up, but we'll be fine."

"I guess we should exchange information." They walked back to their car and I started to take out my driver's license from my left pocket, but my left hand protested, so I used my right. That was awkward and took a while, but I did it. While I was doing that, they drove their car into a parking spot.

By the time I got my driver's license and my car registration documents ready to share with these guys, they were walking away. I followed them and said, "Hey! I need your driver's license and stuff to report this accident."

They kept walking, but the tall one, probably the driver, said, "I'm terribly sorry, but I don't have my driver's license on me. It's at home."

"Could you send it to me?" I asked.

"Of course."

I walked along with them, tagging behind. "You can send it to my email address, Jeff at omniscient dot software."

He smiled. "I'll be sure to send it to you."

"Good. Thanks." I stopped walking. For some reason I didn't feel good about this arrangement, but what could I do? I wasn't sure I could trust these guys. I would have to write down their license plate number myself. I walked back to the scene of the crime and took pictures of everything. Then I inspected my car. The door was dented in, but nothing seemed to be touching the front tire. It might still drive. I crawled in again from the wrong side and found a place to park.

By then it was late, and I had probably missed our morning meeting. I'll report this accident to the police and deal with my damaged car after work. Right now I need to go to work. No, first I need to get some drugs for the pain, then I'll go to work. It's too bad I missed the meeting. I hope I didn't miss anything important

8:39 AM

"Hi Jeff," the receptionist greeted me.

"Hi Luanna," I said.

I walked past her, then peeked into the board room to see if the morning meeting was still going. It was not, so I made my way to my desk. On the way, I stopped by the cubicle of Cheryl Bankowsky. I smiled at her and said, "Hi Cheryl."

She returned the smile and said, "Hi Jeff."

The room I worked in was in the corner of the building of our floor. Our company, Omniscient Technologies only had this one floor, and only half the floor at that. When I got there, Doug was already there. I gave him a, "Hi Doug," and he replied with a "Good morning Jeff." Doug was older than I was, and not very talkative, which was fine with me.

Before I sat down, I checked the Joke of the Day, which was written down on a little white-board by another co-worker, Garth. It said, "How many programmers does it take to change a light bulb? None. That's a hardware problem." I chuckled. Ah yes, hardware, something I probably should have known more about, but didn't. I was a software guy, as were the rest of us in this room. Our company made a product called Omniscient, which handles email and almost all other forms of communication. We wrote the software. I was a computer programmer, and I loved it. I could do it all day long. In fact, I did.

Then Garth came in, holding a can of Dr. Pepper. "Hello Jeff Davis," he said. "You are at work, I see. You were absent earlier." He eased his large form into his chair.

"I had a car accident in the parking lot."

He raised his eyebrows. "Nothing too serious I hope."

"Well, some places still hurt."

"If you require anything of me, please do not hesitate to ask."

"Thanks."

He turned around in his chair toward his computer and I did too. Then Scott came in.

"Jeff! You're here!" he said.

"Yup. I had a car accident in the parking lot."

He looked at me. "Are you OK?"

I shrugged. "I guess. Some things still hurt."

"How's your Honda?" he asked.

"The driver's side door is smashed in."

"Oh! That's terrible. A man's car was taken out, and the man hurt. It is a sad day. But you need to get rid of that thing and get a real car anyway, Jeff. Something with more power. Your Civic was s little gutless."

"I liked it," I said.

Doug threw out a comment, "I wouldn't dare to suggest a man's vehicle is an indication of his character."

Garth snorted with laughter, and I half expected Dr. Pepper to come out his nose. "Are you suggesting young Jeff here is gutless himself?"

"I didn't actually say that."

Scott said, "Hey, don't insult my friend here. Jeff is not gutless. I'll remind you all that he took down a whole pack of hackers, not that long ago. When was it? Two weeks ago?"

"Four", I said.

"That's right. A month ago. So he deserves our respect. Even if he seems a little passive or timid at times, he still got the job done. So well done to you, Jeff."

"Thanks, I guess," I said. I was about to ask him if he was serious or just kidding about being me being passive and timid when Randal, our boss, walked in.

He went up to Garth and extended his hand to him. He said, "It was good working with you, Garth."

What?! Is this what I missed? Is Garth quitting? He didn't get fired, did he?

Garth shook it. "And you too, sir," he said.

Then my phone rang–the one in my pocket, not my desk. It was my mom. I answered the call on my way out of the room. "Hi, Mom."

"Jeff," she said. "Did you get my text?"

I didn't have to think long to remember. It was the one about losing money. "Yeah. About you losing money? What's that about?"

"Oh, honey!" She started crying. "It's gone. They cheated me! They... I... I'm so stupid! I'm so stupid!"

"Mom! What happened? Tell me what happened."

"I... I called a phone number I saw on my screen, and..." Her voice was still quivering. "This is too hard over the phone. Can we get together for lunch?"

"Of course, Mom. Any time."

"Good. I'll stop by at noon. I need to tell you what happened."

"And I want to know what happened too."

"I'll tell you everything. Oh, I'm so stupid. I'm sorry, Jeff. I'm sorry your mother is so stupid."

"Stop saying that, Mom. We'll talk later. I'll see you for lunch."

"I'll see you later Jeff. Bye."

"Bye".

I disconnected the call, then walked back to our room. Something happened this morning and I still didn't know what it was.

9:10 AM

Back at my desk, I rolled my chair closer to Scott and whispered to him, "Did Garth quit?"

He leaned in to me and whispered back, "What?"

"Did Garth just quit this morning?" I repeated.

"No. Randal."

"Randal what?"

"Randal quit."

"Randal quit?"

"Yeah."

"Why?"

"Sailboats, remember? He explained it all at the meeting. Weren't you? Oh right, you weren't there. And why are we whispering?" Scott sat back up and said out loud, "Randal quit this morning."

"Randal said he wanted to talk with Jeff," said Doug.

"That's right." Scott pointed at me. "Randal said he wanted to talk with you, because you weren't at the meeting, and you just skipped out of the room. He wanted to talk to you about upcoming changes."

Changes. I hated change. Why can't people just settle down and let me live in peace? I kept my feelings to myself and instead said, "OK, I'll go find him right now."

I walked next door and found Randal sitting in his office. His usual mess was already half gone, and he was packing more stuff into boxes. He said, "Jeff, have a seat." I sat down.

He began. "You weren't here for the meeting this morning."

"I had a small car accident."

"Oh! Are you alright?"

"Yeah, I guess. A bit sore. My finger on my left hand hurts." I held up my hand, not that anyone could see the pain, but that's just what you do. I didn't bend it, though. "I took some drugs, so I'm good for now."

"I hope you get better soon, Jeff. But the reason I wanted to talk with you is that I made the announcement today in our morning meeting that I will be leaving Omniscient."

"Why?" I asked.

He sat back and scratched his head. "Because... being a manager is stressful. And I don't like the stress. I can't handle it. I used to be a ship captain. I sailed yachts and boats for rich people mostly. So after last month's drama with everything around here..." He made some hand gesture. "And me going to the hospital for my bicycle accident, I decided to look into maybe changing careers."

I sat there, looking at him. He was probably waiting for me to comment, but I had nothing to say, so he continued.

"And I found something. Someone was looking for a pilot to bring a yacht from California to Honolulu. That's exactly my fit. And he hired me."

I still said nothing.

"Of course I talked with Peter, and he has already found my replacement."

"When will he start?" I asked.

"This morning some time. I guess we'll see him soon enough."

Wow. This was a big change. I didn't like change, but what could I do? I said, "OK."

"Do you have any questions about that?" my boss asked.

I thought for a moment, then said, "Nope."

He stood up, and so did I. He held out his hand. "It was good working with you, Jeff. I wish you a long and successful career."

I shook his hand. "Thanks. You too."

As I left the room, I wondered to myself that two big things had already happened today–my car accident and my boss quitting. What else could happen?

9:26 AM

Then I almost bumped into Luanna, the receptionist, who held something out to me and said, "Somebody dropped this off at the front desk. I don't know who to give it to, so you can have it."

I took it and said, "OK, thanks." She left.

It was a USB stick that had our Omniscient Technologies logo on it. When I looked closer, the logo was a sticker that was stuck onto the USB stick, not printed directly onto it. But clearly this belonged to us.

Five steps later I was in our room. "Does this belong to anyone?" I asked, holding it up.

The guys turned around to look. Scott and Doug said, "Nope". Garth said, "Not I."

I continued. "Luanna gave it to me. She said someone dropped it off."

"Perhaps it belongs to the artist down the hall," said Garth.

I turned around. That could only mean one person. I knocked on Andy's door, and when he shouted for me to come in, I did. He was wearing a lime green button shirt with a lighter green flower print on it, and a dark green bow tie. His walls were lined not with the traditional black-and-white Dilbert comics which come standard in a programmer's office, but with colorful posters. One said, "Sgt. Pepper`s Lonely Hearts Club Band", and another said, "Creme Disraeli Gears," and one said, "Born in the U.S.A. / Bruce Springsteen." His one window was not to the outside of the building looking out, but to the inside, looking into the hall.

He said, "Hey Jeff, what's up?"

I showed him the USB stick. "Is this yours?" I asked.

He took it and scowled. "Ugh. This is our old logo. And it's not even centered. Absolutely not." He gave it back. "By the way, why do you ask? Are we ordering USB things now? Because I certainly wasn't asked to design them."

"Uhhh... no. Someone just found this."

"And you're wondering who's it is?"

"Yeah."

"Well, let's just take a look at the files." He motioned for the stick back, so I gave it back to him. "If they are .xcf or .svg files, or even .aud or .ogg they are probably mine. But .ods or .odt probably belong to a manager. Let me think here..." He popped the USB drive into his computer. "What do you work with, Jeff? Zip files? .html?"

"Yes. And... a lot more," I said.

Just then we heard a tumpety sound coming from his large expensive speakers and he stared at his screen in surprise. I went over to see too. There was a large blue window that said, "You've Been Hacked!"

"What in the world is this?" he said. "Hacked?! And by a shade of blue from the '90s! Do you know anything about this, Jeff?"

"No. I have no idea. But..." It just occurred to me. "If your computer just got hacked, we should probably take it off the network before it infects everyone else."

Andy stood and put his hands up. "I don't know anything about that. You do it, Jeff."

I climbed under his desk and unplugged the network cable with my right hand, because my left still hurt. Then I yanked the USB stick out. I said to Andy, "I'll go talk with Ronja."

"Good. Thanks. And I'll go get a latte."

I sighed. How many of us just got infected with this thing? I looked at the USB stick. And where did this thing come from anyway?

9:44 AM

Ronja Wolff was our system administrator, so she was the person to talk to about a possible local infection. I found her at her desk and said, "Andy's computer might be infected with a virus."

"How do you know this?"

"We plugged in a USB stick and then a window popped up saying 'You've Been Hacked.' So I unplugged it from the network so it won't infect anyone else."

"Did it say anything besides that?"

"No."

"It didn't say your files were hijacked? Or where to send money to get them back?"

"No. Just that message."

"That sounds odd. Malware usually tries to be very silent. Or it does something malicious. To be loud and peaceful is very unusual."

"Yeah, well, you're the system administrator, so can you take care of it?"

"I will."

"And it may have infected everyone else, too."

"I could check, but I don't think so."

"Why not?"

"Because we have software that sniffs the network looking for viruses. If it found any, I would have received a message by now."

"Oh. OK. That's good."

"Do you have the USB drive so I can analyze that also?" she asked.

I handed it to her.

"Where did this come from?" she asked.

"I don't know, but I'm going to find out."

I walked over to the reception desk and found Luanna there. I said, "Hi Luanna."

"Hi, Jeff! Are you having a good morning?"

"Ha. Um... Well, I've had better."

"What's up?"

"Well, besides having a car accident this morning, and my boss quitting, it seems this USB stick you gave us had a virus on it or something."

"Oh! Someone just handed it to me and said they found it outside our door. I just assumed it was one of yours."

"Well, it's not. It infected Andy's computer. Can you tell us anything about the person who gave it to you?"

"Sure. It was Peter Steele, the CEO. He's the one who found it."

"Thanks, Luanna!" I made my way straight for his office. His door was closed and I could see him talking with someone inside. His visitor just stood up, so I hung around waiting for them to be done. I glanced over at Randal's office. He was in there, finishing up packing. All the walls were bare and all the desk space was empty. It looked a little lonely.

While I was looking through the window into his office, I noticed my reflection in the glass. My 5' 10" frame was not much to notice, especially with my boring brown hair and being a little skinny. At 28 years old I should have had a girlfriend or been married by now, but not me. Well, Cheryl and I have gone out for lunch a few times, and I enjoyed spending time with her, but I don't know what you would call that.

"Hey, Jeff!" Randal called to me. "What's up?"

"Oh, I was just waiting for Peter. It seems we have been infected by a virus that came from a USB stick that he found outside."

He seemed in a good mood, considering the news. "Wow. Well, have fun with that. That's another reason I'm out of here."

I probably should have been sad or something about Randal leaving, but I didn't know if I was. I wasn't a very emotional person. Well, except for that one time I got mad at my dad a few weeks, but I try not to think about that. Besides, he's in jail now anyway.

Just then Peter's door opened and a large man walked out. He must have been six feet three or four. He didn't smile as he walked past me. I didn't say anything to him either, because my life is hard enough without more grumpy people in it. I went in to see Peter.

"Ah, Jeff! What can I do for you?"

"Hi, Peter. It seems Andy's computer has been infected with a virus of some sort, and it came from the USB stick you found outside our door this morning. I was wondering if you could tell me anything more about that."

"A virus?" he said. "On one of our devices?"

"I think it might not be one of ours. Maybe somebody put a virus on it and put our logo on it and left it around our office for us to plug in."

"To try to infect us by disguising it with our logo?"

"Yes."

"That's terrible. What do you know about this so far?"

"Nothing," I said. "I was hoping you could tell me something about where you found this USB stick."

"I just found it outside our doors. That's all I know."

"OK, thanks, Mr. Steele."

"You're welcome. And you should tell your boss what's going on."

I smiled. "Randal doesn't care. He's leaving."

"Oh, I don't mean Randal. I mean your new boss."

"I haven't met him yet."

"I believe you have, outside my office just now. He was the man I was just meeting with."

CHAPTER 2

9:53 AM

When I got back to my computer, I saw an email waiting for me.

From: victora@omniscient.software
To: developers@omniscient.software
Subject: Your New Boss
I am Victor Akulov. I am your new boss. Be in the board room for a meeting at 11:00.
—

Victor Akulov
VP of Development
Omniscient Technologies

I noticed this guy wasn't very wordy. That might be OK. Perhaps he wasn't very polite either. That might not be good.

"Well, that's it." I turned around to see Randal holding a box. "Goodbye, everyone."

Scott said, "Enjoy the water."

"Oh, I will," he replied.

"Goodbye, Randal," said Garth.

Doug and I just said, "Bye," at the same time.

With that, he turned around and left.

The three others turned back around, but I sat there and contemplated the end of an era. I wouldn't have called Randal my friend, but he wasn't a bad guy. I don't know how good a manager he was either, but he got the job done I guess. But about the new guy, I'm not sure how he's going to work out.

Scott piped up. "Hey, how do you think you pronounce the new boss's last name? Ah-kulov or Ay-kulov?"

"We'll find out in an hour, I guess," said Doug.

"It matters not to me," said Garth.

Just then Victor himself showed himself at the entrance to our room. He scowled and announced. "We're having a meeting in one hour. In the board room." Then he spied Garth's little whiteboard. Without pausing, he wiped out the joke with his hand, grabbed the near-by marker, and wrote: "Meeting. 11:00 in the board room."

As he turned to leave, Garth spoke up and said, "Excuse me, sir. That is mine."

Victor turned back and glared at Garth. "If it is property of Omniscient Technologies, it is not yours, it is mine. If it not property of Omniscient Technologies, take it home." And without waiting for a response, he walked away, leaving Garth speechless for perhaps the first time in his life.

Garth stood, grabbed the whiteboard off its hook on the wall, and furiously wiped out the note. Then he threw it under his desk and sat down again. I think he was mad. I don't blame him.

We were all kind of in shock. Who could be that rude? It just wasn't possible.

Scott said, "I think I'll call him Ay-kulov, as in Adolf."

Just then I remembered that Peter Steele told me I had to talk with him about the USB stick that infected Andy's computer. "And I have to go talk to him," I said.

"About what?" Scott asked.

"Haven't I told you? Peter found a USB stick outside our office door, and when we plugged it into Andy's computer, a window popped up saying we've been hacked."

"I trust you took his computer off the network," Garth said.

"Yes."

"Has our system administrator been notified?"

"Yeah, I told Ronja. And Peter says I need to talk to our new boss about it."

"While you're there, kick him in the shins for me."

I'm sure Garth was kidding. Well, no he wasn't, but I wasn't going to kick anyone. I stood up and walked over to Randal's old office, now Victor's office. Nothing was hung on the walls. Nothing decorated his desk space. He was staring at his computer and not looking happy.

His door was closed, so I would have to knock. I noticed my heart beat faster and my breathing increased. This was like conflict, and I hated conflict. I took a deep breath. Then another one. Then I mentally pushed my anxious thoughts to one side as my hand came up and knocked on the door.

Victor looked up and said, "Come in."

I opened the door and walked in. As quickly as possible, I sat down on a chair opposite his desk. I subconsciously pulled my feet under the chair and held my hands on my lap with my elbows close to me.

"What is this about?" he asked.

I said, "This morning Peter Steele found a USB stick outside. When we plugged it in, it said 'You've Been Hacked.' Now we might have infected the whole network, but Ronja doesn't think so."

"Why did you do that?" I didn't dare make eye contact, because his eyes were drilling into me.

"Do what?"

"Were you familiar with this USB drive?"

"Ah... no."

"So why did you plug in an unfamiliar USB drive into your computer?" I thought he was going to come up with a plan to sanitize Andy's computer and the network, but instead he almost sounded angry.

"Well... it had our logo on it."

"But you admit it was unfamiliar to you."

"Well... yeah."

"That was your mistake. Don't put anything in your computer that you don't trust."

"OK, but what about Andy's computer and the network?"

"I will deal with it." He turned back to his computer and waved me away with the back of his hand like a fly. "Dismissed."

I considered asking what he was planning to do, but for some reason I didn't feel like spending any more time there. I stood up and left the room, but not before I dropped the USB stick onto his desk.

Back at my desk, Scott asked, "How did it go?"

I said, "Terrible."

"Why?"

"He basically said it was my fault."

"Your fault for hacking us?!"

"Something like that."

"That's crazy."

Ronja appeared and said, "I have started scanning Andy's computer for viruses and malware. We should know in an hour if it finds anything."

"Thanks," I said.

"Has anyone in here noticed anything unusual that I should look at?" She addressed the room.

We all said no.

"Garth, is your computer working for you? Would you like me to take a look at anything?"

Garth kept staring straight at his screen. "Everything is fine, Ms. System Administrator. "

"Good. But if you notice anything, please come see me."

"Thank you for your concern," he said.

It amazed me how Ronja could keep trying to get past Garth's rock-solid shell. Didn't she know that he just puts up his wall even higher when she is around? But then again, I suppose she was free to try.

I looked at the time. In a few minutes, we were going to officially meet our new boss. I'm not sure I was looking forward to it.

11:00 AM

The giant table in the middle of the board room would have been the first thing you saw, except that everyone expects to see the table. Instead, the art on the wall is what gets your attention. They were beautifully framed photographs of airplanes, mostly old airplanes, and mostly black and white. It turns out that our CEO, Peter Steele, had a pilot's license and liked planes. Rumor has it that he still flew a glider once in a while.

On the opposite wall were portraits of the board members. I've never studied them, because they were mostly old people, and in a social class far removed from me. However, as I was sitting there with everyone else waiting for the meeting to begin, my eyes fell on one board member. He was the stereotypical thing: old white male, gray hair, but he did seem to have a friendly smile and a peace on his face that most others lacked. He appeared strangely familiar somehow, but I almost spit out my coffee when I read the small plaque underneath the frame. It said, "Darryl Bankowsky".

Then Victor Akulov walked in. He didn't seem happy to be there, but I was beginning to conclude that he never looked happy.

He stood at the end of the room and announced, "I am Victor Akulov, the new Vice President of Development." He pronounced the A in his last name like Apple, not like Adolf, but for some reason, I already associated this man with the word "Adolf". He continued. "The first thing I am doing as boss, is to clean up and fill in the holes left by my predecessor. In the news, last month, I read that hackers were trying to hack into Omniscient Technologies." He grew stern. "This will not happen while I am here! The first thing I am doing is to mandate a list of security rules you will all obey." He held up a piece of paper with black words printed on it.

I pondered this idea. Security might be a good thing, but I don't think anybody likes obeying rules. I sat back and listened to his rules.

He began reading them. "Rule number one. Don't put anything into your computer such as a USB drive, CD, etc, that you don't trust."

Well, I broke the first one already.

He continued. "Two. Never open attachments from people you don't trust." Wow. That's going to severely limit communication.

"Three: Never download anything from websites you don't trust. Four: Never send private data by unencrypted email, chat, or web sites."

Wow. That's going to slow down productivity around here.

He continued. "Five: Use long passwords, random upper and lower case letters, numbers, and symbols. At least 16 characters long, preferably 24. Never use the same password twice. Change it every 4-6 months. Use 2-factor authentication if available. Six: Always use a VPN on networks you don't trust. And finally, seven, Never trust anyone by phone or in-person that you don't know."

We sat there, staring at our new boss like people who just had straight jackets thrown onto them and were now expected to get to work.

He said, "I will send these rules to everyone. I also have a list of rules for the network that I will send to Ronja. He pronounced Ronja's name with a jay sound instead of the proper German yeh sound. I looked at Ronja to see her reaction.

She said, "It's pronounced Ron-ya. It's German."

He waved his hand. "Whatever. Before I take any questions from you, I should mention that someone already broke one of these rules this morning. It was Jim. He plugged in a USB drive he did not recognize into Andy's computer."

He was referring to me, and he got my name wrong. Now my friends looked at me to see if I would correct him. Not on your life. I sat there, not moving a muscle on my face. The less communication with this guy the better.

"Now, does anyone have any questions about this list of rules? Does everybody understand what they are supposed to do?"

Scott spoke up. "Yeah. What are we supposed to do if we see a USB drive with our company's logo on it?"

Adolf glared at Scott. "Do we have USB drives with our logo on it?"

"Well I didn't know of any until now, but when I saw one, apparently we do."

Now Victor wasn't just grumpy. He looked a little angry. "Your problem is that you trusted something you should not have trusted. You were gullible and you were deceived. Stop being gullible. It is gullibility like this that will get us all hacked. This is how we invite viruses and malware into our network and onto our computers. This will not happen with me in charge. This sloppiness stops now." He hit the table.

Now Garth spoke up. He wasn't one to walk away from a fight. He said, "But the question remains, sir, what are we supposed to do?"

Victor relaxed. He said, "A good question. Ronja will set up a computer that is not on the network. Whenever you receive anything you don't trust, anything at all, bring it to that computer. You can scan it there for malware."

Ronja said, "We don't have a spare computer available."

Victor said, "You'd better get one. Your delay is holding up work."

Garth said, "And how will we bring it to that computer if it is not on the network."

"Use a USB drive."

Scott asked, "Will it have our logo on it?" Scott had a lot more guts than I did.

Victor stared at my friend and pointed at him. "I don't like your impertinence. You will respect your boss, and you will respect these rules." He stood up and started monologing. "I run a tight ship, and good rules are what define a good company. You can judge a company by the rules they live by, the same way you can judge a person by the rules he lives by. Even whole countries and religions are judged by their rules. A good country has good rules. And a bad country has bad rules, or no laws at all. That's why Christianity is the best religion, because it has the best rules. I'm referring to the ten commandments of course."

I was in shock. I couldn't believe he said that last thing. I just couldn't believe it. You can't say something like that. You just can't say it. This guy's crazy. He's not just crazy, he's a religious nut. I work for a religious nut job.

There were a few other questions, and Victor answered them. Then we were dismissed.

11:49 AM

Back at our desks, Doug spoke first. "So, what do you think of our new boss?"

We all reacted. Scott rolled his eyes and groaned. I frowned and thought unpleasant thoughts. Garth said, "Not so loudly. He's not that far away."

It was at times like this that the chat feature on the software we made, Omniscient, came in useful. It was available as an app on our phones, but also as a website. Garth started typing, and soon we were all in the chat.

Garth: Victor Adolf
Scott: He's not very cheerful, is he?
Me: I don't think I like him.
Scott: Can you believe that thing he said? Christianity is the best religion?
Doug: Should we all become Christians like our new boss?
Me: I certainly won't
Garth: The Jews have more rights to the ten commandments than Christians. He was actually promoting Judaism.
Scott: Poor, confused man
Garth: Religious wackos are the worst kind of wackos
Just then we all received an email from Victor with an attachment.
Scott: I don't trust this email from Adolf. I'm going to put it on a USB stick and stick it somewhere.
Doug: Careful!
Scott: OK, I'll carefully stick it somewhere

Then I saw Cheryl walk past our doorway. I checked the time and guessed maybe she was on her way to lunch. I stood up. "I gotta go," I said to the room.

"Have fun with your girlfriend," said Scott.

"She's not my..." I stopped talking and ran to meet her instead. Her reddish-blond hair looked amazing from the back. And her face looked good from the front too. "Cheryl!"

She turned. "Hi, Jeff."

"Are you going for lunch?" I asked.

"I was thinking of it."

"I could join you, if you wanted."

She smiled. "OK"

We walked together. As I pushed open the big glass door of Omniscient Technologies, I used my left hand and winced. My pinky finger still hurt, and the pain wasn't going away.

"Are you OK?" she asked.

"Oh. I had a small car accident this morning. I'm a bit sore, and this finger is bothering me."

"Let me see," she said. I gave her my battered hand and she took it in her soft, warm, feminine hands. "It's red, and turning purple. You should get it looked at."

I was so distracted by her physical touch that I simply replied, "OK." Then she let go, so we had to keep walking.

Once we were outside our building, known as the Johnston Terminal, we made our way toward another building, the Forks Market, that contained some shops and restaurants. That's when I got a text message. It was from my mom. It read, "I'm here."

CHAPTER 3

12:05 PM

I stopped walking, not knowing what to do. I forgot that I told my mom we could go for lunch. But Cheryl and I were already going for lunch. I paused and hesitated.

"What?" Cheryl asked.

"Ummm…" I considered my options. There were none. "I just told my mom we could go for lunch, and she said she's here." I looked around.

"I haven't met your mom yet. Let's all go together."

"Yeah." I didn't know if I wanted my Cheryl world and my mom world to collide just yet. It was all undefined. It was all unknown.

"Is that her?" Cheryl asked. I saw my mom walking toward us. At 49, she didn't look old yet, but having a hard life had taken it's toll. My dad, her husband, left us when I was fifteen, and she had to work hard to support two kids.

I said, "Yup."

Cheryl started toward her so I followed.

I think my mom would have given me a hug, but Cheryl got to her first and stuck out her hand. "Hi. I'm Cheryl," she said.

My mom looked at her, confused, then at me, then back to Cheryl. "I'm Julie," she said. "Who are you?" She looked at me again.

I said, "This is… ah… this is Cheryl. We… we work together."

My mom said, "Oh. Oh! Well, I don't want to interrupt you if you're going out together."

Cheryl laughed, good-naturedly.

I said, "We weren't going out, we were just… grabbing a bite to eat."

"Please join us, Julie," said Cheryl. "I would love to meet Jeff's mom."

Mom said, "And I would like to meet you. You know, Jeff hasn't told me about you."

She said, "Really?", and glanced back at me. I shrugged.

12:20 PM

After ordering at the KYU Grill, we sat down with our Heroshima grilled-skewer sandwiches. It was one of those places that said they were Japanese, but you never knew how true that was. The food was still good though.

"So, Cheryl," Mom began. "Did you meet my Jeff here at work?"

"Yes. I used to tend the plants at Omniscient Technologies."

"They hired someone to just do that?"

"I actually started a small business tending plants. I went around to a number of businesses in town and they hired me."

"But you don't anymore?"

"No. I sold that business. Now I'm working as a Customer Service Rep."

I paused my eating and interjected. "The plant business was your business that you started?"

Cheryl said, "Yeah. It was my dad's idea. He's pretty good at business."

I asked her, "Is your dad's name, perchance, Darryl Bankowsky?"

She looked guilty. "He told me not to tell anyone."

I said, "Don't tell anyone your dad is on the board? He probably owns part of the company too, doesn't he?"

"He said I should be rewarded for my own skill, not because of a family connection."

Mom said, "Speaking of family, Jeff, you should go visit your father."

I put down my sandwich. "Not interested."

"He's your father. You should go see him."

"He's in jail."

"He's still your father."

"My father? He tried to kill me, Mom. I mean literally. He told his guy to kill me. Those were his exact words. 'Kill Jeff.' That's what he said. And you want me to go visit this guy? What for?"

"He has something he wants to tell you."

I laughed. "I'm sure he does. 'Come here and I'll try again.' That's what he wants to tell me."

Mom scowled. "It's not like that. He's... he's changed."

I rolled my eyes. "Oh yeah, he's a different man now, is he?"

"Stop it! Why can't you just go visit him? He's your father, and wants to tell you something."

I sighed. "What does he want to tell me?"

"I promised him I would let him tell you himself."

"So you've been talking with him."

"Of course. We used to be married, you know."

I pushed more skewered sandwich into my mouth.

"I think you should go," Cheryl said. "I'd go with you."

That made me pause.

Mom looked at Cheryl, then back at me. "I like this girl. You should listen to her, Jeffrey, if you don't listen to your own mother."

I said, "What did you want to talk to me about, Mom?"

Her composure changed. Instead of fighting me to do something, she wilted on her chair. "I got scammed. Yesterday evening. I called a phone number on my screen because my computer said I got a virus and I should call this number to get rid of it."

"Mom, I would have helped you."

"I know. I should have just let you help me. I was just trying to show you I could help myself."

"What happened?" Cheryl asked.

Mom looked up at Cheryl, drawn to the compassion in her eyes. Cheryl was like that. She had some sort of compassion inside of her that most people didn't. I didn't know where it came from. Maybe she had loving parents or something.

Mom said, "The man I talked with on the phone said he had accidentally transferred fifty thousand dollars into my account."

"Fifty thousand!" I said.

She continued. "He said they were going to give me five hundred, but accidentally gave me fifty thousand."

"How did they do that?" I asked.

"They didn't. They just transferred money from my savings into my checking account."

"You had fifty thousand dollars in your savings account?!" I said. "Where did you get that from?"

She studied me briefly, then said, "You don't need to concern yourself with that right now." She turned back to Cheryl and said, "And then they said I could keep five thousand of it if I gave forty-five thousand back to them."

"So you did?" Cheryl said.

She nodded. "I went to the bank and transferred it in person. You need to do that in person because it was such a large amount."

"So you gave them your own money." Cheryl looked genuinely sad for this woman she'd never met before.

Mom nodded.

Then Cheryl shuffled her chair over to my Mom's and gave her a hug. The women embraced each other, and I felt like a third wheel. I sat there like an awkward man while the women were sharing a moment.

Finally, Cheryl moved back and my mom sighed. "Thanks for that, dear," she said.

I don't think I'll ever understand women.

Then my mom turned to me. "Jeff," she said, "Will you get my money back?"

"Me?"

"Yes. You're a computer guy. I read about how you brought those hackers to justice a while ago. What did they call themselves? The Information Organization?"

"The Information Underground," I said.

"Yes. You got them, Jeff. You brought them to justice, and now you can help me. You can help me bring these bad people to justice. Will you help me, Jeff? Will you do it?"

Before I could respond, Cheryl added, "If your mother got scammed, think how many other people are also getting scammed. You might be able to stop them."

I saw Cheryl looking at me with her large eyes, as if I were the hero, her hero. I didn't know if I could live up to her expectations, but somewhere inside of me it felt good to be admired by a woman. If this is how she saw me, maybe this is who I am. I also looked at my mom, who loved me and had got scammed out of a large amount of money. There was no way I could say no to her. But I briefly remembered the last time I tried going after criminals. I got kidnapped, threatened, and shot at. I may have even shot someone too, or at least I tried. Did I really want to go through that again? Looking at these two women, I knew I had no choice.

I took a deep breath. "I'll do it. I'll get them for you, Mom."

"Hey! That's my Jeffrey! I knew I could count on you."

We stood and she came and gave me a big hug. When I embraced her, I winced as I flexed my pinky finger.

Finally, she said, "What should I do?"

I said, "You could start by going to the police."

"OK, who should I talk to?"

I said, "It turns out I know a detective. His name is Joseph Wakefield. I'll send you his information."

She said, "Good. You do that." I pulled out my phone and sent her Joseph's information.

Cheryl said, "It was good meeting you, Julie."

"You too, Cheryl. Let's get together again some time."

"I would love that."

We heard a noise coming from my mom's purse. She said, "That's your contact information coming through. I'll go see him right now." She waved and walked away, leaving Cheryl and me together again.

1:12 PM

Cheryl and I slowly wandered away from the eating area.

As we passed by Sweet City Candy, I asked her if she wanted anything. She shook her head and asked if I did. I also said no, but she noticed that I was staring at something.

"What is it?", she asked.

"Oh, nothing."

She looked where I had been looking and tried to guess what it was. "You were looking at those chocolate bars."

I shrugged. "I sometimes like a good eighty-five percent dark chocolate."

She smiled, then walked over to it, picked it up and went to pay.

"You don't need to do that," I said.

She just grinned, and when it was paid for, broke a corner off and popped it in her mouth. Then she gave the rest to me and mumbled, "It's for you."

"Um... thanks," I said. I also ate a piece. "Mmmm... dark chocolate. The chemicals do things to my brain."

"You should take good care of your brain. It's what makes you money."

We laughed.

After leaving the Forks Market, when we were in the open air, Cheryl asked me, "So does God still send you email?"

I shook my head. "No. Not since that day you started in Customer Service, when he said he was going to give me a new assignment."

"That was weeks ago."

"Yeah."

Then she stopped and turned to me. "Hey, you don't think..."

"You think my mom's scammer is my new assignment?"

"Maybe," she said.

I considered it. "Maybe it is. Maybe it is. And someone tried to... do something to us this morning with a USB drive."

"What?"

"We found a USB drive with the Omniscient logo on it, and plugged it in, but a window popped up saying 'You've Been Hacked'".

"Maybe they're related."

I shrugged. "Maybe. Maybe not. But maybe. But right now we should get back to work."

"I think you need to go to a hospital, Jeff Davis. Your finger is purple."

I looked at it. It was.

I sighed. "OK, I'll go to a hospital. See you around, Cheryl."

I turned to go, but Cheryl said, "Jeff."

I turned back, and she said, "I just wanted to say thanks for doing this for your mom. You know she looks up to you and admires you." She paused briefly, then said, "And so do I." Then she turned and went back to work.

With a strange and wonderful feeling in my chest, I walked out to my car, at least what was left of it.

1:21 PM

I didn't know what the doctor would say about my finger, but I'll give him the opportunity to say it.

I tried yanking on the driver's door of my car, but it was stuck shut. Maybe it should stay shut, because if I got it open, it might stay open. I'd rather have it shut. So I climbed in from the opposite side, making sure to spare my left finger from too much work.

The engine came to life and sounded fine, so I backed out of my spot and started driving. So far so good. I headed straight for the hospital, where I parked and scrambled out again.

As I stood in line at the emergency desk, I looked around at the people. They looked fine. I didn't see any missing limbs or blood or anything. Maybe it was a slow day.

When it was my turn, I presented my hand to the nurse like a cat presenting a dead mouse to its owner. I said, "I think I may have broken my finger." She examined it underneath her thick spectacles and declared, "It might be broken. Or maybe it's just sprained. Either way you should see a doctor. When did it happen and how?"

I said, "Car accident. About eight o'clock this morning." She wrote this all down.

"It took you a while to come in, huh? That was what, almost five and half hours?"

I shrugged. "The pain didn't go away."

"Better now than when it's too late. Some people come in only when it's too late."

"That doesn't sound very smart."

"Oh, smart has nothing to do with it. It's stubbornness. They don't want to ask anyone for help. They want to stay independent. Take care of themselves." She handed me a clipboard. "Have a seat and fill this in. Then give it back to me."

I sat and started jotting down my name and address. She may have said pride keeps people from asking for help, but I think it's just stupidity. Of course you need to go for help if you need it. Then again, who knows?

As I was sitting there, I saw a poster that said "Triage" in a large font. The word was blue, and I wondered if Andy would consider it a color from the 90s. I didn't know anything about that.

The top word on the poster said, "Emergency" and was followed by smaller words. "Cardiopulmonary arrest, severe respiratory distress, major burns, major trauma, massive uncontrolled bleeding, coma." I was pretty sure that wasn't me.

The second word was "Urgent" and then "Abdominal pain, non-cardiac cp, multiple fractures, lacerations, renal calculi." I had no idea what "renal calculi" was, but it sounded like math.

The third was, "Non-urgent", which was "Rash, chronic headache, sprains, cold symptoms." That wasn't me. I searched again for "broken bones," but couldn't find it in the list. That was pretty dumb.

I finished filling out information and handed back the clipboard. While I waited, I emailed my new boss.

From: jeffd@omniscient.software
To: victora@omniscient.software
Subject: At the hospital
Hi. I was in a small car accident this morning, and now I'm at the hospital getting my finger looked at.

I soon got this reply.

From: victora@omniscient.software
To: jeffd@omniscient.software
Subject: Re: At the hospital
Next time come to me and ask before you leave work.

Wow. I didn't like my new boss. There was just something about him that rubbed me the wrong way.

While I was there, I decided to try to email God.

From: jeffd@omniscient.software
To: god@heaven
Subject: Hi
Hi God. This is Jeff. You said a while ago that you were going to give me a new assignment. Is it to catch the scammer that scammed my mom out of lots of money?

To my delight, he replied. This is what he said.

From: jeffd@omniscient.software
To: god@heaven
Subject: Re: Hi
Hi Jeff. I love you very much, my son. I love when you come to me. I love talking with you. I love that you ask me about how to live your life. I will certainly meet with you. I will certainly answer you when you call to me. I am always here for you, Jeff, my son. Always.

These people who stole money from your mom have been operating too long. It is time to stop them. I want you to do it, Jeff. I want you to stop them. Find them. Track them down. Put an end to their business. Stop the evil they are doing. I don't like when innocent people lose their money. I hate injustice. I want you to stop their injustice. Put an end to it. This is what I'm calling you to do, Jeff Davis. I'm calling you to track them down and stop their evil ways.

I love you Jeff, my son. I know you can do this. I'm not calling you to something you can't do. You can do this. I know you will.

As I read, that familiar warmth that always came with God's words flooded into me. There was just something about his words, something about him, that made me come alive inside. I decided that I would have to put more practice into hearing from him the normal way, without technology. Over the weeks I tried to do just that, but it was hard, and I didn't always get anything. But I'll keep trying.

Then the nurse called for me and I got up and went with her.

2:29 PM

I sat in the small sterile room when a man in white came in. "And how are we today? Could be better, or you wouldn't be here, right?" He laughed.

I tried to laugh with him. "I think I broke my finger," I said. "May I see it?"

I handed over my discolored, swollen, and painful hand to him, hoping he could somehow make it better. I wasn't being stubborn. I wanted it fixed. It was broken, so I presented myself to the doctor. That's just smart. Why someone wouldn't go to a doctor if they are broken is beyond me.

He examined it, and even moved my finger around, which caused me obvious pain. "It's impossible to say if it's broken or just sprained. We'll have to get it X-rayed." He turned to his computer and started doing stuff.

I also turned and watched him. He did some typing, then moved his mouse and clicked, and did some more typing. I said, "You could probably just hit Tab to get to the next field."

"What?"

"Instead of clicking on the next text field, you could probably just hit the Tab button. The cursor should go to the next field by itself."

He paused. "I don't know what you mean."

So I showed him. "Take your mouse and click there." I pointed at one field. He did. "Now on your keyboard, press Tab." He did. And the cursor moved to the next field.

The doctor smiled. "Hey! I learned something!" He kept pressing Tab and the cursor kept advancing. "But what if I want to go back?"

"Shift Tab," I said.

He shift-tabbed and the cursor skipped backwards. He smiled again. "Thanks." Then he said, "Are you a computer guy?"

"I'm a computer programmer."

"What kinds of things do you do?" He asked, then kept on entering information.

"I write software."

"Like this software I'm using?"

"Well, no. Our software has a web component and a mobile component. Your software is obviously not mobile friendly."

"I don't know what that means, but you're the professional."

"The buttons are too small. To be mobile friendly, you need nice big buttons for big fingers."

His printer started printing, and he handed it to me. "Go down to X-ray and give them this. They will X-ray your finger. Come back when you're done." He glanced at the time. "We might have time to cast it when you get back."

"Thanks." I left the room and went in search of X-ray.

I finally found a room called X-ray, and I handed over my paper to a very tall and skinny man. I waited for him to say something, but he just studied the paper and finally said, "This way." I followed him, of course, because when you're in an unknown place, the best thing to do is to follow someone in charge.

He lead me to an X-ray room, where he told me to place my finger in several positions on a table while he left the room each time. I did as I was told and didn't ask questions. He didn't tell me anything. When he was finally done, he said, "Someone will be in touch with you. Good day."

I said, "Thanks," and left.

Chapter 4

3:24 PM

As I sat waiting for the doctor again, I decided to start investigating the scammers. I emailed my mom, asking her for details. Where did she find these people? Or how did they find her?

Soon she replied and said she was searching for a good anti-virus program, and found a phone number on a website. She said she couldn't remember the phone number, but she gave me the address of the website. I went there on my phone. It looked cheap. And there were lots of ads. Maybe the scammers put an ad there, and my mom thought it was a legitimate help service. I scrolled up and down looking for a phone number, but couldn't see one, so I emailed my mom again, asking her to check her phone's dial history for the number. I might have to call these people myself.

But what would I say to them? Ask them nicely to give the money back? Threaten to call the police? And speaking of police...

Just then a nurse called me in to see the doctor.

So I went with her and sat in the same room as last time, waiting again. But the doctor came in very soon, carrying some stuff. He said, "Well, it looks like you've fractured your fifth intermediate phalange." He pointed to that part of his hand.

"Great," I said. Well, at least I know what's wrong.

"So let's put it in a splint." He held a thin strip of metal with foam on one side. He bent it around my finger so I couldn't move it. Then he taped it on. He said, "With this kind of injury, I'd say you're looking at four to five weeks to fully recover."

"That long, huh?"

"Oh, you'll have this thing off before you know it."

"Well, thanks for your help anyway."

"That's why I'm here. My motto is 'You break 'em, I fix 'em.' And speaking of, I have other patients. Have yourself a good day."

"Thanks."

He left the room, and so did I. I pondered this thing on my left hand as I walked. I could still make a fist, without my pinky finger of course, but if I need to scratch my face, I would have to make sure I didn't poke myself in the eye. That shouldn't be a problem.

As I passed the food shop, in the hospital, I got a text message. It was from God. It said, "How much money do you have in your pockets?"

What? God is asking me how much money I have in my pockets? I'm pretty sure he is God and already knows the answer. So why is he asking me?

I replied and said, "20"

He said, "Buy a slice of pizza for Garth Fonte."

That made me stop. Yeah, I'm sure Garth would love pizza, just like he loves chips, burgers, and Dr. Pepper. I know that much. I also know that he was the one who, just four weeks ago, accused me of being the hacker who was trying to blackmail the company. I almost got fired because of that. We've never talked about that incident, and I don't want to. I also don't want to buy him pizza.

I must have been standing a little too close to the shop and staring, because the person inside asked me, "Can I help you with something?"

I shook my head and walked away.

At the car I checked the time. It was nearly quarter after four. It looks like the afternoon was gone. I may as well forget about work and bring my car to the garage too.

My phone rang. It was my mom. "Hi Mom," I said.

"Hi Jeff. Are you going to visit your dad this evening?"

"I wasn't planning to."

"Do you have anything else more important than visiting your father in jail?"

I thought about my evening plans, which consisted of nothing, followed by more nothing. "No."

"So you're going to visit him?"

"No."

"Well, I have something for you that might help you change your mind."

"What is it?"

"I'll come bring it to you. Where are you? At work?"

"I'm actually leaving the hospital, on my way to the garage to get my car fixed."

"Oh! What did the doctor say?"

"My finger is broken, and he put a cast on it."

"I hope you get better soon, son. What garage are you going to?"

"I was thinking of J.W. on Bannatyne."

"I'll meet you there. I'll be there in a few minutes."

I paused. That was kind of weird, but whatever. I said, "OK."

"OK. Bye."

"Bye"

4:29 PM

J.W. McDonald Auto Service was a small garage on Bannatyne Avenue that had probably been there for fifty years, maybe a hundred. It was nestled between two ancient brick buildings that were probably built before electricity was invented.

But the service was friendly, and they knew how to fix cars. While I was standing in line to talk to the person behind the service desk, I looked around at the shelves of oil and fluids and miscellaneous car parts. There was a poster that said, "We fix what you break." I chuckled. It sounded like my doctor. "You break it. I fix it." Maybe he gets his car serviced here. No, I'm sure he goes somewhere a lot nicer than this.

"Can I help you, sir?" It was a woman's voice and it came from the other side of the counter. Her name tag said, "Becky" on it. I was a little surprised to see a woman working at a garage, but after reminding myself to not be sexist, I went with it.

I said, "I got into an accident this morning, and my car is beat up."

"Do you have it here?" she asked.

"Yes."

She came around and we walked outside. I gestured to my beat-up Honda Civic.

"Ooo... doesn't look good," she said to me. "Were you in it at the time?"

I held up my left hand and nodded. "Can you fix it?"

"Absolutely we can. We are very good at fixing broken things."

"I seem to have my share of broken right now."

She kept inspecting the damage to the car. "Hey! Look at this! You shouldn't be driving this."

"Why not? It drives."

She pointed. "Your tire touches the panel here when you turn." She rubbed the tire. "And your tread is... gone. You need a new tire right now. I wouldn't drive this thing home."

"Well, that's why I'm here I guess."

"And you probably want an estimate for insurance."

"Ummm... yeah. Thanks."

"I'll get started on that right away."

"Thanks."

As she turned to go inside, we both noticed a car drive onto the lot. It was a beautiful silver Mercedes Benz.

Becky said, "I'll be right back."

I kept staring. I recognized this car. And I recognized the person getting out of it. I walked over and said, "Hi Mom."

"Jeff!" she said, as she got out. "This is your dad's car. Do you like it?"

"Pfff... of course."

She held out the key to me. "It's yours."

I paused. "Seriously?"

"It's a gift from your dad."

I grinned as I reached out for the key. Just as my car was going in for repairs, I get this one. I could drive this thing. I sure could. Today wasn't turning out so bad after all. That is, until she pulled her hand away. "Go visit him."

"Ah! Mom!" I lifted my hands. "You're bribing me? You would bribe your own son?"

"And you would refuse to visit your own dad? Don't you guilt me, Jeff, if you can't go say 'Hi' to your own father. He wants to see you. He wants to say something to you. Go visit him." She dangled the keys at me.

I didn't respond, so she said, "Just one visit."

"Just one?"

"Just one. If you promise to go tonight, you can have this car right now. Do you agree?"

I sighed. "Fine. I agree. I'll go tonight, if they are open."

"Yes they are." She put the keys in my hand.

Becky reemerged carrying a clipboard. "I'll give you the estimate in a minute!" she said to me, as she started poking around the damaged vehicle.

"Thanks!" I replied.

My mom said, "When you're done here, you can give me a ride home, then go see your dad."

"OK."

Suddenly she got happy and gave me a hug. By reflex I put my arms around her too. "You're a good son, Jeff."

"OK."

"I love you."

"I love you too, Mom." Moms. You have to love them. Even if they don't give you luxury vehicles, you still have to love them.

Soon Becky was done with the estimate and gave me the paper.

"Can I keep this car here for now?" I asked.

"Absolutely."

"I'll let you know about fixing it when I hear from insurance I guess."

"Good. I'll need your key."

I gave her the key, then I wrote down my contact information on another paper on her clipboard.

"Thanks. Have a great day..." she looked at what I had written, "Jeff!"

"You too."

She went inside, and then I sat down in my new car. The last time I was here I was sitting in the passenger's seat. Now I'm driving it. This wasn't bad at all. "Is this mine, or is he just lending it to me?" I asked my mom in the passenger seat.

"It's yours. It's a gift from a dad to his son."

"Nice."

I drove my mom home in luxury, then I made my way to Headingly Correctional Centre. It wasn't something I was looking forward to. I had no desire to see this man again at all. If I ever saw him again, it would be too soon.

5:46 PM

"I'm here to see John Davis."

After producing identification and filling out a large amount of paperwork, the guard at the front desk finally allowed me past the main waiting room into another waiting room.

The guard that met me there treated me like he suspected me of smuggling in drugs and an iron file, but there were rules about how to treat visitors, so he couldn't do all the things he probably wanted to do. I was glad for the rules at that point. I suppose rules had their place, sometimes. Then I was patted down and metal detected. I had to leave my phone with them. Then with my arms and legs out, a large dog came and sniffed me in places that made me very nervous. The guard looked almost disappointed that he didn't find anything, so he had to let me through.

I was escorted to a small room with a table and chairs, vending machine, and a coffee maker. I briefly considered drinking some coffee, but then I changed my mind. I didn't like this place.

The door opened and my dad came in. Gone were the dress pants and crisp white shirt. His green tie was nowhere to be seen. Instead, his body was covered with a drab gray t-shirt and sweat pants. But what was most surprising was his face. Instead of the sleazy salesman smile on his face, it was relaxed. His smile looked genuine. He looked like he had just been relaxing on a grassy hill soaking in the warm sun, instead of rotting in a jail cell. It was startling. It was confusing.

I stuttered. "Dad?"

His smile got even brighter. "Jeff! It's good to see you. Thank you so much for coming." He sat down opposite me.

The guard said, "Let me know if you need anything," then closed the door from the outside.

My dad stared at me briefly, then took some deep breaths, blinked, and almost started crying. He said, "I'm... so... sorry, Jeff. I was not a good dad, was I?"

I didn't respond.

He continued. "I didn't treat you well. I didn't treat your mom well. I did so many things wrong." He looked at me meekly. "Do you think you could find it in your heart to forgive me?"

"You tried to kill me."

"I know. It was wrong. I'm sorry."

"You're sorry?"

He nodded.

I wasn't buying it. I'm not going to fall for this guy's empty words anymore. After all he did, he's going to say a few words and make it all better? You've got to be kidding me! The idea made me sick, and I let him have it. "You abused Mom. Then you abandoned her. You abandoned me. I had to grow up without a dad, while you were out doing who-knows-what. Selling drugs and blackmailing people. Maybe killing others."

"I didn't kill anyone."

"Then you had Max do it for you, whatever."

He almost got angry then. "Jeff, I'm not that person anymore."

Here it came. He might be able to hide his temper for a little while, but it always came up. Now he was going to explode and all my distrust of him was going to be justified. I pushed him a little more and I enjoyed it. "Yes you are! You were a bad person then, and you're a bad person now. I don't buy this 'Oh I'm so sorry now that I got caught' nonsense for one second. I know what you really are."

"And what am I?"

I leaned forward and said the words to his face. "You're an abusive, unfaithful, unscrupulous, murderer."

Then I sat back and waited for the inevitable, but instead of flaring his temper, he sat quietly. Finally he spoke. "You hurt me,

Jeff. But then again, I deserve it. Yes, I was all those things. You deserve to be mad at me. I deserve it. I don't know if you'll ever trust me again, but..." He looked at me again. "I'm sorry. Will you forgive me?"

Then I got mad. "How dare you?! You are the bad man in this room, not me! It was you who did those bad things, not me. It was you who hurt me. How dare you ask me to forgive you?!"

Instead of yelling back, his eyes almost brightened. "That's why I wanted you to come, Jeff. That's what I wanted to tell you. I became a Christian!"

I was horrified. "You..."

"I'm a Christian, Jeff. And you should become one too!"

My world started swimming. This man I hated was now a Christian, just like my new boss Victor Adolf was a Christian. And he had the nerve to ask me to be one too? That's the last thing I would ever do with my life. I would sooner die. I stumbled to my feet and pointed a self-righteous finger at this horrible man. "I. Will. Never! Ever! Be like you."

He may have said something after that, but I didn't hear it. I threw the door open, and almost ran out of the building, trying to control my breathing and my emotions.

7:28 PM

I wouldn't say I was a momma's boy, but she did raise me, and that included teaching me to cook. So I enjoyed a spaghetti and meatball supper. While I was sitting at my small table, chewing, I thought about my mom and the people who scammed her. I would have to find them somehow. I kept chewing.

I checked my phone. She had replied to my email giving me the phone number she had called when she got scammed. I considered calling it. I cleaned the last of the pasta off my plate, then sat back. What would I say to them? I stared out the window.

I don't even like talking to people on the phone.

While I cleared the table and washed the dishes with a busted finger, I consoled myself with the thought I couldn't call them anyway, because I wouldn't know what to say or do with them. Maybe I should talk with the guys at work first. Maybe I should call police officer detective Joseph Wakefield first. Maybe I should talk to God about it first. Maybe I'm just making excuses. Pfff. Of course not. OK, I'll talk to God first.

I sat down on my sofa and said out loud, perhaps in an awkward and formal way, "God, what do you want to say about me calling these scammers?" Then I tried to remember the how-to-hear-from-God recipe I got from the guy on the bus.

The first step was to quiet yourself down, because it's hard to hear when your brain and emotions are racing. I closed my eyes and breathed in and breathed out. I don't know if the guy specifically mentioned breathing, but whatever.

The next thing was to look for pictures. I tried to imagine something, but in my relaxed state, I could feel my finger bothering me, so I saw myself at the hospital. Then I remembered standing in front of the food shop at the hospital and God told me to buy pizza for Garth. The thought came to me that if I would have obeyed that command, I would already have help.

The fourth step was to write it down. Yeah, too bad I had nothing to write down. Oh, I suppose I could write down that last thought. Step three was to listen for spontaneous thoughts, and that was spontaneous I guess.

I took out my phone and wrote a note. "If I would have obeyed that command, I would already have help." Then I wondered if that was really from God or not. Would God say something like that? I don't know. Sure, why not?

I sighed. If this was really from God, and God was trying to help me catch these scammers, and if he thinks Garth could help me, maybe I should listen. I didn't want to, though. I checked the time. Was there time to go out and buy a frozen pizza? Yes, but maybe it would be better to get something hot tomorrow morning. Tomorrow was definitely better.

Then I received an email from God.

From: god@heaven
To: jeffd@omniscient.software
Subject: Help

Hi Jeff, my son, whom I love. It pleases me and warms my heart when you try to listen to me. It is like a young child trying to take his first steps, and his mom is right there and is so proud of her son. I am so proud of you, Jeff, my son. Keep trying to walk. You will get better and better at it, and one day it will be second nature for you to hear from me all the time.

I will help you catch these scammers. I will bring you wisdom and counsel. But you will need more than that. You also need hardware, a computer. I am bringing you a server. When you receive it, give it to me. It is mine. From it, I will give you success.

Jeff, listen to me. I am showing you your path. Walk in it. Follow closely. Don't wander off by yourself. When I tell you to do something, do it. You will have success when you obey my words.

It was very good of you to visit your dad. Thank you for that, Jeff. You did very good. You need to go back. You need to build a relationship there. He has given to you his car. You also need to start giving to him. Start with your time. Go back to visit him again.

You also need to work on your relationship with Garth. Mend what was broken. Buy him a pizza.

When you go to work tomorrow, you will notice something new. Go check it out.

I contemplated what God said, and contemplated if I wanted to do all those things. No, I didn't, but maybe I should. Maybe tomorrow.

I put my phone away and took out my laptop and watched some shows the rest of the evening.

As I was falling asleep, I wondered what in the world God wanted a server for.

CHAPTER 5

Wednesday 7:59 AM

"Morning Jeff!" my friend Scott said to me as he joined me in the elevator. We were on the ground floor of the Johnston Terminal, the building our company was located in. Omniscient Technologies was on the third floor, hence the need for an elevator.

"Hey Scott," I replied, and I pushed the button labeled "3".

"Have a good evening yesterday?"

"Sure. I visited my dad in jail."

"Yeah? How was that?"

"Ehhh." I scowled.

"Well he did try to kill us. I wouldn't expect it to go well."

"Yeah."

The doors opened and we walked out. Scott looked to his right and said, "Oh, that's something new. Let's check it out."

I was about to decline and get to work, when I remembered what God said in the email last night, something about a new thing. So I said, "OK."

To our left was our office, behind large glass doors. In the middle of the floor were the stairs if we had chosen to take them. On the other side of the floor were smaller doors with a new sign above them that read, "Tech Solutions".

"It looks like a new company," Scott said, on his way. I followed behind.

He burst through the doors and beamed at all his new friends. "Hey! a new company! Welcome to the Forks! What is this place? What do you do here?"

The place didn't look very new. It didn't look very expensive. The desks were old and nothing matched. There were two or three desks around the room and on the far wall were several offices behind closed doors. There was much less floor space than we had on our side.

Two of the desks had people behind them. The one in front of us looked like the main receptionist. The man behind the desk looked a little Asian. Maybe from India. He said, "Welcome to Tech Solutions. How can I help you?" He had almost no accent, but something about him seemed familiar.

"Oh, we're not looking for anything. Just looking around and greeting our new neighbors. But what do you sell here?"

"We provide help for all your computer needs."

Scott laughed. "We probably don't need much help. We're computer programmers ourselves."

"Ah. We deal mostly with consumers."

"Fair enough. What do you sell to consumers?"

"Antivirus software, telephone tech support, some books, some training videos."

"What kind of training videos?", Scott asked. I let him do all the talking.

"Basic internet security. How not to get infected. How not to get scammed."

This got my attention, so I stepped up from behind Scott and said, "You have a video on how to not get scammed?"

He glanced at my finger, then back at me. "Yes."

"How much is it?"

It's only two hundred and ninety-five dollars.

"Wow!" Scott laughed. "It looks like you're the ones doing the scamming. Ha ha!"

"I assure you, sir. If it will keep you or someone you love from getting scammed, it's well worth the price."

"Oh, I'm just kidding!"

I noticed someone walk in from farther down their hallway, then immediately turn around and go back. I thought that was odd.

"Well, have a great day!" Scott turned to leave and I followed him out.

"Those seemed like nice people," he said.

"I guess so."

He greeting our receptionist on the way in, then asked me, "What was her name again? Luella?"

"Luanna."

"Right."

Scott kept on talking, which he does, so I couldn't pull myself away to go say "Good morning" to Cheryl. Maybe I'll catch her later.

When we got to our room, our new boss Victor was there and said, "You two are late."

"What?" said Scott. "No we're not."

"The time is 8:06. Work begins at 8:00. You're late."

"Whatever."

We sat down and tried to get to work, but Victor said, "We will have to address this." Then he left the room. I didn't know what he was going to do, but I wasn't expecting to like it.

I glanced through my list of email messages and replied to one or two. Then I spun my chair around to ask my friends for ideas on how to catch a scammer. As I did, Victor came back in, and I immediately felt like I was caught not working, so I kept my chair spinning, and made a complete circle, facing away from the doorway and my boss.

"Jim, come to my office."

That meant me. I sighed. Nobody likes being called into the principal's office, especially if the principal gets your name wrong. I followed him slowly, afraid of what might happen to me.

8:12 AM

Victor's office was perfect. His desk was clean. His books were arranged. And all papers were exactly where papers should go, tucked away somewhere out of sight.

I sat there, with my hands on my lap, not daring to make eye contact, because he was staring at me.

"As you know, the software we make, Omniscient, is open source."

I nodded my head.

"That means any public person can download and edit it."

I nodded again.

"It also means we need to have our code well documented, in case someone wants to compile it for themselves."

I didn't nod again, because I saw where this was going, and I figured I didn't need to nod all the time.

He continued. "It's not well documented. It's terrible! That's your new job from now on. Documenting."

I looked up. "What?!"

"You're doing the documentation from now on."

"Why me?!"

"Because I need someone who is familiar with the code. You are."

"But I'm a programmer."

"From now on you're documentation."

Fear and panic took hold of my stomach. I found it hard to breathe. I could only think of one way out. "Why can't someone else do it?" I asked.

"I have to pick someone. I picked you."

"Why?"

His eyebrows furrowed. "I say you are doing documentation. You will listen to me. Now, do you have any other questions?"

I shook my head.

"You are dismissed."

I stood up dragged myself back to my desk and fell into my chair.

Scott asked, "What's wrong, Jeff? Did Adolf transfer you to the Russian front?"

"He's making me do documentation."

"What? Full time?"

I nodded. "I think so."

"So what, you're just not going to do programming anymore?"

I shook my head. It hurt. Computer programming is what I went to school for, for a long time to learn. I loved it. And now it was taken away from me. I felt pain. I felt loss. I didn't know how to handle it.

Doug turned around and said, "Documentation isn't that bad. You still need to be familiar with the software. And it's relaxing. Words don't throw errors at you like code does. You can't accidentally break anything. Think of it like a pleasant vacation."

Garth also commented. "The act of documentation is reserved for the lowest of the life forms. Documentors are like the plants that photosynthesize sunlight into energy, then cows eat the plants. Then us lions feast on the cows. You have fallen far, Mr. Davis. Far indeed."

Wow. For a moment I wondered if Garth himself suggested me to Victor.

But I didn't want to think about this now. I couldn't think about this now. I went out to the staff kitchen to find some coffee. I grabbed a mug from the cupboard. It was white and with a logo on it. The logo was the top half of a man's head. The hair was spiked and he was wearing square glasses. I stared at it, wondering where this thing had come from, but then used it for its purpose. I filled it with coffee. I took coffee like I took my chocolate: dark, with no fillers like milk or sugar.

I turned around and leaned against the counter, staring out the large windows overlooking the Assiniboine River. I didn't know how I was going to handle this loss. Programming is what I loved. For it to be taken away was like... I don't know... when a loved one dies? When your girlfriend you love leaves you?

Just then Cheryl walked into the room. My heart lifted slightly. I was about to unload on her when she asked me something out of left field.

She said, "Jeff, what is six?"

I stared at her. "What?"

"Like the Roman numeral six. It must be some computer thing."

I thought out loud. "Six? Like in binary? It's one, one, zero."

She said, "No, like the letters v,i."

I thought some more. "vi is a command-line text editor." I pronounced it like two letters.

"Maybe that's it." She cocked her head at me. "How do you close it?"

"How do you close vi?"

"Yeah."

"Escape, colon, q, enter."

She laughed. "Yeah, that's it."

Now she had me curious. "What are you talking about?"

"Haven't you read Garth's joke of the day? I went there to find you, but you weren't there, so I read his joke of the day."

"No I haven't. What did it say?"

"It said, 'How do you generate a random string? Put a Windows user in front of vi, and tell them to exit.'"

I laughed. It felt good. Then I explained. "vi gives absolutely no hints on how to close it. Once you've opened it, there are only two things you can do. Look up the documentation on how to close it, or press any and every key you can think of."

"Randomly."

"Yeah, like a random number generator, or a random string generator."

She moved closer to me. "I enjoyed going for lunch with your mom yesterday."

Not knowing how to respond, I simply said, "Good."

"So I was thinking, maybe you want to meet my parents too some time."

For some reason I suddenly felt nervous, and it must have shown.

She chuckled. "They're good people. You'll like them."

"Your dad's on the board. Isn't that some sort of conflict of interest or something?"

She laughed again. "Of course not. People are allowed to meet and talk."

I couldn't think of any way out of this one, so I finally just said, "Sure."

"Great!" She smiled and walked away, leaving me with my coffee that was getting cold. I took a sip. Life was moving fast. Too fast. And something told me this was only the beginning.

8:39 AM

I sat at my computer, looking through code. There was a class called "Connection" with a method called "open" that was completely uncommented, so I added a comment on top of it.

```
// This opens the connection.
```

I stared at what I just wrote. This is what four years of computer science at a University gets you. You study operating systems, data structures, non-imperative programming language concepts, even advanced analysis of algorithms. And here I am, adding comments that a ten-year-old could write.

I found another uncommented method, so I commented it.

```
// This closes the connection.
```

This was so painful, I would even be willing to take a phone call instead of doing this. Then my phone rang. I hesitated, wondering if I was actually serious. But it rang again, so I had to answer. It was only an internal call, so it wasn't that bad.

I picked up. "Hi. This is Jeff."

"Hi Jeff." It was Cheryl. I smiled. Her voice was a ray of sun shining through the bars of my dark prison.

I said, "Hi! What's up?"

"I just took a call from someone who is having trouble using the Identity settings page in Omniscient. He said he is going to send me a screenshot and said I should get a tech guy to look at it. Would you like to look at it?"

"Sure."

"OK, I'll send it to you."

"OK, thanks."

She chuckled. "I think I should be thanking you."

"OK, go ahead."

"What?"

"Thank me, if you want."

"Thanks, Jeff. I have to go now."

"OK."

"Bye."

"Bye."

I hung up and sighed. Five seconds of pleasantness. Maybe the screenshot might be interesting. Was it going to be a real bug or user error? I was pretty sure I knew the answer. Most problems are a result of the "nut behind the wheel."

Her email arrived at the same time my phone rang again. It was no contest to me which one I would choose. I opened her email and saw it had an attachment. It was a pdf, not a jpeg like I was expecting. I double-clicked it to open it, then picked up the phone.

"Hi. This is Jeff."

"Jeff, don't open it!" It was Cheryl.

But it was too late. I stared at a large, blue window on my screen with the words, "You've Been Hacked!" laughing at me.

I said, "Uh oh."

She said, "I just opened it too, and I got the blue window. What do we do now?"

I rested my forehead on my hand. "Uhhh... I'll ah... Don't do anything. I'll take care of it."

"OK. I won't touch anything. I'll wait for you."

"Bye."

"Bye."

I hung up and wondered what to do. I certainly didn't want to talk to Adolf, so I guess I'll go see Ronja.

8:59 AM

Ronja's desk was in one of the cubicles in the middle of the room. I said, "Hi Ronja."

She said, "Hello Jeff. Is everything all right?"

I said, "I opened an email attachment and I got the blue window saying I've been hacked."

She scowled. "You were supposed to open all attachments from people you don't trust on this computer here, off the network." She gestured to a lonely computer sitting at the end of her desk.

"Really?"

"Victor says so. It is his rules. And it is good for security."

"It's a pain."

"Yes, but it is good for security, and it is the rules."

"So what do I do now? Do you want to scan my computer for malware or something?"

"Mmmm… I think I should." She opened a cupboard door and started rifling through things. "I will come to your desk and run a scan. Your computer will be down for some minutes."

"Cheryl's computer also got hit."

"OK then, I will scan her's too."

"Thanks Ronja."

She looked at me. "You need to tell Victor."

"I don't want to."

"You must. It is the rules. You must follow the rules, Jeff."

"I don't want to."

"We are employees. We must follow the rules of our company. That is natural. That is the way it works. They hire us, and we do what they say. This is the agreement, no?"

I reluctantly had to agree. "Yes." But maybe I don't like the agreement. Maybe I didn't like working here that much anymore at all. "I'll talk to him."

"While you do that, I will scan your computer. And Cheryl's."

I left her cubicle and went to see my boss and his rules. His door was open, so I stood in the doorway and said, "I think someone is trying to hack us."

He looked at me, not very pleasantly. "Why do you say that?"

"We received another blue window saying we've been hacked."

"On your computer?"

"Yes."

"Did you open something you weren't supposed to?"

"I opened an attachment from… from a user who was having trouble."

I couldn't tell if Victor was unusually upset or if he just always looked that way. He said, "You broke rule number two."

I didn't say anything.

"You broke rule number one yesterday, and rule number two today."

I didn't want to be rude and tell him what he could do with his rules, so I continued to say nothing.

"You must learn to follow the rules! They are here for a reason. They are important for security. You are an employee of this company, and you will do as the company says. Now, will you follow the rules from now on?"

I said, "Fine," and I walked away. He probably wasn't done talking, but I was. I went to my desk, but Ronja was there doing stuff, so I went to see Cheryl.

Cheryl was at her cubicle on her phone. I said, "I don't like my boss."

She put the phone away. "Why not?" She rolled her chair back, then pushed a rolling stool at me. I sat on it.

"He's irritating," I said. "He has these rules."

"What's wrong with rules?"

"Ah! They get in the way of me doing stuff."

"You don't think they're good for you?"

"Ah, I don't know. Maybe."

"Then maybe you should follow them." She looked at her computer screen. "I guess I should have."

"Oh, about that. Ronja is going to stop by and scan your computer. It will take a few minutes."

"In that case, I will try to do my work on my phone. And maybe you should go for a walk to try to calm down or something." Then she came close and whispered in my ear, "Or talk to God about it."

I said, "Yeah." Then I said, "See ya", and started walking.

I went out our main doors and saw the "Tech Solutions" company across the way. Their door was open, and when I looked in, I saw somebody walk past who almost looked familiar. Where did I remember seeing that guy? Then I remembered. Yesterday morning. He was one of the guys who drove into me on the parking lot. He was supposed to give me his driver's license and stuff. And never did.

I ran over and went in. The man at the desk asked if he could help me. I ignored him and looked around. I said, "Where was that guy who was just here?"

"What guy?" he asked.

"I just saw someone in here. Where did he go?"

"He might be in the back, but only employees are allowed there. I could pass on a message to him for you."

I looked back at this man talking to me. "Um... Yeah... I think he may have been in an accident with me yesterday morning. If it was him, I need his driver's license and vehicle registration."

"Yes sir, I will pass certainly pass that on to him."

I said, "Thanks," and turned to go.

When I was almost out, he said, "Jeff!"

I turned around, wondering how he knew my name.

He said, "I wouldn't mess with those guys if I was you."

I looked at him, wondering if he just threatened me.

He said, "It's just friendly advice."

I still didn't know what to make of what he just said. He didn't look angry. He didn't look mean. I turned and walked away.

On my way back to my desk, I thought of something I could do, and should do. I decided that it was time to talk with Doug and Scott and Garth about how to go after my mom's scammers. It was time to make that phone call to them. It was time to start scamming the scammers.

CHAPTER 6

9:31 AM

Ronja was not in my office, but my computer looked busy, so I sat in my chair, turned to face the room, and said, "I need advice."

Doug, Scott, and Garth swiveled around toward the middle. Scott said, "What's up?"

I was about to say something, then realized I should back up a bit. So I started again. "A few days ago my mom was scammed out of lots of money."

Doug said, "That's terrible, Jeff."

Scott said, "Stupid scammers!"

Garth said nothing.

I continued. "I want to get these guys. I want them put away and locked up."

Scott said, "Yeah! Go for it!"

Doug said, "How did they find your mom?"

"She found their phone number and called them."

"Do you still have the phone number?" Doug asked.

"Yes."

"You haven't called them?"

"I... don't know what to say."

"Swear at them," Scott suggested.

"Call the police?" Doug suggested.

Finally Garth spoke up. "Gentlemen, in such a situation, there can only be one answer. We must ask ourselves this question: What is our goal? What is it we want to see happen? If we swear at them, or if we threaten to call the authorities, they will simply disconnect the call, thus sweeping us away like so many Oreo crumbs, tasty though they may be. I'm sure these scammers are used to such threats and have a well-documented flow chart on how to handle it."

I listened.

Scott said, "Instead we shoot for what?"

Garth answered. "Full network penetration."

We chuckled. Garth certainly shoots big.

Scott said, "OK, what does that look like?"

"Software installed on at least one of their workstations, preferably many if not all of them. We need access to their local files and network files. We need to be able to turn on all their webcams and microphones. We need their Wi-Fi passwords. Everything. Once we have that, they can't hang up on us, or run away, because whatever they do, we will be watching them."

Scott said, "Wow."

I said, "And then we call the police?"

Garth replied, "End it however you like, but if it was up to me, I'd consider taking back what belonged to me."

"That's still theft," I said.

"Call it what you like, Jeffrey, but it has the ring of justice in my ears."

"We can't stoop to their level."

Scott replied, "They started it."

I looked at my friend, wondering what side he was on, but then Doug continued the conversation. He said, "How would we get this software installed on their computers?"

"Simple," Garth said. "We prey on their desires. Everybody wants something. Jeff's mom wanted something. Now Jeff wants something. Even the scammers want something."

"I didn't know you were a Buddhist, Garth," said Doug.

"Buddhism is not a religion; it is a philosophy. And the Noble Eightfold Path is simply good advice, no matter which religion you subscribe to. And as learned as I am on all matters religious, I subscribe to none of them."

This made me curious. Considering the fact that I've been talking with God himself, I should probably look into this religion thing. Maybe Garth can do my research for me. I said, "Why not?"

"Because, dear Jeffrey, all religions are a slap and a Band-Aid. In Hinduism, you are born into a low class. That's the slap. But if you are a good person, you will be reborn into a higher class. That's the Band-Aid to make you feel better. Islam teaches that you must be a devoted servant of Allah. That's the slap. But if you obey the five pillars, you can consider yourself a good Muslim to make yourself feel better. That's the Band-Aid."

"And Christianity?" I asked.

Garth seemed a little agitated. "Christianity is the worst offender of all! It teaches that no matter how good a person you are, everyone is still a sinner. But Jesus can save you, to somehow make you feel better about being a sinner. Religion is just a slap and a Band-Aid. It might make you feel better, but in the end, everyone still dies."

"And you don't feel like being slapped, huh?" Scott asked.

Garth took a breath and regained his composure. "You are correct, Scott Stark. I don't need someone to tell me I need to submit to Allah, or I need to perform certain rituals, or obey Moses's arbitrary ten commandments. I choose to see myself as good enough, not by anyone else's standard, but by my own. I reject the label of sinner and instead view myself with acceptance. Isn't this what healthy self-esteem is all about, the opposite of religion?"

As I sat there, pondering this perspective, Doug commented. "There are those who would take issue with some of that," he said.

Garth rolled his eyes. "Nothing new there."

After a short lull, Scott said, "So, at the risk of not discussing religion, what exactly do the scammers want?"

"I'll tell you, Scott," said Garth. "They want your passwords. They want your banking information. They want your name, address, and telephone number, so they can steal your identity and make bank loans in your name."

I said, "Wow." Then I said, "So... we write software that gets installed on their computers?"

"Oh, my naive friend. Such software has already been written. We are not the first computer programmers to go on the offensive. There is plenty of software out there to choose from."

"On the dark web?" I asked.

"The dark web is a treasure trove for the nefarious at heart."

"But how do I get this software onto their computer?"

"On that, I have some ideas."

The four of us discussed strategy for a few minutes until Victor stopped by to look around and prod us back to work as if we were minimum wage workers on an assembly line, and he wanted to maximize our number of lines of code per hour.

My computer was done doing its thing, so I got back to work. As I sat there, typing up documentation, my mind was busy with ideas on how to go on the offensive with the scammers. Ideas were forming. A plan was taking shape. This evening, after work, Jeff Davis was going to do... something.

10:37 AM

In the silence of work, Scott piped up. "Hey! I just got an email from a contributor with a zip file attached. Should I open it or what?"

I leaned over to look. I didn't recognize the email address. "Do you know this person?" I asked.

He said, "No."

"What does he want?"

"He wants to contribute a change to the UI and is asking what we think of his idea."

"And he zipped the images?"

"I guess so."

"Sounds suspicious."

Doug said, "I often zip a pile of images if there are a lot of them."

"I'm going to open it," said Scott.

"You're risking the wrath of the VP of technology," said Garth.

"You think this is someone trying to scam us?" asked Scott.

"No. That's not what I said. I said Sir Victor will be upset if you open it on your desktop without following proper protocols."

Scott rolled his eyes. "What am I supposed to do? Open this on a different computer?"

"Ronja has a computer set up to test these things," I said.

"Can I send it there over the network?"

"No. It's not on the network."

"So then how? Sneakernet?"

I grinned. "Yeah. Put it on a USB drive and walk over there."

"You want to do it for me, Jeff?"

I contemplated my options. I could do more documentation or I could do anything else. And in this case, I would be following the rules, so Victor couldn't harass me for it. "Sure I will."

"Thanks buddy."

I went and found a USB drive and gave it to Scott who copied the zip file onto it. Then I brought it to the computer Ronja had set up. It was an old laptop in her cubicle. She was there too. I sat down on a footstool and plugged it in. "Scott received a zip file by email, so I'm checking it out."

"Good. That's what the laptop is there for."

I double-clicked the zip file to open it, and when I did, I was greeted with the familiar blue screen with words, "You've Been Hacked!" along with that trumpety sound.

I said, "Uh… Ronja… I got the blue screen again."

She turned around to see too. "What did you do to get this?"

"I just double-clicked the zip file. That's it."

"Where did this file come from?"

"It's Scott's. It got emailed to him."

"It is obviously malware. He needs to permanently delete that email message."

"OK. I'll go tell him. But what do we do about the people trying to hack us?"

"Nothing."

"What?"

"We won't do anything about these blue screens."

"Why not?"

"They're not malicious. They are not doing any wrong. There is no crime happening here."

"Then what's going on?"

"As our boss Victor says, we will obey the rules."

I unplugged the USB drive and stood up. This didn't make sense to me. I walked back to my office to tell Scott.

When I got there, I saw someone I didn't know sitting in my chair. He was older than me. He looked calm and friendly. Victor was saying to everyone, "This is where Nigel will sit." When Victor saw me approaching, he said, "Jim, this is Nigel. He's a new programmer. He will sit in your spot."

I stood there, not saying anything, so he continued. "You will join Andy in his office. It's big enough for two. Bring your computer and equipment there immediately, so Ronja can get this spot set up for Nigel." I didn't move right away, so he pointed at my spot and said, "Go!"

Nigel jumped out of my chair and I walked out there to start unplugging my monitors, keyboard, and mouse. Nigel tried to be friendly and said, "Hi!" to me. I replied with a quick "Hi" back and left it there. My job at Omniscient Technologies was becoming less and less fun.

When Victor had taken the new guy away, presumably to continue the tour of the building, Scott said to me, "It's been good working with you, Jeff."

Doug added, "Yes, it has been, Jeff. Enjoy your time with Andy."

I didn't even know how to respond. Yesterday morning I had a fun job with fun people. This morning I have a grouchy boss. Now, I'm no longer even doing the work I love, and I won't even be sitting with my friends. Life was moving too fast and in the wrong direction.

I gave the USB drive to Scott and said, "Oh, don't open the zip file. It's infected with something."

"With what?" Scott asked.

"That blue screen that says, 'You've been hacked!'. But apparently, nobody cares that someone is trying to hack us."

"That's still a mystery to you, Jeffrey?" Garth asked me.

"Yeah."

"I am surprised."

I didn't know what he meant by that. Was that supposed to be a compliment or not?

I made the short walk from my office, I mean my old office, to Andy's office, I mean my new office, a few times, carrying equipment. It reminded me that my left pinky still hurt. Andy wasn't even in his office. At one point I threw out a "Bye" to the room, and Scott and Doug responded. Garth remained silent, but maybe I didn't care.

After I set up my workstation in Andy's office, including my chair, I looked around the room at all the colorful posters and pictures and art. I thought to myself that I might not be able to concentrate on coding in such an environment. It was too... too... right-brained. Programming is very left-brained, and all this right-brained, colorful, art stimulation might be very distracting. Then I remembered. Oh yeah. I'm not a programmer anymore. I'm doing documentation. I tried not to think about that.

Just then Andy came in, to his own office, carrying a latte. He was wearing a black felt hat with a colorful band around it that looked like pictures of red flowers. Nope, it was pictures of soup cans. When he saw me, he said, "What's up, Jeff? Are you moving in?"

"Yeah. Victor told me to move here. They... they got a new programmer."

"What, someone to replace you?"

I shrugged.

"Well, you and I can create together here. Instead of creating sound and graphics and visual layout and design like I do, you can create code! We'll call this the Creative Cube!"

"I'm not coding anymore. I'm doing documentation."

"Oh. Is that like a demotion? Did you tick off the new boss or something?"

"I don't know. Maybe. I don't think he likes me anyway." I looked to see if anyone was around. "And maybe I don't like him either."

"It is what it is, I suppose. Life throws things at you sometimes." He sat down and put on some expensive-looking headphones.

I looked at the time. Maybe I should go for lunch. I'll see if Cheryl is free.

11:46 AM

On my way to Cheryl's cubicle, I got a text message. I stopped and read it. It was from God. He said, "Go buy a slice of pizza for Garth." I checked the time. I was looking forward to going for lunch with Cheryl, perhaps the last good thing left in my life. Besides God, of course, but that was different.

I put my phone back in my pocket and kept walking toward Cheryl's cubicle. I got another text message. It was from God again. It said, "Do it now." I should probably obey this, but as I was considering not obeying, I got a third text. It said, "Remember, Jeff, I love you very much and I only want what is good for you. I'm trying to help you. I would never lead you into anything that is only bad for you. You can listen to me when I tell you to do something."

I sighed. Then I turned around and headed for the door. I walked down the stairs, out the door of the Johnston Terminal, across the empty pavilion, and into the Forks Market, where I looked for somewhere to buy pizza. I found a place called Red Ember Common, which had a huge stone oven. While I was standing in line, I replied to God and said, "What kind of toppings?"

He replied, "You pick. It's from you."

I thought maybe Garth liked everything, but then again he could be opinionated and like nothing. I played it safe and got pepperoni. In only a few minutes I was holding a small, piping hot pizza in a box. I walked quickly back to our office and placed it on Garth's desk, beside him. He looked at me and said, "What are you doing?"

"I... bought you a pizza."

He looked at it, then back up at me. "For what reason?"

I shrugged. "I was just out there at the food court... and... I had some money on me... and... so I bought you a pizza."

He stared at me some more. Suddenly I got warm and I started fidgeting with something in my pockets. This was probably a bad idea. I wish I could just walk away.

"What kind of pizza is it?" he finally asked.

"Pepperoni."

He kind-of snorted and nodded his head, which I took to mean agreement, or at least he wouldn't argue with me. So I walked away. That was awkward, and it was embarrassing. If the command hadn't come directly from God, I would have said that was the dumbest thing I've ever done in my life.

Soon I would be eating lunch with Cheryl and I could tell her all about it. Just when I reached her cubicle, so did her boss, Kaleisha. She said to me, "No, Jeff, you can't have her. She needs to come to a meeting."

I wouldn't dream of arguing with this woman, so I didn't say anything.

Cheryl came out, carrying a clipboard. She said, "Oh, Hi Jeff. Did you want me for something?"

"Go for lunch?" I asked, quickly, trying to avoid the rebuke of the head of Customer Service.

"Uh uh," Kaleisha shook her head. "We've got a meeting in the board room. You birds will have to wait."

As Cheryl walked away she said back to me, "Oh, Jeff. Remind me I need to ask you something later."

"What?" I asked, but she was gone, and I was left standing alone.

On my way back to my office, Victor spied me and called me into his. I didn't want to talk to this man, but I had no choice. I went in and took a seat. He said, "Have you been doing documentation?"

"Yup." I nodded.

"Good. It is necessary. Keep on doing documentation. You don't need to talk to your friends anymore, unless it is work-related. You may ask them questions about how things work. That is all."

"What if they want to ask me how things work?"

He scowled. "You are not a developer anymore. You do documentation. They are the developers."

I didn't dignify that with a response, so he finally said, "Do you understand?"

I said, "Yes," because I understood exactly what he was saying, even though I hated it.

He continued. "You have broken several security rules here, Jim, so I will now repeat to you the security rules." He went on to repeat the seven rules to me. I nodded once in a while. Then he said, "Do you agree to follow these rules? You must."

I said, "OK."

"Good. You are dismissed. Go back to your documentation."

Without another word, I stood up and left. As I walked past my former office, I noticed nobody was there. They must all be gone for lunch.

I ran out the door, hoping to catch them and join them. I might not be a programmer anymore, but I can still have lunch with whomever I want. They were nowhere to be found.

12:51 PM

I searched the whole Forks Market for my friends but couldn't find them anywhere. I finally grabbed some food from Fergie's Fish 'n Chips and went and sat on a bench by the river.

I was going to take out my phone and write an email to God about what was going on, but instead I decided to do it the old-fashioned way. I just spoke out loud.

When nobody was coming, I said quietly, "God, as you know, Victor is making me do documentation. But I don't want to do it. I want to be a developer. I want to be a programmer."

Then I sat back, closed my eyes, and imagined God sitting next to me on the bench. I could see him smiling at me. He was not upset or mad. He was at peace, and his peace seemed to radiate out toward me. I tried to soak it up like a sponge. It worked a little.

I said, "Do you want to say something about this?"

I could imagine God speaking, and some words came to my mind. They were, "It's OK for life to be hard sometimes, but I am with you. It will be OK."

Those might not be the words I wanted to hear. I would have preferred, "I'll get rid of Adolf for you, so your life can be happy again." That's what I wanted to hear.

I went on to the next topic. I said, "I gave Garth a pizza, like you said to." Then I closed my eyes and imagined God next to me.

He seemed to radiate even more love and acceptance. The words "Well done!" came to my mind. That made me smile. It always felt good to please your boss. I mean God in this case, of course, not Victor Adolf. Victor was impossible to please, and I didn't even want to. But God loved me so much, it felt good to please him. Victor could learn a thing or two from this God of mine on how to be a boss.

I continued, "What about the people trying to hack into our network?" The thought occurred to me that if we had been following Victor's rules, we would have stopped every single one.

I was about to get back to work when I had to bring up one more thing. I said, "I'm going to try to scam my mom's scammers this evening."

Nothing came to me for a while. I imagined God beside me grow sad or something. Finally I these words came to me, "I love all people. I love you, Jeff. I love your mom. I even love the people who scammed her. And I want justice. Justice means your mom gets what she deserves."

I said, "Then why do I sense you are sad?"

He said, "Because justice also means the scammers will get what they deserve, and that makes me sad. I don't like when my children experience pain, even though I know it is the right thing."

I didn't dare say out loud, but I thought to myself, "If you want both good and bad for someone, doesn't that make you schizophrenic or something?"

He said, "No, it means I have both a head and a heart."

I said, "So what do you want me to do?"

He said, "Do the right thing."

"Yeah, but should I follow my head or my heart?"

"Follow wisdom. Work for justice, on both the positive and negative sides. Rejoice with those who receive positive justice, and mourn with those who receive negative justice."

"And my mom should receive the positive and the scammers should receive the negative?"

"That's right. Do that, Jeff."

CHAPTER 7

1:43 PM

I sat down at my computer and checked my email. There was one from Victor that said he was calling a meeting for 1:45 in the board room. That was in two minutes, which gave me enough time to ask Cheryl what she was going to say to me.

I got up to go, but at my office door, the guys were all coming back–Scott, Garth, Doug, and the new guy. They looked happy. Scott said, "Jeff! You should have come with us. We went to The Old Spaghetti Factory."

"I didn't know you were going out."

"Ah, that's too bad. Next time."

"Yeah."

"Hey, have you met Nigel yet? He's a great guy!"

"No, not really."

"Well, say 'Hi' to him. He's friendly. He won't bite."

"Victor called a meeting for right now. In the board room."

"Did he? Oh. OK. We'll be right there."

Scott walked off and I heard him say, "Nigel! Come. There's a meeting in the board room."

I went to see if Cheryl was back from her meeting. She was, so I said to her, "Hi."

She turned around and said, "Hi Jeff."

"You wanted to ask me something."

"Yes. How was lunch?"

"Fine. I grabbed some fish and chips."

"Hey, I wanted to say that my parents were planning on coming over for supper this evening to my place, but..."

Right then all the developers walked past on their way to the board room, and so did Victor. He said to me, "Come, Jim. I have called a meeting." Instead of walking past me, he stood there, waiting for me.

I said, "OK" to him, and to Cheryl I said, "I'll catch you later".

When we were seated in the board room, Victor began. "It has come to my attention that people who work here don't appreciate the fact that their work hours belong to the company. They think they can do whatever they want—go for lunch for as long as they like, or to the hospital, or garage, or even on dates during company time."

Garth had the nerve to reply. "We are salaried employees. We don't work by the hour."

Victor got mad. "It's still company time!" Then he composed himself again. "Yes, you get paid biweekly, but that is no excuse for wasting company time. You are still employees, and you still must put in a full day's work each and every day!"

Nobody dared to say anything. It wasn't fun to be belittled like children. We were professionals who were good at our jobs. We worked hard and produced high quality code. Well, I used to anyway. But I didn't like being talked down to like this. I tried not to get angry. I took some deep breaths.

Victor continued. "I run a tight ship. From now on, you will all log your hours. I have found online software that we will use. When you arrive at work, you will check in. When you leave for a lunch break, or at the end of the day, you will check out. The software will send you each a unique URL to click on where you can register. I will receive reports on your hours. If you have less than the full number of hours at the end of the week, I will talk to you, and it will be noted in your personnel file, and discussed at your annual performance review." He looked at us all. "Are there any questions?"

Garth dared again. "How long will these odious restrictions on our dignity remain in effect?"

Victor hit the table with his hand that time. "As long as it takes for you to start respecting the rules."

Nobody had any other questions, probably because nobody wanted to talk to him. At least I didn't. So we were dismissed out of the board room. By habit, I followed everybody to our room, but I stopped and stood there as my friends sat down and got to work.

I heard the new guy, Nigel, ask what the god account was, so I answered. "It's like God-mode in a computer game. You can log in to anyone's account and do whatever that user can do."

"So God has an email address and password?"

"Yes, he does," I said.

"And if someone logs in as God, and selects a user, is he that user or is he God?"

"Well, you're still God of course. But at the same time, you're limited to what that user can do. So... kind of both God and a regular person... at the same time."

"I guess that makes sense," Nigel responded.

Just then Cheryl showed up at the doorway. "Who?"

"What?" I asked.

"Who are you talking about?"

"Nobody. Just some user who logs in with the god account."

"Oh, I thought you were talking about Jesus."

Every head in the room turned to look at this woman beside me bring up religion. But I suppose by now we should be used to it.

Garth commented. "Are you suggesting, Ms. Customer Service Rep, that Jesus was both a man and God at the same time, in the same way someone can log in to Omniscient using the god account and selecting a user to act as?"

"I… wasn't exactly suggesting that. I just heard people talking about someone being both God and a person. That sounded like Jesus to me, that's all."

Garth said, "We are well familiar with the claims of Christianity, especially the claim of the divinity of the Nazarene."

"Good," Cheryl said, with a touch of confidence. "Everyone should know about Jesus."

Garth, who up till now, had simply turned his head to us, now swiveled his chair and faced Cheryl full on. He said, "We are the computer programmers. We are the ones who understand how computers think. In fact, we think better than they do, because we are their masters, and they are our slaves. We, who are the masters, who create and run the entire world, don't need a young customer service representative, like yourself, to tell us how to think. We think very well on our own, thank-you, and your input is not only not needed, but it is entirely superfluous, like a mosquito buzzing around our very large heads. We don't need your religious advice, young lady."

I looked at Cheryl. She didn't say anything. For a second I thought she might start crying, but she didn't. She turned and walked toward her cubicle. I followed her.

She sat down on her chair with her head down and turned away from me. She busied herself with some papers. She must have known I was there, because she said, "What?" I couldn't quite read her emotions. I didn't know if she was sad or mad or what.

"Umm… I… Garth can be rude sometimes."

"Yes."

"I… I'm sorry."

She turned to me. She looked sort of emotional. "You could have done something."

"What?"

"You could have said something. You could have defended me."

"I..." This was new. What? She is expecting me to defend her? Is she that weak? Is she my damsel in distress? Am I supposed to be some sort of knight in shining armor here? I wasn't used to this. I thought women were strong. For one to submit to my strength, or lack there-of, was a new concept. I mentally tried on the concept. Could I be a man who stood up and defended his woman? The thought almost felt good, but I don't know if I could pull it off. But maybe. "I'm sorry," I said to Cheryl, and I meant it. "Maybe I should have."

My choice of words must have been the right ones, because she nodded. Then she took a deep breath and seemed to recover, which surprised me, because I didn't know an emotional woman could recover so quickly. Maybe she was stronger than I thought.

"I was going to say to you before," she began, "that my parents are coming over to my place this evening for supper. Maybe you would like to join us?"

"Ummm..." I wanted to yell 'No!', because this relationship was going way too fast for me, but instead I said, "Sure." But then I saw her smile, and that brightened me up so much that I was glad I agreed.

"I should get back to work now," she said. "I'll see you at six?"

"OK." I smiled too.

"Great! See you then."

I said, "Yup," then turned to go. This evening I was going to meet Cheryl's parents, including Darryl Bankowsky, her father and part-owner of the company. I wasn't sure how I felt about that. No, scratch that. I knew exactly how I felt—extremely nervous.

3:31 PM

I had been busy documenting code and features, a truly soul-sucking thing to do. In my research, I had pulled out my phone and was examining the UI of the Omniscient software, when I came across an email from God from the previous night. One paragraph jumped out at me.

God said, "I will help you catch these scammers. I will bring you wisdom and counsel. But you will need more than that. You also need hardware, a computer. I am bringing you a server. When you receive it, give it to me. It is mine. From it, I will give you success."

I paused to consider this a moment. God was going to give me a server?

Just then, Garth the heathen darkened the doorway to my room. He looked less than his usual confident self. He almost looked nervous, as if that were possible. He said, "I appreciate, Jeff, your gift of pizza earlier today. It turns out that I do appreciate a good pepperoni pizza."

I said, "You're welcome." Maybe this guy wasn't that bad after all.

"And also, from our discussion this morning, I am aware that you are trying to scam the scammers. In so doing, you will need to install some sort of malware on their machines, and this malware will want to connect to a server in the cloud somewhere to report to and give you access to their computers."

I didn't say anything, because I was busy trying to understand what was going on.

"It turns out," Garth continued, "that I recently began renting a new server in the cloud for my personal purposes, and the server I had been using until now is paid up until the end of the year and I don't need it."

I was in awe.

"And so…" he paused to scratch his armpit. "You can use it if you want to."

"Really?" It must have sounded like I was amazed that Garth would give me something, but really I was more amazed at the fact God told me he was going to give me a server and it just came to me through the hand of Garth Fonte.

"Yes. I will email you the IP address and user name. Here is the password." He handed me a piece of paper with the password. I guess he didn't want that transmitted in plain text by email.

I took it. "Well, thanks, Garth."

"You're welcome." With that, he turned and left, and I was still processing what had just happened. God said he was going to give me a server, and now I have one. And what did he say? Oh yeah, "When you receive it, give it to me. It is mine."

I whispered out loud, "Well God, I have a server now, and… I… give it to you. It is yours. But you probably want me to do something with it, so let me know… or something."

My computer let me know that I just received an email from Garth. It had the details of the server: the IP address, and the user name. I connected to it using SSH, which is a way of talking to a remote computer. It asked me to authenticate, which I did. Using the terminal alone, I checked the RAM, hard drive space, and CPU information. The specs weren't amazing, but it would certainly do.

I couldn't spend my work time playing with my new server. I had to get back to work. But after work this evening, I would… no. Wait. I was going to Cheryl's for supper. Hmmm… and also, I was going to start hacking the scammers this evening. Agh. So many things to do. I looked at the time. And I have to finish work, too.

I got back to the dismal job of documenting when Cheryl poked her head into my room and my personal phone rang at the same time. It was my mom. I said to Cheryl, "It's my mom." She smiled and said, "Take it," then as she was leaving, added, "Say 'Hi' from me."

I answered the phone and said, "Hi Mom."

"Jeff. How are you?"

"I'm fine Mom. Oh, Cheryl says 'Hi' too."

"Cheryl. It was lovely meeting her yesterday. Give her my love too."

"OK."

"Did you meet your father yet?"

Ah yes, memories of that came flooding back. They were not fun memories. "Yes I did."

"And?"

"And what?"

"Did he tell you he became a Christian?"

"Yes," I scowled.

"And?"

"And what?"

"And what do you think?"

"I think if he wants me to be like him, he's got another thing coming."

"But Christians are good people."

"Ha!" Then I said it again. "Ha! My dad, the criminal who tried to kill me. My new boss, who is a jerk. These are not nice people, Mom. They are the dregs of society. No thank-you."

"I thought you would like that he was trying to turn his life around."

"Labeling yourself with your favorite religion doesn't make you a better person. I'll believe it when I see some actual change."

"He gave you his car."

"He's just trying to buy votes."

"Jeff, give him a second chance."

"Did I mention he tried to kill me?"

"Everyone deserves a second chance."

"He can take his second chance in jail where he belongs."

My mom paused, then said, "Well, I would still like you to keep visiting him."

"I don't see why I should."

"Because he's your father, and that's all the reason you need." I didn't reply, so she said, "At least consider it."

"Fine, I'll consider it."

"Thank you." Then she said, "That's all I wanted to say. Have a good day, Jeff."

"Thanks. You too."

"Bye"

"Bye"

I hung up the phone and got back to work.

A few minutes later, Cheryl came back and said, "Jeff."

"Yes?" I turned and replied to her.

"It turns out my little brother is home from University, so my parents want to have supper at their place with him... and me... and you."

I felt my stomach scrunch up. Now I'm going to meet Cheryl's parents at their house? It's probably a huge mansion. I won't be able to relate to them at all. My nervousness just leveled up, but I managed to pluck up my courage and said, "OK".

She smiled. "Great! I'll see you there at 6:00. It will be fun!"

"Yeah."

She told me the address and left. I looked it up online. Yeah, it was a large house, on the river. I sighed. Maybe it wouldn't be that bad. I could hope.

5:06 PM

I sat at home on my laptop. I didn't have to bother making supper, so I got busy preparing for the scammers.

I hadn't checked out of our fancy new time tracking software, because I hadn't checked in at all. That would start tomorrow.

Tomorrow I would have to check my minutes like a child for his mama.

Right now, I had a few minutes before I had to go for supper with rich people. I wanted to use those minutes getting my new server ready, I mean God's new server ready, for use in scamming the scammers, but I forgot the piece of paper with the password on it, so instead I worked on the malware I would use to gain access to the scammer's computer.

Malware is not exactly a virus. A virus does something nasty on your computer, then duplicates itself and tries to send itself everywhere else it can, usually over your network or by sending email from your address book. The thing I was making wouldn't duplicate and spread. It would only do something nasty, and the nasty thing is everything. If I could get it installed on someone else's computer, it would give me complete control of their entire computer, in every respect. First, it would connect to my new server, so I would know it was there. From that point on, I could control that computer as easily as my own.

The hard part was getting the scammer to install the software. I thought about how I would be able to do this. Then it occurred to me that all the ways I thought of were exactly against all of Victor's safety rules. I grinned to myself. Instead of following the rules myself, I would be hoping that the bad guys wouldn't be following the rules themselves. If they followed all the rules, there was nothing I could do. But if they messed up, like I messed up once or twice already, I would gain access to their computer. And once I have their computer, that's only one step away from the people themselves.

All computers try to make themselves secure—they put on armor. In order to break through the armor, one needs to find a chink in the armor, or a gap between the plates. A system that is fully patched with all the latest software updates shouldn't have any of these security holes.

My choices were few. Maybe I could find a very recent security hole that had only recently been discovered, before the responsible party has had a chance to patch their software. This was called a zero-day vulnerability. They are very hard to find if you are looking yourself. But there might be some out there, hiding on the dark web, that are for sale for the right price. I decided to not spend money trying to buy knowledge of a zero-day, mostly because people who sell these vulnerabilities are by definition completely unscrupulous, and they would have no problem taking my money and giving me nothing in return. I didn't want to risk being treated like a sucker. And besides, I might not have the expertise to create functioning malware from it.

The other way to hack into someone's computer is to use a known vulnerability and hope the owners of that computer haven't applied the security updates yet. This happens, and it happens all too often.

There are other ways to gain access, of course. The famous virus Stuxnet used many ways to do its thing. For one thing, it used stolen public key certificates from two well-known companies, JMicron and Realtek in Taiwan. Of course, Stuxnet took a team of programmers many years to develop. I didn't have nearly that time, nor the required resources.

I decided on using a known vulnerability, and hoped I could sucker the scammers into opening it.

I wasn't done getting everything ready, but pretty soon it was time to leave. If I wanted to be on time for supper, I would have to leave now.

I would get back to this soon, maybe this evening. My plan to scam the scammers was coming together. But first I had to plunge myself into the unknown and confusing world of human social interaction.

6:02 PM

I pulled into the driveway at 373 Kingston Crescent. Kingston Crescent is a road that curves around the inside of a loop of the Red River. They are all riverfront properties. It's where rich people live.

In the driveway, I noticed a red Porsche, a tan Toyota, a Mazda, and a Pontiac convertible. If I had to guess, I would guess that Cheryl drove the Mazda, and her brother drove the Porsche, and her mom drove the Toyota, and her dad... nah, I gave up.

I parked and walked slowly toward the door, feeling a deep pressure on my chest. It was most likely just stress, but still, it didn't feel good.

To my intense relief, Cheryl met me at the door so I wouldn't have to knock or ring the doorbell. "Hey Jeff!" she beamed. "Welcome to my home, well, my childhood home." She held the door open for me.

"It's good to see you too, Cheryl."

An older woman, presumably Cheryl's mom, came to welcome me. She didn't share her daughter's red hair. It was brown. She was no taller than Cheryl, and even slimmer. "You must be Jeff. We've heard all about you." She held out her hand and I shook it. She stopped talking, as if I were supposed to say something, but I couldn't think of anything to say, since she didn't ask me a question, so I said, "Yeah." She chuckled at that, as if I made a joke. "Come in, we all want to meet you."

We walked out of the entrance into the rest of the house, which was quite open. To our right was the living room. I recognized Darryl from his picture at Omniscient. His hair was even grayer, and not red either. I didn't know where Cheryl got her red hair from, but when I saw her younger brother, he had it too.

Darryl seemed friendly. He smiled at shook my hand. "It's good to meet you, Jeff. Welcome here. We have a good meal planned."

I said, "Thanks." It will certainly be easier to get along with these people, since they seem friendly. My parents were never this friendly. It must have been nice to grow up with parents who were nice instead of parents who fought each other and one of them leaves.

"Come join us in the living room," Darryl said. "We were just talking."

I went and sat down with them. Cheryl's brother, who was already sitting there, looked like a younger, male, version of her.

Darryl said, "That's a nice car you're driving there, Jeff. We must be paying you well at Omniscient."

He was referring to my dad's Mercedes. "Oh. Thanks. It... a... was a present from my dad."

"Sweet deal," Cheryl's brother said. "It must be nice to have a dad who buys you a Mercedes." He was looking at his dad, with the slightest hint of a smile.

"Yeah, yeah," his dad replied to him. "Your car if fine. Besides, you're twenty and you don't need me to buy you cars."

"Hey, I'm just saying that the car I drive directly reflects on your skill as a businessman, that's all. When people see me driving a Mazda, they might think that you aren't successful enough to buy your son a real car. I'm looking out for your reputation here, Dad."

I couldn't tell if he was serious or not, but I guess he wasn't because his dad said, "Ha. Ha. Nice try." I guess that means Darryl drives a Porsche. That's not bad. I could respect a man who drives a Porsche.

Then Darryl turned to me and asked, "What is it your dad does for a living, Jeff?"

I stammered. "He... uh... he ran a business."

"Ran? What happened?"

Meeting Cheryl's dad was one thing. The fact that he was rich was another. But admitting that my own dad is in jail–that was a new level of uncomfortable. "He... ummm... went to jail." I'm pretty sure the sweat was soaking right through my shirt.

"Oh! Oh. That's too bad. What for?"

I may as well come clean now. "He was selling private information, including corporate espionage and blackmail."

"Oh! That's right! I read about that. That was your father?!"

"Yeah. That part didn't make the news, thankfully."

Cheryl's brother, whatever his name was, said to me, "So hang on here, Jeff. I read about this too, obviously, since it's the family business."

"Not really," Darryl interjected.

"So you're telling us that this Jade, that you helped to put away, is actually your dad?!"

I nodded.

He grinned at his dad. "Just think how much more you love me now, knowing that I have never put you in jail. Doesn't that just strengthen our relationship?"

"Our relationship is already strong, and I have never done anything that deserves jail."

"That we know of."

"I haven't, and you know it."

"You just keep saying that in front of our guest."

"Do you want me to disinherit you?"

What was even more shocking than these words was the fact that these two men were completely joking. They seemed to be having a great time poking each other. They weren't just trying to not tick each other off, it seems like there was nothing to be ticked off. I didn't know that was possible. Up until that day I had never witnessed such a father-son relationship in my life. It was fascinating. I was almost a little jealous.

Cheryl came to us and announced, "Supper is ready." She stayed around me and we walked to the table together. We sat down on one side. Her parents were at either end, and her brother was opposite us.

I looked at the salad and lasagna and said, "This looks delicious." It was a bold move for me, to say something out loud unprovoked, but I was trying to be social.

"Thank you," Cheryl's mom said.

Then Darryl said, "Let's pray," and everyone bowed their heads. I did too, of course, because everyone else did. Then he said some words, as if talking to God, then ended it with "In Jesus' name, amen."

That's when the penny dropped. I couldn't believe I had been so blind, so stupid. Why had I not seen this sooner? These people were Christians! These people were the very thing I just railed at Mom about. I had yelled at my dad that I would never be a Christian like him. My boss Victor was one of these people. Didn't I make a vow that I would never be like these people? I did. And now I was here in their home. And Cheryl was one of them. I froze. I didn't know what to do. Should I leave? Should I stay? I had no idea. I was confused.

Then I noticed everyone was staring at me, and Cheryl's mom was trying to hand me the salad. I woke up from my stupor and took the salad.

"Jeff," Cheryl said. "Is everything OK?"

"Yeah," I lied. "I'm fine." Just when I was starting to enjoy this evening, I wanted to leave. But I still wanted to stay. Maybe we should change the subject. Thankfully, someone did.

CHAPTER 8

6:26 PM

"I thought we were going to have tuna casserole," Darryl said, as he helped himself to lasagna.

"No, Daddy, " Cheryl said, "I was going to make tuna casserole, but Mom made lasagna since we're eating here." She took some salad.

"It's all because of me," Cheryl's brother said. "I'm sorry you didn't get your tuna casserole, Dad."

"Oh, it's no problem. I don't like fish that much anyway."

"Tuna isn't fish anyway, Dad. I'm sure you know that."

"What?" said Cheryl.

"You haven't heard? It's actually vegetation that grows on the seafloor."

"Seaweed?" asked his sister.

"Something like it. You see, when they send the ships out to supposedly catch tuna, they actually harvest the vegetation and bring it back to the canning factory where it is processed."

"Really?"

"Haven't you ever wondered why you can never buy a whole tuna fish? Because they don't exist."

"I've seen videos," Cheryl said.

"Oh, those fish they show you in the videos are actually a species of marlin. They don't taste a thing like tuna. That's just PR."

"It's a giant hoax?"

"Well, it's not really a secret, per se. It's just that the secret has gone on so long that nobody cares anymore. The packagers put pictures of that marlin on the can, because that's what everyone expects to see. I had a buddy who worked in the plant out in Nova Scotia. He told me the whole thing."

"And you believed him?"

"I looked it up myself on the Internet. Wikipedia has the whole thing in black and white. Most people just don't care to look it up. You all should be happy I told you now. Can you believe how embarrassing it would be to tell your friends you actually thought tuna was fish?" he laughed. "It's funny when you think about it."

Cheryl's mom said to her son, "You're a goofball."

Cheryl turned to me. "Don't believe him, he has a vivid imagination." Then turning to her brother, she said, "Tim, you should be a writer with all your crazy ideas."

"A writer, huh?"

"Yeah. You could make yourself the main character of a book."

"Oh, I would never do that. If I did that, everyone would say, 'Your main character is so much like you!'. No, if I wrote something, I'd make myself an obscure minor character in the second book or something.

"Do what you like," Cheryl said.

"Thanks. I was planning to."

After a small pause, Cheryl's mom broke the silence by asking me, "So, Jeff, you work at Omniscient Technologies?"

I said, "Yes," and she kept looking at me, so I tried thinking of something else I could say. Then I added, "I'm a programmer." Then I remembered that I wasn't a programmer anymore and was going to mention it, but she continued.

"That's interesting. Omniscient is a good app."

"We make clients for smartphones and a web client too."

"Clients? You mean apps?"

I thought about that then said, "Yes."

"And these apps all talk to each other?"

"Yes. Well, they talk to the server that coordinates everything."

She looked at me and said, "I often hear people talking about servers. What is a server?"

I started to say something, then backed up. I sat up and finally said, "A server is something that serves."

"Serves what?"

"Well, print servers serve you a printer. And a file server serves you files. And a web server serves you web pages."

"Don't forget a food server," said Tim.

I smiled. "A person at a restaurant who gives you your food would be a food server."

"Like a servant?" she asked.

I thought about that. "I guess so. An email server is your servant because it fetches you your email."

"I thought a server was a kind of computer that ran in the server room," Cheryl said.

I replied, "A server could be either hardware or software. If a computer is a server, it means it's not designed to be used as a workstation by a person. It probably has no sound card, and a very poor graphics card, and big fast hard drives. But it's still a computer."

"So a server computer runs server software?" Cheryl's mom asked.

"Yes. But you could run server software on any desktop or even a phone if you wanted to."

"Well, I guess I'll leave that stuff up to the professionals. You know that Darryl here owns part of Omniscient?"

"Yes, I… saw his picture in the board room."

"Oh. I thought Cheryl would have told you."

"I decided not to tell anyone, remember Mom?" Cheryl said. "I don't want to get preferential treatment because my dad owns the company."

Right then Tim started half coughing half choking, but he was faking it. "Sorry," he said. "I'm fine. It's just that the thought of not using your dad's wealth and position to get ahead really startled me there. I've never considered that before." He shivered. "It's a crazy idea. Are you feeling OK Cheryl?"

Cheryl rolled her eyes. "I got my job fair and square."

"Suit yourself," he said. "But I think when you're climbing the ladder, it's fair to use any handle or leverage you can get."

"I like to think I raised an honorable son," Darryl said, with a grin. "But I wonder sometimes." Everyone else laughed at this. Where I came from, this would have been a painful wound. I was amazed that these people could talk so freely with each other without getting offended. They were somehow... different.

Tim put his hands over his heart in mock pain. "I am wounded, father."

"I'm just kidding, Tim. You are a great son, and very honorable."

"That's more like it," he replied and got back to eating.

That was probably the highlight of the evening. It went downhill from there.

6:49 PM

The rest of supper consisted of small talk and Tim being goofy. I was doing quite well at socializing, I thought.

Then something happened that I was not expecting. It rocked my world.

At one point, when we were eating pie, Cheryl's mom asked Cheryl, "Do you work with many Christians?"

Cheryl replied, "Not many, except Jeff." Then turning to me, she said, "Right?"

Then all eyes were on me, waiting for me to casually agree, except that the thought of being a Christian like my terrible boss and like my murderous dad was not something I could handle. I couldn't even bring myself to lie. I could have justified an answer by rephrasing the question in my mind to mean "There aren't many Christians at work, are there?" If I convinced myself that that was the question, I could respond in the affirmative, as if to say, "Yes, there aren't many." But I couldn't even bring myself to say that. And by the time I had considered that, there were so many eyes on me, I had to say something.

And when I didn't immediately answer this question that should have been the world's quickest answer, the room got quiet. I finally said something like "The Director of Technology is a Christian."

Cheryl's parents slowly looked away, as if I had personally hurt them. Cheryl kept staring at me with some strange expression on her face. I couldn't explain it. Was she sad? Hurt? Confused?

After a few minutes, everyone seemed to recover, much like Cheryl had recovered after Garth said those mean things to her. But it wasn't the same after that. They were a bit too polite.

It was one thing to be awkward at a social gathering, but I didn't want to make other people feel awkward too, so early into the evening I thanked everyone for having me over. They were gracious and said kind words back to me. When I made my way to the door, Cheryl came with me. She walked with me to my car, then got in and sat down on the passenger's seat.

We sat there for a while until she finally said it. "So, you're not a Christian?"

"My boss, Adolf, is a Christian. My dad who tried to kill me is a Christian. I'm not going to be like them."

"But what about God? His email address? Talking with him? You obviously believe in God, don't you?"

"Yes. I can't help that."

"And don't you feel something inside when he talks to you?"

"Yes."

"So what's the problem?"

"I... I don't know. Maybe I just want to be my own man. Maybe I'm tired of everybody trying to make me do things. Adolf is making me do documentation, and my dad wants me to become a Christian like him, and my mom wants me to keep visiting my dad. And now you... you want me to become a Christian too. I'm sorry. Maybe I'm going to do what I want to do, not what everybody else wants me to do. I... there's just too much pressure. I can't take it."

I was surprised by her answer. She simply said, "OK," and got out of the car. Then she shut the door.

As I drove away, I thought about the evening. Her family seemed nice enough, but I couldn't handle it right now. Part of me was glad to leave early, because that gave me more time to plan my attack on the scammers. I still needed to configure my new server. I could log in from home and install the right software I needed on it.

Then I remembered that I didn't have the password. It was written on a piece of paper, and I had forgotten that at work. No problem, I could stop by the Forks on my way home.

8:24 PM

I parked my car in the parkade and walked out the back toward the Johnston Terminal. It was dark out, but it was only because of the clouds. A storm had rolled in. It wasn't raining yet, but the wind had picked up.

I had just left the protection of the parkade when four men ran up and surrounded me. They were wearing ski masks and dressed in black. I had no idea who these people were, and expected that they didn't know me either. I, of course, stopped and looked around at them, wondering what was going on, hoping that nothing bad was going to happen.

To my surprise, one of them said, "Jeff Davis?"

I didn't know if I should respond or not. If people knew who I was, would they be more likely to hurt me or not hurt me? I didn't have any enemies, that I knew of, so I said, "Yes."

He said, "We have a message for your dad."

If this was going to be a words-only exchange, I could probably handle it. I hoped it was. I hoped it wouldn't get physical. I wouldn't know how to handle that. I said, "What's the message?"

He said, "This." Then the three others rushed at me. The first one hit me on the jaw, and the one behind me kicked my legs out from under me. I went down to the ground. My jaw hurt, as did my leg. I didn't have much time to ponder this or feel sorry for myself, because they didn't stop. When someone kicked me in my stomach, I doubled over and grabbed myself. I also closed my eyes, which means I didn't see all the other blows and kicks that were coming. I cried out when someone's foot landed on my back. My vision got blurry when someone kicked my head. Blows began landing all over my body.

I had never been in a fight before. I had never gotten beat up before. I didn't know what to do. In my distress, in my mind, I cried out to God for help. I prayed to the one who said he loved me, who claimed he was my father. The blows kept landing, and God wasn't answering. My head hurt. My face hurt. I was in pain all over. And God wasn't answering. I opened my eyes and looked up into the sky. There was nothing but darkness.

Another kick rolled me over onto my side and instead of looking at the sky, I was looking at the bushes next to the parkade. Then I remembered what had happened here three weeks ago. With all the strength I had left, I started crawling toward the bushes. This allowed my attackers to kick my ribs and stomach, unhindered, which they did. I got knocked down twice on my way to the bushes, but I finally made it there. Another kick to my head brought me down to the ground again, but I had arrived. I reached out my hand and felt the ground behind the bush. Nothing. Then I reached with my other arm and closed my hand around the thing I had tossed into these very bushes not that long ago. It was a gun, the same gun I had shot my father with.

When my fingers closed around that weapon, something changed inside of me. Something snapped. Suddenly I was no longer the Jeff Davis that people bossed around. I was done being bossed around. Now I had the power. Now I was the boss. Suddenly the world answered to me.

Up until that moment in my life, I may not have ever, not even once, told anybody what to do. That old me was weak. This was the new me. I pointed the gun at my attackers and yelled through my bruised and bloodied face, "Stop!" Now I was giving the orders. Jeff Davis was the boss. "Stop it! Get away from me!" When they saw my weapon and heard my threat, every one of these men stopped their assault, turned, and ran away. And when I saw that they did, something inside me sparked. I felt something new, something I've never felt before. It was the feeling of power. It was glorious. It numbed all the other pain in my life. It was a drug, and it felt good. It saved my life. This was the new me.

When I had caught my breath, the old me might have rolled around on the ground or called an ambulance for help, but not the new me. I stood up. My feet were wobbly, my head was spinning, and I had to steady myself as if I were drunk. But at least I was up. Nobody helped me. I did it myself. See? I didn't need anybody. Jeff Davis was all I needed.

I made my way to our building limping, but in control. As I swung this gun in my hand I wondered what other people might think. They would conclude that there goes a powerful man, and they would be right. If they called the police, I wouldn't care. I could take care of myself. I took care of myself with a pile of attackers, and I could take of myself with the police.

It hurt to walk all the way to my desk and pick up the piece of paper, but I did it. It hurt to walk all the way back to my car, but I did it. On the way it started to rain, but I didn't care. I pointed the gun up at the sky and pulled the trigger a few times. It just clicked, because it was empty. I knew that. It doesn't take bullets to control people. It only takes power, and I had that.

When I got into my car, I considered going to the hospital, but then caught myself thinking like the old me. I didn't need more people telling me what to do, and waiting in their lineups. I was my own man. I didn't need any nurses to do that for me. I'll go home and clean myself up.

I got into my Mercedes and gunned the engine. I drove fast out of the parking lot and swerved while turning onto the road. I ran a few stop signs and red lights, and drove as fast as I liked. The new Jeff Davis did whatever he liked.

9:42 PM

I parked slightly crooked in my parking spot outside my apartment simply because I could park however I wanted to.

As I was getting out of the car, my phone told me I got an email. It was from Cheryl. With the door open, I sat and read it.

From: cherylb@omniscient.software
To: jeffd@omniscient.software
Subject: Us
Hi Jeff.

I don't know how to say this, so I'll just say it. I have enjoyed going for lunches and talking and spending time with you for these last few weeks. I admit I have grown close to you. Until this evening I wanted our relationship to progress even more, and I was looking forward to it. In some ways I still want that, but it can't be. Jeff, I can't pursue a romantic relationship with someone who's not a Christian. As much as I like you, I can't.

I'm sorry.

If we see each other at the office, we can still talk of course, but we can't go on dates, not even just for lunch.

I'm sorry again.

—

Cheryl Bankowsky

I read the whole email, then read it all again. Multiple strong emotions mixed inside of me. I said out loud, "Fine. I don't need you. I don't need anyone." I was about to put my phone away when I received another email. It was from God.

Anger rose up inside me. "You?!" I punched the phone with my finger to delete the message, then got out of the car. It was raining, but I didn't care. I shouted at the black sky. "You?! You think you can waltz in here now and speak some cute words to me? After I get beaten up? After you let me get beaten up? You didn't do anything to stop that, did you? No! You let this happen. Not only that, it's your fault Cheryl broke up with me. She only wants to date Christians, so I guess I'm out, huh? And now you think you can just send me a cute email and we're buddy pals again? I don't think so. So why don't you just stay in your Heaven and I'll stay on my Earth, and we'll both get along just fine?"

My phone didn't make any more noise all the way inside, and that suited me just fine.

By the time I dragged myself up the stairs, I was in no mood to work on a server. I popped a pile of painkillers, had a shower, and lay down gently in bed. I didn't sleep well, if at all.

Everything hurt despite the drugs, and I kept having this one thought. Who in the world would send a message to my dad by beating me up? Whoever it was, was going to pay.

CHAPTER 9

Thursday 8:04 AM

I was late checking into work, because I was still limping and I hurt pretty much all over. My face was scratched up and red in places. All the bleeding had stopped, but I still didn't look good. My left hand still had a cast on it. I didn't walk past Cheryl's cubicle on my way to my desk.

I sat at my new desk, typing documentation, when Adolf poked his head in.

"You're late, Jim."

I swiveled around to face him, and when I did, I could see he was shocked to see me.

"What happened to you?" he asked.

"I fell down the stairs," I lied, and I didn't care. I noticed he had something on his face, beside his nose. It may have been a piece of egg or something. I didn't say anything. I hoped it would be embarrassing for him. The longer it stayed there the better.

He regained his composure. "Make sure you finish a full day today."

"Of course."

Then he left and I said to myself, "...mein fuhrer."

Andy came in too. He looked at me and said, "Oh, dude! What happened?"

"Got into a fight."

"Really? You didn't strike me as the fighting kind."

"You should see the other guys," I said.

"Yeah. Right. Well, remind me to stay on your good side."

"That's a good side to be on."

Scott walked past and yelled, "Hey Jeff!"

I said, "Hi!" Then I heard him laughing. I wondered what was so funny, then I realized that Garth probably has his Joke-of-the-Day up.

I went to read it. It said, "Your mama's so FAT, she can't save files over 4 GB." I laughed too, despite my misery. Garth was already there, and so was Doug. Scott just sat down. Then the new guy, Nigel, showed up.

He said, "Good morning, Jeff," to me, so I said, "Hi" back to him. I may as well be polite.

Nigel read the joke, sat down, then said, "I know FAT stands for File Allocation Table. Does it have a file size limit of 4 GB?"

"Yes," said Garth. "It does. FAT's file size limit is four gigabytes. More modern file systems have more. EXT4 has a file size limit of sixteen terabytes, and NTFS has a file size limit of sixteen exabytes."

"That's good to know," said Nigel.

"Except nobody uses FAT anymore," said Doug. "Exactly for that reason."

Victor came in and said, "Scott, you're late. I expect you to still put in a full day."

Scott shrugged. "I'll try, but you might need to remind me later in case I forget."

Victor pointed at him. "Remember!" Then he left.

When he was gone, Scott said, "Wow, did you see the booger on that guy's face?"

We laughed.

"Speaking of faces," Scott said again, "What happened to yours, Jeff?"

"It turns out that my dad still has some enemies out there."

"Aren't you one of them?" Garth asked.

That was a good question, and I didn't have an answer. "These guys didn't think so. They were sending a message to Jade through me."

"Take care of yourself, Jeff," said Doug. I remembered he was the one who gave me the gun, and may have been referencing that fact in his words.

I looked at him. "I will."

Just then Kaleisha, the head of Customer Service came up to me and said, "Jeff, I have something to say to you." Then she looked at me and said, "Eww! What happened to your face?"

"I got into a fight."

"By the look of that, I hope you won."

"In a sense I did." I was of course referring to the fact that I ended up chasing all my attackers away.

"Anyway... I wanted to tell you something."

"What?"

"When I came into work today, I was walking in with Cheryl." I didn't know if I wanted to hear this, but she continued. "I said to her that the other day I saw a man drop something on the floor outside our office and when I told him, he denied that it was his. Cheryl thought you should know that."

"Cheryl said I should know this?"

"Yeah. She said I should tell you. I don't know why she just didn't tell you herself." Then her eyelids narrowed and she pointed at me. "You didn't do anything to hurt her, did you? Because nobody hurts my girls."

"No!" And this woman had some nerve to accuse me. "Can you describe what this man looked like?"

Kaleisha relaxed her accusatory stance. "He had darker skin. Not as dark as mine. I'm guessing India. He had a slight Indian accent. He hung around for a while, then went into that shop on the other side of the stairs."

"Would you recognize him if you saw him again?"

"Probably."

I took a deep breath and tried to chase away the nervousness and terror of what I was planning to do. I said, "Please come with me."

"OK, where are we going?"

As we walked past Victor's office, I saw he wasn't in, but the USB stick was lying on his desk. I grabbed it, then kept walking down the hall. Kaleisha followed.

We walked past Cheryl's desk, but I didn't even stop to see if she was there. Well, I couldn't help myself. Yes she was, but I had something to do.

We marched out of our office and past the stairs.

"We're not going in there, are we?" she asked.

"Yes we are."

I pushed through the door and we stood there. The receptionist man was in front of us. "Can I help you?" he asked. I ignored him. I scanned the room and saw other desks with a few people behind them. There were other offices with closed doors, and we couldn't see people in there.

"Do you see him?" I asked Kaleisha.

"No."

I turned toward the receptionist. "Can we speak with your manager please?"

He said, "Do you have an appointment?"

"No."

"Then I'm sorry. I can't help you."

"I'd like to make an appointment with him."

"I'm sorry. He is not in today."

"When will he be in?"

Kaleisha said, "Maybe he doesn't work here."

The receptionist said, "It's hard to say, sir. He doesn't have a set schedule."

I said, "What is his name?"

"Who's name, sir?"

"The name of your manager. Don't you have a boss here?"

"Of course, sir."

I felt like I was losing control, like the previous night. Then I remembered that I was in control. I put my hands on his desk and leaned forward. "Tell me his name."

He paused, then said, "Yash. Yash Nagi."

"Maybe I'll stop by sometime to talk with him."

When I stood up again, he said to me, "It looks like you've been in an accident, sir. You should take care of yourself."

I stared at him for some time, and he didn't look away. Finally he said, "Is there anything else I can help you with, sir?"

I said, "No." Then Kaleisha and I left and went back to work.

9:20 AM

I dragged another hour of documentation out of me before I received an email from my mom.

From: Julie Davis

To: Jeff Davis

Subject: Message from your father

Your dad said your meeting yesterday didn't go very well. Are you OK Jeff? Is there something you should be telling me?

Anyway, he said I should pass on a message to you to be careful. That's what he said. He said you should be careful. I don't know any more than that, because that's all he told me. Maybe you should see him again yourself. I get the feeling he isn't telling me everything either.

I hope everything is OK with you. I'll see you soon.

Love, Mom.

I leaned back in my chair and contemplated this. I should be careful? What does that mean? Is he threatening me? Is he trying to protect me from other people? Yeah, he's probably trying to warn me to not get beaten up. Somehow I got caught in the middle of a feud between my dad and some other monster. They are getting to Jade by beating me up, but he knows about it somehow and is trying to warn me. It's a little late for that, buddy.

I closed my eyes and remembered the previous night, getting kicked and hit and abused. I remembered crying out to God who claimed he loved me and yet did nothing. I remembered closing my hand around a firearm and pointing it at bad people. That felt good. It felt good inside. And it felt good to tell people what to do and they did it. It was a powerful feeling, this feeling of power. And it was mine. This was the new me. I didn't need anyone except me.

Just then my boss came in and said, "How's the documentation going, Jim?"

I spun around and said, "Terrible!" I noticed he still had something on his face. I hoped it was embarrassing for him.

He said, "Why?"

"It's stupid! Documentation is stupid! It's a waste of time! I should be writing new code and developing the software, instead of writing about it. And it's dumb to even ask me to do it. It's a waste of my time."

He scowled. "We've had this discussion before."

"I still don't like it."

"You will do as you're told."

"Maybe. Maybe not."

He shook his head as if not sure what to do with me. Then he ducked away. Pretty soon he was back and said, "Fine. If you don't want to do this, you can work for Ronja. She needs help cleaning the servers."

"I would love to!" I said.

"Good. Go report to her." He left.

I stood up and walked around a while until I had cooled off a little. I didn't know what was going on with the servers, but at least I wasn't doing documentation anymore. Then I found Ronja in the server room and said, "Victor wants me to work for you."

She was standing behind the server rack, fiddling with something. "You can hand me a new network cable from that box."

"The box labeled 'network cables'?"

"Yes. This port is flapping. It might be a bad cable."

I didn't know if she was serious. I'd never heard of a flapping port. It sounded like one of those things you say to a noob who doesn't know anything, just to make fun of him. As I rummaged through the box, I asked, "What's a flapping port?"

"If the network goes up and down many times a second. It's usually a bad network cable. At least I hope so."

It sounded reasonable, and she wasn't laughing, so I handed her a cable.

She looked at it and said, "No, I need a yellow one. It's inside the firewall."

I didn't know her color scheme, so I kept rummaging. I finally found a yellow network cable and gave it to her. She plugged it in and went to the workstation in the server room and set the KVM (Keyboard Video Mouse) to the correct server. After running a command and looking at the text output on the screen, she smiled and announced, "Good. That fixed it."

While I stood there doing nothing, she looked at me and said, "So, what else can you do, Jeff?" Then, "Yes, I can think of something. It is on our yearly maintenance task list to clean out the servers."

I said, "What needs to be done to them?"

"They get dusty. They need to be taken apart and dusted."

She pointed out to me which servers needing cleaning, and how to open the cover while leaving the machine running. She showed me the cans of compressed air to blow out the dust. If that wasn't enough, there was isopropyl alcohol and the toothbrush I should use to scrub the caked dust.

I got to work. I dusted and cleaned. I took apart and put back together.

At one point Scott came in and asked what I was doing. I said, "I'm cleaning the servers."

"Wow. You really got on Adolf's bad side, huh?"

"I guess so."

"I hope it all works out for you, Jeff."

"Thanks."

Then he left and I was all alone again. Pretty soon I was done cleaning the servers. Instead of going to Ronja for something else to do, I had to go see Victor.

11:09 AM

I walked into my boss's office and sat down.

"Are you done cleaning servers?" he asked, without looking up.

"Yes."

"If you need more work, go talk to Ronja. You work for her."

"I don't suppose," I began, "that you care that I may have found out who is trying to hack into our network."

He looked at me. "What are you talking about?"

I was surprised he didn't know, or didn't care. "It all started with the USB stick two days ago, with malware on it. Then Cheryl got a PDF, then Scott got a zip file. People are trying to hack into our network."

"Don't worry about that. You just follow the rules."

"We need to find these guys."

"No."

"No?"

"No. Don't concern yourself. I say so."

I threw my hands up. "Of course. Why should I care about security around here?"

"If you really cared about security, you wouldn't have plugged in that USB drive, and you wouldn't have opened those attachments. That's the security you should be worried about."

"And what about finding the people doing this? What about bringing these people to justice?"

"Forget your justice. It's not important."

"Justice is important! It is... critical. Without justice, we... have nothing! We can't just let the bad guys do whatever they want. They must be stopped."

"I've told you many times now. Do not think about it. Do not go there. Focus on obeying the security rules. Do not put your time into finding anyone. This is not your concern. This is not something you should care about."

"I do care about justice, but you don't. You don't care about finding who's trying to hack into our network. You don't care about us managing our own time. You don't care about what skills I have to offer. You don't care about anything except your stupid rules."

"Rules you will follow."

"No I won't."

"Yes you will."

"No I won't, because I quit."

"You're quitting?!"

"Yeah. I can't take this anymore. I can't take it."

"You can't quit unless I say you can, Jim."

For a split second the room became very quiet. Then I stood up and yelled in his face, "My name's Jeff!"

I turned around and stomped out of his office. Everywhere I looked, people had their heads out of their cubicles and were staring. They obviously heard our conversation. I didn't care. I marched down one hallway, right past Cheryl without saying a word, turned a corner, and proceeded down that hallway too. I left our office, and took the stairs down. By the time I got to the main floor and out the door, my heartbeat had slowed down but was still going.

I didn't know where I was going. I didn't know what I was doing. I walked out to my car, my Mercedes, and got in. I started driving. I drove out the parking lot and down the road. I was gone. I was free. No more Victor Adolf. No more documentation, no more servers, no more... people I didn't need anyway.

I drove around the city for a while, even exceeding the speed limit, half hoping I would get pulled over, but nothing happened.

Then suddenly I knew what I had to do. It might be dangerous, but that bridge had already been crossed. It might even be illegal, but maybe pursuing justice was a higher calling. It was something I had never done before.

I pulled out my phone and searched for just the right store. When I found it, I headed out there right away.

1:05 PM

It was a small store in a strip mall on the edge of town. The sign read "Mike's Tatoo and Guns".

All over the wall to the left were photographs of tattoos. Some were on people, and some were just sketches on paper. Some were black outlines, some were colorful flowers or abstract. Some looked exactly like photographs. The one in the middle caught my eye. It was the word "broken" in a style that displayed the very essence of the word. The word was split almost in half, and bricks were falling out of it, like a building was coming down. I found it irritating. Why someone would willingly put this on their body was beyond me. Shouldn't we try hard to keep ourselves together? To display this was like admitting defeat. It was stupid.

On the right were shelves of guns, all behind glass. I had never seen so many guns before in my life. Some were small handguns like I had, and some were rifles for hunting I supposed. Some appeared to be military grade. I had no idea it was even legal to own those. I tried to pick out something that looked like mine.

By the time I got there, a man came out from the back and said, "Can I help you find something?"

His appearance surprised me. I guess I was expecting someone with a scraggly beard and an eye patch, and missing a limb or two. Instead, this man wore a white shirt and tie, and he was cleanly shaved. He also had a tattoo of a lion's head at the base of his neck on one side, but I guess that shouldn't surprise me either.

I said, "I... I'm looking for bullets for... for my gun."

He went behind his desk near the back, glanced at his stock behind more glass, and said, "Sure. What kind of bullets do you need?"

"I... uh... for a handgun."

He said, "Twenty-five? Forty? Forty-five?"

"I don't need very many. One small package will do."

He looked at me in a funny way then said, "I meant caliber," then he said, "What size of ammunition do you need?"

"Ummm..."

"What kind of firearm do you have?"

"I could show it to you."

"Sure. Bring it in."

I went out to my car and reached into the glove box. When I put my hand around it, I could feel the same feelings of power I had last time. It occurred to me that I could probably rob this place by waving it in his face. I could. I had the power. I wouldn't of course. But I could.

I glanced inside the building to see if he was calling the police on me. Maybe if I hurried I could buy the bullets and take off before they got here.

I didn't know how to bring it inside. Just hold it by the handle like I was going in to rob him? That might be taken as an act of aggression. Should I hold it by the barrel? That also felt silly. Maybe I should conceal it somehow. But I had nothing to hide it in. I gave up thinking and just walked inside with it. He was there waiting for me.

I placed it on the counter, and without touching it at all, he said, "That is a Glock 19. Gen four or so. It takes nine millimeter ammo." Turning around and gesturing to a package behind locked glass, he said, "I recommend American Eagle 147."

I said, "OK, I'll take it." And when I said that, I congratulated myself. I had done it. I just went to a gun store and bought bullets. I pulled it off.

But then he turned back and said, "You got a pal?"

I had no idea what he was talking about. When I didn't reply right away, he said, "Possession and Acquisition License?"

I still had no idea what he was talking about, but I didn't want to admit I didn't have one, so I lied. "Oh yeah. It's at home. You don't need to see it, do you?"

He smiled to himself, then said to me. "All handguns are restricted. You can only fire them at a gun range. And you need a Possession and Acquisition License to even own one. I can't sell you anything if you don't have one of those."

So he saw right through my lie. But maybe there were other ways of doing business with this man. I tried to think what Jade would do. He is my father after all, like my mom likes to say. He would start with positive motivation.

I smiled at him like only my dad could, or at least I tried. "There must be some way of doing business without you having to lay eyes on it. I don't mind paying extra, perhaps a lot extra."

His pleasant demeanor turned hard. "It's a fifteen thousand dollar fine to do what you just asked me to do." He shook his head. "I'm not going there."

I knew the next step. After positive motivation came negative motivation. I wondered what I could do. Threaten him with violence? I've never fought anyone in my life, and my gun isn't even loaded. Besides, he could probably protect himself very well. Hmmm... maybe I could threaten to break his windows or something. No, I couldn't imagine me doing that. Wow. This was hard. After thinking about it some more, I couldn't come up with anything, except to say, "Please?"

He said, "No," quite firmly.

So I took my gun and trudged back to my car.

As I drove home, I knew there were other ways of getting what I wanted. There was a large Internet out there, and I was quite sure someone would be willing to send me bullets, legally or not. Shipping might take some time, but I had no doubt I could find what I wanted. What did the man suggest? American Eagle 147? Yes. I looked at the time. Pretty soon I would find what I needed, perhaps on the dark web. I would pay with BitCoin, probably. Hopefully. Then in a few days, I would have bullets for my gun, and then I could defend myself with force, not just with intimidation. I was looking forward to it already.

CHAPTER 10

1:49 PM

I sat on my sofa, munching left-over pizza, browsing the dark web.

I had to install a special web browser that could connect to the dark web via TOR, or The Onion Router. It's called that because each message sent over the Internet is wrapped in multiple layers of encryption, like an onion, so neither the sender nor the receiver can know where each other are.

Once I got it going, I did a quick Google search to find out a search engine for searching the dark web. Its domain ended with .onion, as did everything in this God-forsaken place.

Bullets weren't the only thing you could buy here. I also found sites selling weapons of all sizes, credit cards, driver's licenses, passports, PayPal accounts, child pornography, drugs, and people selling services of every kind you could care to think of. There were also services laundering BitCoin, so your BitCoin purchases and sales can't be tied back to you. If the guy we paid BitCoin to, a few weeks ago, for his bug report would have used this service, he wouldn't have got caught. But I limited myself to bullets.

And speaking of BitCoin, that was the preferred currency of trade, so I had to first go buy some. I did that on the clear web, because you could trust it more. I used the same service we used last time and paid for them with my credit card. When that was done, I made bullet purchases from three different vendors, because honestly I didn't trust any of them.

Then I decided to clean my gun. After looking up a video on how to do it, I followed along.

I held the gun backwards from the top with one hand and squeezed to pull the slide back. Then with my other hand, I pressed the release button on the side. The slide detached in my hand. Then once that was off, I could remove the spring and the barrel from underneath the slide. Then I just scrubbed everything until it was as clean as I could get it. I didn't have any grease, but I found an old can of WD-40, and that seemed to work. The video said Glocks don't rust very easily, but mine did have a spot or two on it. I guess that's what happens when it sits outside in a bush for a few weeks. I was surprised at how well it still operated.

When it was done, I practiced loading imaginary bullets. Then I practiced shooting. I stood with the gun tucked into my pants in the back. I practiced reaching around, grabbing it, and bringing it out front and pulling the trigger. I did that for a while until I was reasonably proficient with the process. These are the tools you need when you go up against bad guys. Fight fire with fire. You have to play their game in order to win. And I was done losing. It was time to start winning.

I whipped out my Glock 19 and pointed it at a calendar hanging on the wall. It was a free calendar about cars I got from a hardware store. The picture for this month was of a cherry red 1968 Ford Mustang Cobra Jet 428. I pointed the gun at the Mustang and said, "No! Stop that!". Then I nodded and put the gun back. Then I whipped it out again. I was practicing being the opposite of a push-over. What would you call that? Leadership, that's what it was. I was practicing my leadership skills. I pulled the trigger and the gun clicked. That's what you call it when you boss people around. Leadership. I used to have a boss. Now I am the boss. I pointed at the Mustang again. "Stop! Get over here! Get out of here! Because I say so!" Click, click.

Suddenly the lamp in the corner pulled a gun on me, but I was faster. I swiveled to it and shot it. Bang, bang. It fell over, or so I imagined. I put my gun back behind my back. I had won again. I was the hero. I saved the day. I saved everyone. I was everyone's savior, including mine.

And speaking of that, there were some scammers out there that I needed to deal with. I spent some time getting my plan together and software ready, then it was time to act. After finding their phone number, I took a deep breath, rehearsed in my mind what I would say and do, and then I called the number.

3:43 PM

"You have reached Tech Support Services. How can we help you?"

"Hi. I just got a pop-up on my screen saying my computer has a virus. Can you help me?"

"Of course we can, sir. Are you on your computer now?"

"Yes."

"The first thing we're going to do is install some software for me to access your computer, is that alright?"

"Sure."

"Excellent. First, may I have your name please, sir?"

"My name is... Jim."

"Jim, I'm going to tell you a website to go to, so we can get the process going. Can you do that?"

"I think so. That's the Internet, right?"

"Yes, the Internet." He told me the website of a legitimate company that provided software that lets one person control another person's computer. There would be no way I would ever give control of my computer to anyone I didn't know, but in this case I followed along dutifully. There was nothing malicious about the screen control software. The malicious part was the guy talking to me on the other end of this phone call.

I got the screen-sharing software set up as per his instructions. The reason I didn't mind doing this was that, although I was using my laptop, I had another operating system running inside of mine. I could let this scammer do anything he wanted in that virtual operating system all he liked. And I could keep a close eye on everything he was doing.

When I was done setting it up, and he had access to my virtual desktop and mouse, I said, "Oh! Someone's at the door. Can you hang on a minute?"

He said, "Yes, I will hold."

I stayed sitting exactly where I was and watched my screen, because on my virtual desktop, I had conspicuously left a file called "passwords". At least I tried to be conspicuous about it. I was really hoping he would notice it. As I sat there, I saw him looking around with his mouse. The mouse cursor went over to the passwords file, and then a menu appeared. He must have right-clicked it. Then he selected "copy" from the menu. I smiled. He was taking the bait. Then the mouse moved off the screen. I assumed he was pasting the file somewhere on his own computer. That's exactly what I was hoping he would do. The plan was working.

Then he found his way to my system log and opened the window to display the log of all the harmless things that happened on my computer, even though some of them had yellow warning icons next to them, which might look scary if I was an ignorant user who trusted scum like this.

I said, "I'm back. Sorry for the interruption."

"That's no problem. Jim, I have opened up the window that shows you all the viruses on your computer. All these warnings and errors are viruses that your computer has found."

I rolled my eyes at those words, but said out loud, "Oh! No!" and I tried to sound convincing.

He continued. "Yes. It is a good thing you contacted us. Jim, I can take care of all these viruses for you, but first I have a deal for you. This doesn't happen all the time. Because you are our one hundredth caller today, instead of paying two hundred dollars for our virus removal software, we will pay you the two hundred dollars."

I said, "No thank you."

He paused briefly, then continued. "Sir, this is a wonderful deal I am offering you. Normally this virus removal software costs two hundred dollars, but if you take this deal you will receive it for free, and I will remove all these viruses from your computer, and we will actually pay you the two hundred dollars. You should take the deal. Do you accept?"

"No I don't. No thank you."

"Sir, what are you planning to do with all these viruses on your computer? They are terrible things. They will steal your information and delete all your files. You don't want that to happen to you, do you?"

"I'll take my chances."

"But sir, Jim. You called us for help. I'm trying to help you."

"You know, I've changed my mind. Maybe I'll just buy a new computer. This one's old anyway. Thanks for your help."

"Sir..."

I hung up.

As I continued to watch my screen, the man was still connected and doing things. He activated a setting on the screen sharing program to black my screen out, which he did. At least he thought he did. My virtual desktop could still be seen by me. I watched this scumbag go all over my system, looking in drawers and cabinets and rummaging through all my files. There was nothing to find of course, but it was still a violation of my personal property. I'm sure he had done this very thing to many people before me. That was not acceptable. This man was going down.

The only thing of interest he found was the file named "passwords" on my desktop. It was a pdf file. Inside this PDF I had hidden some code, that if run on an unpatched PDF viewer, would infect the system with some malware of my choosing. The malware I chose to infect him with was nothing too bad. It would simply hide in the background and connect to my awaiting server. When it did that, I also could connect to my server from anywhere and thus connect into his machine. It would also give me complete control of his computer. I could do anything I wanted. It wasn't bad if you used it to hunt bad guys.

I shut down my virtual operating system, thus kicking him out. Then I fired up a web browser and browsed to a website running on my server that allowed it to receive connections from my malware. It told me that nobody has connected. That meant that either the guy's PDF viewer had been patched against that vulnerability, or that he simply hadn't double-clicked it yet. I hoped for the latter.

I looked at the time. I was still hurting from my encounter with some bad people yesterday evening. Maybe I had time for a quick visit with someone who could help me find them.

4:36 PM

I sat in the waiting room of Headingly Correctional Centre without my gun, because I'm not a complete idiot. It waited for me in the car.

Soon my dad came in. He dragged himself in slowly. When I saw his face, I was shocked to see what it reminded me of–the face I saw in the mirror that morning. It was red and puffy in places, and one eye had a dark patch underneath it. He still smiled at me. "Hi Jeff..." Then he saw the condition of my own face, and he became more serious. "I see they found you."

"Who found me? And what happened to you?"

He dropped himself into a chair and leaned on the table. "So, you want to know all about your dad's past sins, huh?"

"I want to know what's going on."

"I'm sorry for dragging you into this, Jeff."

I sat there, waiting for the story.

He took a deep breath, then glanced at the door.

I said, "We have to assume they're listening. Don't give anything away."

"Yeah." Then he began. "When I first got started in business, I found a guy who had connections, and he had supplies of various kinds."

I could guess what kind of supplies these might be. Drugs and weapons, probably. That gave me an idea of where I could get bullets, but he continued.

"Over the years of doing business with him, I moved a lot of product, but I also had a good amount of accounts payables."

"You owed him money."

"When I got arrested, Vesuvius—that's what they called him—got nervous and thought he was out that much money."

"How much money?"

"Not much. Only three hundred fifty."

"Thousand?"

"Yeah." He watched the coffee maker across the room. "I would have got it for him too, if the Omniscient thing would have worked out."

"Sorry about that."

He whipped his head back at me. "You're sorry?! You're sorry?!"

"Well... you know... I don't want people mad at us. If people come after you, you have to fight back. I just want us to win, that's all."

He stared at me as I had had a third ear growing out of my forehead. Finally he said, "Are you OK, Jeff?"

"Yes I am," I said, maybe still a little angry at life for beating me up. "I'm doing great. Maybe for the first time in my life, I'm finally living. I'm done with being beaten up and bossed around. I quit working for my boss who was an idiot..."

"You quit your job at Omniscient?"

"Yes."

"Why? I thought you loved being a programmer."

"My new boss was a jerk. I'm living my own life now."

"Nobody is ever really on their own."

"You were. You ran your own company."

"You don't want to run your own business, Jeff. You're just tired of being at the mercy of stronger people around you."

"Pfff. That's right I am."

"Well you can't get away from that."

"Yes I can." I was referring to my handgun, which gives me instant power over people stronger than me.

"No. Even if you were stronger or more powerful than everyone around you, there's still the government."

I frowned, thinking about not being about to buy bullets because of the government.

"Jeff, look at me. Do you see these clothes I'm wearing? Do you see where I am right now? I'm in jail. Why? Because I thought I could get around the government's rules. I thought I was above them. Nobody is above rules."

I didn't respond.

He continued. "And there's God, too."

I raised my voice. "Don't talk to me about God."

"Why not?"

"Because..." I was going to say because God abandoned me when I needed him most. Because it was his fault my girlfriend broke up with me. "Because I'm tired of his rules too."

"Really? Which one of the ten commandments do you have a problem with? Stealing? Murder? Is not killing people cramping your style?"

I briefly considered clicking my gun at the calendar and lamp this afternoon, but then I remembered who I was talking to. "You're one to talk."

He looked tired again. "Jeff. I've apologized for that and I'll do it again. I'm sorry for trying to kill you. It was bad. I'm trying to live better now. And besides, I think you tried to kill me too."

He was probably looking for an apology there, and I almost gave him one. I may have mumbled "Yeah" or something. We sat in silence for a little while until he said, "How did you get beaten up?"

"I was walking back from work and some guys came at me. They said they had a message for my dad, then they beat me up."

He looked me in the eyes. "I'm sorry."

"Yeah, so am I."

"No doubt they were sent by Vesuvius, or one of his guys."

"He has guys?"

"Everyone reports to someone, as I was trying to say before— if not another person, then the government, or God. Yes, Vesuvius has a number of guys who report to him. He is quite the entrepreneur. He has his hands in a lot of pies."

"I want to take him down."

Then to my surprise, my dad threw his head back and laughed. Then he kept on laughing. Finally he calmed down and said, "Jeff, Jeff, Jeff. Vesuvius is a vapor. He is a shadow."

"What?"

"I've never personally met him. He only works by sending messages. You would do well to even take down one of his guys. Hey, you got me, didn't you? And I was hard to catch. If you want to get the guys who beat you up, then go after them. At least they exist."

"I also want to get the guys who scammed Mom."

"That, my son, is a good thing to do. I would help you there if I could, but I'm not a techie. But I wish you all the luck I can. Oh, I mean, what am I supposed to say? 'I'll pray for you?'"

"Sure, whatever." I stood up to leave, then said, "Oh, you haven't heard of a guy named Yash Nagi, have you?"

He looked stunned. "I have. He's one of Vesuvius's guys."

4:47 PM

I sat back down and said, "Yash Nagi runs a shop next to Omniscient, called Tech Solutions. They sell some software and stuff and do tech support."

"It's probably a front for something."

"For beating people up?"

"Jeff, be careful. These people are dangerous."

"I can handle myself."

"I don't want you to get hurt."

"It's too late for that, isn't it?"

"These guys are professionals."

"I'll be careful."

"You say those words, but I don't think you mean to be careful. I think you mean to be dangerous."

"You can't accomplish anything just sitting around. You have to get out there and do something. And besides, I have a..." I lowered my voice and looked around. "...a way of persuading people."

"Oh Jeff, you can't just go around waving a gun at people."

"You did."

He threw his arms out. "And now I'm in jail!"

"Be careful, Dad. I'm almost getting the feeling you care about me."

"Of course I do."

"Don't worry. I've got it covered. Now, what else can you tell me about this Yash guy?"

"Well, I can't describe him to you, because I've never met him. All I know is that he was into tech and software. And of course, he had a bunch of guys who worked for him. He was the boss. They say he likes to run a tight ship."

"A tight ship, huh?" I knew someone else who likes to run a tight ship.

"How do you know Yash runs the shop?"

"One of his guys told me."

Dad scowled.

"What?" I asked.

"Did you see him?"

"Who?"

"Yash."

"No. The guy said he wasn't in."

"It's just that in this line of work, you don't like to drop the name of your boss too easily, if your boss doesn't want to be known."

"Maybe they're trying to run a legit business?"

"Or maybe they were trying to intimate you. Or me."

"Or maybe Yash doesn't actually work there."

"What do you mean?"

"Nothing. Just nobody has seen him. We don't know what he looks like. He could be anybody. Maybe even somebody we already know."

"Jeff, are you telling me you think someone else you know is actually Yash Nagi?"

"I have no idea. But if I did, how could I prove it?"

"You want to prove someone is actually someone else?"

"Something like that."

"You mean like shouting their other name and see if they look at you?"

"Ummm... yeah. That might work."

"Jeff, what are you doing?"

"I'm trying to hunt down justice."

"Are you sure?"

"What? Yes."

"Are you sure you're not trying to hunt down revenge?"

I considered his words, then said, "The right thing to do is still the right thing to do."

"Perhaps waving a gun around in someone's face is not the right thing to do."

"It worked for you."

"Did it? Maybe you need to sit down sometime and contemplate what exactly worked for me. Where did waving a gun around get me? Is this success?" He gestured to the jail around him. "Is this what you want for your future? If not, then you need to reconsider your actions." Then he settled in and started lecturing me like only a father can. "You need to ask yourself this question. What is it that you want? What is your end goal? First, determine what you want, and then that answer will tell you the steps you need to take. In your case, what is it that you want? Do you really want justice? Or do you want to see other people hurting like you're hurting?"

I didn't answer that, because deep down I knew the answer. And I didn't want to talk about it. "I'm done talking," I said, and stood up.

"Regardless of what you do, Jeff, it was good to see you again."

"Yeah. See you later, Dad." I left the room and made my way back through security and to my car. My dad had given me the information I was looking for. Now it was time to put it into practice. While I had breath in me, I could still fight. And while I had my gun, I could still do something. Even though I didn't have bullets, it might still be effective.

CHAPTER 11

5:17 PM

I didn't park in my normal parking spot, a five-minute walk from the Johnston Terminal. I parked in visitor parking, right outside the building. I tucked my gun into the back of my pants, under my shirt, then got out of the car. I looked around. The world is different when you are carrying a gun. Even though it's not loaded, everything is different. When I walked up to the building, I had confidence. When I stood in the elevator going up, I stood tall, knowing I had an advantage that nobody else did. When I got out of the elevator, I was no longer an employee of a business. I was a man with a gun. That's a totally different story.

But instead of turning left toward Omniscient Technologies, I turned right toward Tech Solutions. But their door was closed. I knocked, but heard no reply. They must be closed for the day. I scowled. I was looking forward to this. I still felt sore from the beating the other day, and my finger still hurt from the car accident. I was hoping I could do something about that pain.

I turned around in time to see someone leave the Omniscient office and head toward the elevator. It was Cheryl. She seemed sad. I was tempted to feel sorry for her and let my heart break for her sadness, but I refused. She dumped me. She should feel sad. She should feel terrible. She should feel the same pain I did.

I watched her get into the elevator, turn around, and press a button. As the doors started closing, she looked up and saw me. For a split second we made eye contact. I hardened my facial features. She could not see how I was feeling. Nobody could. Just before the doors closed, I saw her reaching for more buttons, probably trying to open the door. But it was too late. The elevator started descending.

I figured she was going to try to find me, and that was not a conversation I wanted to have, so I had to get out of there. I could take the stairs. I ran down some steps and looked to see if she was getting off at the next floor. She did not; the elevator continued down. I walked around a bend in the hall and waited in the shadows in case she decided to take the stairs up to find me. Sure enough, pretty soon I saw Cheryl Bankowsky, the daughter of Darryl Bankowsky, ascend the stairs, looking up, searching with her eyes. I stayed in the shadows. Soon she came down the stairs again, looking even sadder, if possible. I watched her. When she was farther down the stairs, I approached the stairwell again and kept my eye on her. Then I went to the window and looked outside, to see her walking away. I wondered what I was seeing. Was this the last time I would see her? Was this good-bye? I frowned.

Something didn't feel good inside of me. I reached around and felt the gun tucked up snugly against my back. Its strength comforted me, at least it tried to. It would bring me relief from my pain, as soon as I used it. The people I wanted to talk with were not here. But they would be in the morning. I could wait until then. I was patient. I could bide my time.

In the meantime, I should eat. I walked across the pavilion to the Forks Market. I bought some Japanese Popcorn Chicken from Kyu Grill, and sat down by myself to eat.

As I was chewing and licking creamy dill sauce off my fingers, it occurred to me that since I was unemployed, I should probably look for work. I mentally added that to my To-Do list for the evening. I reviewed my education and work experience in my mind, and other things I could add to a resume to make it look good. Then when I was finished eating, I stood up and gathered my things.

Just then the new guy, Nigel walked up to me and said, "Hey, Jeff."

I said, "Oh, hi."

"Listen, I've been meaning to talk to you about…"

I interrupted him. "Well, I'd love to sit and talk about it, but I've got something I have to do." I checked at the back of my wrist. "Sorry. Maybe another time."

"Uh, OK. Maybe I'll send you an email."

I started walking away but looked back. "Great idea." Hopefully my email account will no longer be functioning since I don't work there anymore. I walked away from Nigel and soon was at my car. I drove home, because I did have things I had to do. Making a resume was one, and checking to see if the scammers had taken the bait was another.

6:53 PM

I reclined on my sofa with my feet on the coffee table and a drink in my hand. My laptop was positioned correctly on my lap, warming it nicely. My Glock 17 was resting next to me. I had just cranked out a quick resume, threw it onto my website, and onto a few job-hunting websites. Pretty soon the offers will start coming in and I'll go work for someone who respects me.

With that done, I took another look to see if I had caught any scammers. I opened a new tab in my browser and pointed it at my server. I just used the IP address, because I didn't bother to buy a domain name. But it worked fine. The software I had installed just sat there. On one hand, it received connections from hacked computers, and on the other hand, it showed me a website that I could use to gain access into those computers. It was very handy software. I clicked the button that showed me the list of all hacked computers. What I saw made me put my drink down and sit all the way up. There wasn't just one computer listed. There were three.

The scammer I called must have shared the file around and it infected a few computers. Their lack of good security practices was my gain.

However, each of the three computers had red dots to the side of them. That meant they were not currently connected. Maybe they had shut down for the evening or something. But even though I couldn't browse their computers remotely in real-time, the server software did take a snapshot of some of the more popular details and file names.

I started with the IP addresses, but they were all in the private 192.168... range, which meant they were on a local network. I couldn't check their location to see where in the world they were. Then I paused and thought about that. Maybe I could. If I could get a traceroute from their computer to my server, I could trace the path of internet connections, from server to server. This would tell me exactly where they were. I went hunting in the software to see if a traceroute was one of the things it provided me even in offline mode. It was! When I checked it out, the route went from 192.168.1.50 to 192.168.1.254 to 10.0.0.17. The 10 dot range is also local, so no help there. I kept scanning. Then I saw 107.152.104.240. I excitedly looked it up and found the location to be the city of Weehawken in New Jersey. I considered calling the FBI, but then I noticed who owned that IP address. To my disappointment, the address belonged to a VPN provider. These people were using a company that provided a Virtual Private Network, and the company was based out of Weehawken. So the scammers could still be geographically located anywhere. So much for that idea.

But the next time they came online, I would hopefully find out exactly where they were. Then I would contact their local police.

And speaking of police, they will probably want some sort of proof or evidence. I went looking.

I found my PDF file that did the infecting. I was so proud of that file. It was beautiful. It was a glorious file. I found other files that appeared to be logs or lists of people they had scammed. I couldn't look at them, because they were offline, but I looked forward to when these people came back to work. I would help myself to all their data then.

It occurred to me that these people could be located in a completely different time zone, far different from mine. Maybe they were just gone for lunch and will be back soon. I kept the window open and refreshed once in a while, just to make sure.

I kept on exploring their documents folder and desktop folder. I recorded all the file names, just in case. Then I sat there for an hour, refreshing the page, waiting for them to come online. They never did. I concluded they must be somewhere near my time zone, or maybe East of me. But I'll find out soon. In the morning they should definitely be online. And then I'll have them. For a while, I was tempted to think that this was easier than I thought it would be and would soon be over. I would soon have my mom's money back and these people would be in jail.

Friday 7:15 AM

Since I was a bachelor, I had no problem sitting around in my living room in my underwear with only my laptop to keep me warm. This is what I did. I wanted to see if these computers I hacked were online.

Yes they were. The red dots were now green, and I was browsing files on those computers as if they were my own. I downloaded a pile of files that looked incriminating.

One was a spreadsheet of victims' names, phone numbers, email addresses, bank account details, and notes. Near the bottom of the list was the name "Julie Davis", and "$45,000". My fingers clenched into fists and I struggled to control my breathing. These people were going to pay. One way or another.

I got up and started pacing back and forth. I had to calm down and think. Let's see. I already had files that were incriminating. This could be evidence against the company, but not necessarily against any one person. How could I get evidence on a specific person? User name? No. Accounting records? Maybe, if there were any. Then I thought of it. All I needed to do was to snap a picture with a webcam, if there was one. I checked, and there was. I told the software on the server to tell the software on their computer to take a picture with the webcam. Two seconds later a picture appeared on my screen. I sat back, aghast. It confused and startled me, but then again I shouldn't have been surprised.

I was staring at a picture of Victor Adolf.

I said to myself, "I was right. I was right." I got up and walked around. "I was right. Ha!"

Then I wonder where exactly this was. Was it his office at Omniscient? I looked at the image again and didn't recognize the background. How could I find that out? Then it occurred to me. I could check which Wi-Fi access point they were connected to. I checked. It was called "Tech Solutions." Wi-Fi access point names could be very handy sometimes.

I leaned back in my chair and stared at the ceiling. I had done it. I had found who stole my mom's money. And I found their boss, Yash, who went by the name Victor.

Now, to get Mom's money back. Since they didn't have a problem persuading my mom out of her money, I shouldn't have a problem persuading them out of her money either. I looked over to my persuader. The Glock sat on the table, ready to go. It didn't have bullets yet, of course, but I'll bet it could still do the job.

I got dressed, grabbed a bite of breakfast, and headed out the door. It was confrontation time.

8:25 AM

I parked my car in my normal spot, but this wasn't any normal morning. When I got out and started walking, I had a Glock 17 tucked into the back of my pants. As I walked toward the Johnston Terminal, I didn't notice the sun and I didn't notice the people. I noticed the press of steel against my back.

When I thought of marching into their place of business and demanding money, I was tempted to become nervous. I didn't like talking to people on a good day, so why in the world would I do this thing? Then I remembered my source of courage, my weapon, and the nervousness went away. I was left with only feelings of power and control. I was in charge. This was the Jeff that told people what to do. I didn't take orders; I gave them. And I was about to give some orders.

I took one step at a time going up the stairs leading up into the building, like a gunslinger counting out steps. When I reached the top, I pushed open the doors like I owned the place and headed for the stairs. I climbed one floor, then the next. At the second floor, a hint of a thought came into my mind questioning my actions. I pushed it aside. I think my own thoughts here.

At the third floor, I turned left, away from Omniscient Technologies and toward Technology Solutions. At the last second I was tempted with a wave of nervousness, but in my anger I barged through it and through the door.

I stood there, in the room, towering with power over everyone else. The person at the front desk looked up and me and said the words, "Can I help you sir?" but his expression showed contempt. That would change soon.

There were two other people at desks. I declared to the room, "First of all, I want the driver's license of these two guys here." Turning to them, I continued. "You hit my car two days ago and I need your driver's license to report it."

"Of course, right away," they said.

I stood there and waited while they did nothing. "Hurry up, then!" I shouted.

The first guy shook his head. "I'm sorry, I must have forgotten my license in my car."

The second guy said, "I lost my wallet yesterday."

"You're lying!" I yelled. "Give me your driver's licenses!"

"I can't, sir. It's lost." He held his arms out wide. "I can't produce what I don't have."

I pointed at the first guy. "You. You said you had it in your car. Go get it then."

"Excuse me?"

"Go to your car and get it right now."

"I got a ride in with Dani. My car is at home."

I was angry, but couldn't think of what else to do. "The second thing I want," I told the room, "is my mom's forty-five thousand dollars back. A few days ago she got scammed out of a lot of money, and I have reason to believe it came from this room."

The guy at the front desk asked, "What is your mom's name?"

"Julie Davis." When I said that, I spotted what looked like a nervous look between these three crooks. "And I'm not leaving until I get it all back."

"That is ridiculous, sir," said the receptionist. "We don't scam people. We sell useful products, and we serve our customers."

I hadn't thought that a mere demand on my part would get them to cough up the money, but of course I had other avenues of persuasion. I moved my hand behind me and closed my fingers around the Glock. I slowly pulled it out and held it beside me, pointing at the ground. I'll do more with it if I have to, but this might be enough to get things going.

"Now," I began. "I want to talk to your manager. I believe his name is Yash Nagi."

"I'm sorry, sir. Mr. Nagi is not in right now."

"Shut up! I'm tired of hearing that!"

I marched out between the desks, toward the offices with doors and started opening doors. The three followed me. "Sir! You can't go in there." The first office was empty.

I waved the gun in my hand in response. "I think I can."

I kept opening doors. All the rooms were empty.

"I told you, Mr. Nagi is not in right now."

Then I remembered my idea. "I think I might know where to find him." I left the room, tucking the gun back in, and walked across the building to the other business on this floor.

8:49 AM

I paused outside the large glass doors and took a breath to refocus. I set my eyes on one thing, one man. Then I opened the doors and went in.

Luanna gave me a cheerful "Hi Jeff!", which may have slowed me down a little. I said, "Hi" back to her and continued.

I went down the West hall, turned right, past a certain Customer Service Rep's cubicle, which I completely ignored, and found my ex-boss's office. He was inside on the phone, and his door was open.

I considered for a moment how I was going to approach this, then I said, "Yash!"

He looked up at me immediately. "It's you," he said, hanging up his phone.

I jeered. "Yes. And it is you."

"I know what you're thinking, and you're wrong."

"Am I?" I laughed.

"Yes. I'm not Yash. You're wrong about a lot of things, Jim. Or Jeff."

"I saw you in their office. I caught you red-handed."

"I'm allowed to visit a place of business. They have a legitimate business selling a service. I'm allowed to visit them and talk business."

"I'm sure you do a lot of business there."

"That's not your concern what I do there."

"I think it is. My mom got scammed out of forty-five thousand dollars. I think that makes it my business."

Victor looked angry and he didn't reply right away. When he did, he said, "They should not have done that."

"So you admit it?"

He yelled back, "I admit nothing. You know nothing. What are you doing here anyway? I thought you quit."

"I'm investigating my mom's scam. And all the clues lead to you, Victor. That's why I'm here. To get her money back."

"I don't have it."

"I think you're going to find it." I reached behind me with one hand, but Victor saw me and pointed.

"Don't you do it. Keep that thing hidden."

I was slightly taken aback. He seemed to know what I had.

"That was them on the phone just now," Victor explained. "They said you came over waving a gun. Jim, ah, Jeff, you should not be doing that to these people. They are dangerous."

"You would know, huh?"

"Yes I would know, and I do know. You need to listen to me when I tell you to leave them alone. That's your problem. You never listen to me. You never listened when you worked here, and you're still not listening. That's what got you hacked and it's going to get you killed."

"Are you threatening me?" I closed my hand around the handle.

"No, I'm not threatening you! I'm warning you! Listen for once in your life! Leave these people alone. They will hurt you."

"You don't scare me. I can take care of myself."

That's when I heard the sirens. I looked out the window and saw flashing lights. I lost some bravado then.

Victor said, "They said they called the police. You better get out of here Jeff." I stared into his eyes to see if he was bluffing. I saw no indication of deceit, so I backed up and turned around. I walked down the hall, and down the other hall. Looking through the big glass doors of our office, I saw one of the Technology Solutions guys on his phone, staring at me. I wondered if he was on the phone with 911. Suddenly I got nervous.

I ran out the doors and down the stairs two at a time. Then I saw two police officers enter the building through the main doors. I did my best to not look like the guilty party they are there to apprehend. I raised my eyebrows and tried to look friendly, but inside I was sweating and outside my knees were shaking. It seemed to work. They ignored me. I walked toward the back doors as quickly but innocently as I could. As I went through, I saw them running up the stairs.

I shoved the doors like escaping a jail cell and considered my options. I had to expect them to run back down the stairs any second, and they will probably come back here. That means I had to run. I could run left toward where I parked. That would bring me out into the open. Or I could run right through the trees and down to the river. My sense of self-preservation lead me to the safety of the trees. I took off in that direction, hoping... well, I didn't know what to hope for. My plan had nothing in it about running from the police. All I knew is I had to get away, so I ran.

CHAPTER 12

9:09 AM

As I ran, I was surprised that the gun stayed put back there. I considered taking it out and running with it in my hand, but that was probably a very bad idea. If the police saw me with a weapon, they might consider shooting. I didn't feel like being shot at, so I kept it hidden.

When I was almost to the trees I was already breathing hard. I glanced back and saw a uniformed man exit the building, look around, and yell something at me. I pretended not to hear. I ran even faster. Soon I was down by the walkway next to the river. I followed it left, but I knew that at any moment this police officer was also going to be down here on the path, and he'll get a clear look at me. There was nowhere to hide.

There was only one thing I could do. I had to get rid of the evidence. I stopped running and whipped out the gun. For a brief moment, I considered hiding it. I could stash it in the woods or under some leaves or something. But no. If I could come back and find it later, that means the police could find it too. I had to get rid of it in such a way that even I couldn't get it back. That meant one thing. I looked out over the Red River next to me. Then I said goodbye to my strength, reach my arm back, and through the Glock as far into the water as I could.

As soon as it splashed, I heard a "Freeze!" behind me. It was the police officer. I admit he could run pretty well, better than me. Of course, I was just a computer programmer, so that doesn't say much.

Pretty soon he got to me, grabbed my arm behind my back, grabbed my other arm as well, and I felt and heard the chinking of metal. I had been handcuffed. He said, "I am arresting you for pointing a firearm at another person."

I said, "What?! I didn't actually do that."

He started leaning me away and continued his speech. "I wish to give you the following warning: You need not say anything. You have nothing to hope from any promise or favor and nothing to fear from any threat whether or not you say anything. Anything you do or say may be used as evidence. Do you understand?"

"Yeah, I guess so."

He radioed to his partner and explained he had apprehended me and was taking me in. He continued talking to me. "You have the right to retain and instruct counsel without delay. You also have the right to free and immediate legal advice from duty counsel by making free telephone calls. Do you understand?"

"Sure." By now we were up the hill and I could see the car waiting for us.

"Do you wish to call a lawyer?"

"I might."

"You also have the right to apply for legal assistance through the legal aid program. Do you understand?"

"I guess so."

He opened the police car door and guided me inside. It wasn't exactly a push, but it felt like it. He got in the front passenger seat and his partner, who was driving, now drove off.

I was going to jail.

9:50 AM

The police services headquarters on Gary Street had a number of holding rooms in their basement. They had white tile floors, one small bench with no padding, and a stainless steel toilet and sink in the same room. At least my room had these amenities. I assumed they were all alike.

After getting finger printed and my personal belongings removed from me, I was placed here. Nobody said anything more to me about calling a lawyer. That line from the arresting officer must have just been something they say, not that they actually cared about me.

So I sat here, doing nothing. I hated it. It forced me to spend time with my own thoughts. I was forced to remember that I was in jail. But I would fight it! I would get a lawyer and get out and bring people to justice. It didn't occur to me that the people who ran this place also thought they were bringing people to justice. But I had really bad guys that needed dealing with. It didn't occur to me that these police might be dealing with a bad guy right here. I wasn't a bad guy. I was me. I was Jeff Davis. I make my own rules. I take care of myself.

I paced back an forth in my tiny room, keeping these thoughts up, keeping my persona up. I had to continue the fight, this fight to sit on the throne of my life, to be in the driver's seat, because if I let my guard down, if I stopped and thought about it, I might catch a glimpse of something I didn't want to see. I might come face to face with something I didn't want to deal with.

And so I paced, and I planned, and plotted. Without a gun, how would I go after the bad guys? Maybe I should drive into their car like they drove into mine. Maybe I could vandalize their building. Maybe I could get some guys together and beat them up like they beat me up. But where would I find guys to do that for me? Maybe my dad would know. Maybe I could get a message to him somehow, since we are both in the system now.

I sat down on the bench. My dad was in prison. Just like me. Like father like son. The last time I saw him, he tried to convince me to not go to prison, because he didn't want me to end up like him. I stood up and tried to think of something else. I should think about my mom's money. She needs her money back. How will I do that? If these guys aren't going to cooperate, I'll need to get creative. What if I stole one of their cars and sold it? I could get some money that way. I could probably do that. I could find some connections to sell vehicles to. And it would all be fair, since they stole her money. I would just steal enough of their cars, or something, to make back the same amount of money. That's fair. That's reasonable.

The idea of stealing cars made me tired, so I sat down again. I didn't know anything about how to steal a car or where to sell it. I didn't have any connections in that world. Of course my dad probably did. It occurred to me that it wasn't that long ago that I pointed my self righteous finger at him and told him there was no way I would ever be like him. And now I'm trying to be like him. Maybe I was wrong. But then, my dad also became a Christian. Was I wrong about that too?

No! I got up again and paced back and forth. I had so many thoughts in my head, and it was hard to keep away the ones I didn't want to think about. If only there was something in here I could do to keep my mind off of everything. A book? Magazine? I would even settle for a TV.

I walked over to the metal door. It had bars over a small glass window, but I shouted anyway, hoping someone would hear me. "Hey! Is anyone out there?" Then I listened. I shouted again, "Is anyone out there? I'm bored!" I listened again, but I didn't get a response.

I walked around for a while, trying to put something else into my head. I tried to think of something to occupy my brain. Maybe a logic puzzle or something. Then I thought of something. It goes like this. You have a weigh scale that is a simple balance scale. It can only tell you if the two things are equal or not equal. And you have a dozen eggs. Eleven of the eggs are the exact same weight, and one is either heavier or lighter. Can you find out which egg it is, and if it is heavier or lighter, while only using the scale three times?

I set my mind to solving this problem, because there were other things trying to get in. I forced them out by thinking about weighing eggs. Let's see. What if you start by weighing six and six? No, one side would go down and the other up. You wouldn't learn anything. OK, what if you weighed five and five? If they were equal, one of the other two must be the bad one. Then you could... you could weigh one with one of the five to see if it was the bad one and heavier or lighter. That would work. But what if the first five and five were different? How could you get which one of the ten was the odd one in only two more weighings?

I stood in a corner, facing the room, leaning against two walls. I imagined weighing eggs: five and five, four and four, three and three, two and two. Soon I got tired of standing and lowered myself to the floor. I sat in the corner with my knees up, and my arms around my legs, trying to protect myself.

With my eyes closed, I imagined if the first three and three were equal, how could I then pick which of the remaining six was bad in only two more weighings? Two and two? But if they were the same again... Cheryl's email came to mind. "I can't pursue a romantic relationship with someone who's not a Christian. I might like you, but I can't." Focus on eggs. There is no way to determine which one of six is the bad one in only two weighings. You can't start with three and three. Maybe four and four... After supper with Cheryl's family, in my car, she asked me, "So what's the problem?" I said, "Maybe I just want to be my own man." I was my own man, and I liked it that way. Being my own man brought me here. But I was in jail. Stop thinking about that.

Eggs. If the first four and four are not equal, that means the remaining four are standard weights. In the second weighing, you could put some of the bad eight against some of the good four. But how many?

Victor's face came to me. "That's why Christianity is the best religion, because it has the best rules." Then my dad's face. "I'm a Christian, Jeff. And you should become one too!" My response, "I. Will. Never! Ever! Be like you."

What if you weighed three eggs from the heavier side plus one egg from the lighter side against three standard eggs? What would that tell us?

I closed my eyes and saw only darkness. It was the night sky two days ago in the storm. People in masks were kicking me. It hurt. I prayed to God. God did nothing. I cried out to him, but nothing happened. Then I pointed the gun at my enemy and I became my own savior. Then I threw the gun into the river. Was I still my savior without a gun? Who am I now?

I tried to think of eggs again, but realized I was exhausted. I couldn't think about anything, even if I tried. My breathing slowed and I kept my eyes closed. Then I relaxed my legs out and leaned my head against one wall. I fell asleep.

12:10 PM

I was awakened from my rest by the sound of a metal door being unlocked and opened. I opened my eyes and saw a paper plate with two slices of pizza on it. A woman in uniform handed it to me. She said, "While you're in here, we gotta feed ya. So have some pizza. I hope you like pepperoni. Most people do. And here's a bottle of water."

Out of habit I replied, "Thank you." I brought my meal to the bench, where I sat down to eat.

The woman left, then came right back. "Oh, and here is something for dessert, I guess. I don't know right where we got these things from, but you can have one, if you like this sort of thing." She handed me a bar of 85% dark chocolate, my favorite kind too. The chemicals do things to my brain. I smiled.

The door closed and I chewed the pizza in silence. Then, as I started to unwrap the chocolate, a thought popped into my head. It said, "Look. I got you your favorite chocolate. Can we be friends again?"

I put the chocolate down and took a deep breath. I recognized this thought in my head. I have talked with this thought before. I have had conversations with this voice in my head before.

I sighed and then said out loud, "You want to be friends again." I remembered when I first found God's email address and he sent me stuff. Those words of life, of love, touched me deeply. I can honestly say I'm not the same person anymore because of the words God has spoken to me. He told me he loved me, and I believed him. Who wouldn't want to hear that? Did I want that again? Of course I did. But that wasn't everything. I spoke out loud, "You... you left me to get beaten up. You weren't there for me. And now you want to be friends again?" I was tempted to get mad again, to let the self-righteousness and pain come to the surface and manifest as anger. But instead I gave God one chance. Instead of accusing him with a slap to the face, I gave him an open door. It was open just a crack, but it was open and now I would see what he would do with it.

I closed my eyes and tried to remember how to hear from God. Relax. Look, not just listen. Tune in to spontaneous thoughts. And then write it down. Well, I had no phone or even pen to write anything down with, so I might have to skip that part. But I did my best to quiet down and imagine God sitting on the bench next to me. I looked at him and saw, in my mind's eye, a man with white hair. No, it was dark hair. And he was wearing a robe with a wide blue sash around his chest. And he had sandals on. It was the stereotypical image of Jesus, I guess. Maybe it came from my own head, but I didn't care. I just went with it. I said again to him, "You didn't rescue me from getting beaten up."

The imaginary Jesus man looked at me with a peaceful smile. I could tell just by looking at him that he loved me and cared for me, but there was also a hint of sadness in his eyes. The thought came to me, "Jeff, I love you, my son. I would never do anything that was only bad for you. I don't abandon my children. I take good care of those who are mine. Are you mine, Jeff?"

This last question caused me to think. Am I his? Have I ever actually given myself to him? Come to think of it, I don't think I have. I always just thought this relationship was about God giving to me. Now he wants me to give myself to him? But he didn't answer my question. I repeated it. "You weren't there for me when I needed you."

The thought came to me, "Jeff, I gave you a gun. What more could you want?"

This last statement struck me deep. God gave me the gun? But of course. I prayed for help, and then I immediately remembered the gun in the bushes. What more of an answer to prayer could you ask for? All this time I thought I was saving myself, but really God was providing for me all along. I choked back a tear. "I... I'm sorry," I said.

God spoke again, "Are you mine, Jeff?"

"I... want to be. But I don't know what that means."

Suddenly I remembered taking my car into the garage. There was a sign that said, "We fix what you break." And I remembered the doctor who said, "You break it. I fix it."

God said, "Just like you brought your car to the mechanic, you need to bring yourself to me. Just like you brought your finger to the doctor you need to bring yourself to me. Just like you cleaned out those servers, you need to let me clean you too."

"What... what will you do to me?" I asked.

"I take good care of what's mine. Are you mine?"

This was the moment. This was the question that demanded an answer. Who's was I? Did I belong to myself, or did I belong to God? Was I his? Or was I mine? It was the fundamental question. If I belonged to me, I could do whatever I wanted—I was the boss and I called the shots. But if I belonged to God and was his, I would have to do whatever he said. I would have to obey his every command. I would be his employee, his servant. I would have to treat him like I was supposed to treat my boss Victor. Suddenly I wasn't feeling so good about this decision. I was trying to get away from an oppressive boss, not find a new one.

I said, "I don't know if I want to submit to another boss like Victor. He was a Christian, and if that's the way you operate, I wouldn't like it."

I listened for a reply. I heard the thought, "Victor is trying to follow me the best way he knows how. I want you to also follow me the best you can."

"Will you be like Victor?"

"The question is not if I am like Victor. The question is: Is Victor like me? The answer is: He is trying, just like many other people are trying. Are you one of them?"

"Will you be a good boss?"

"I am a very good shepherd. I take very good care of my sheep."

And there in the lonely basement holding cell of the police services headquarters on Gary Street, I closed my eyes, nodded, and simply said, "OK."

I imagined God in the form of Jesus beside me. He was beaming and proud and excited. He said, "Jeff, my son, my friend, my servant. From today, you are mine. You belong to me. I will be your God and you will serve me. You will be my server."

I didn't know how to feel. I felt fine, I guess. I felt kinda warm and at peace, but I didn't know if that was just normal. No, probably not for just being arrested. I thought about my current situation and if I was going to go to jail for real, but even that didn't make me as worried as I thought I should be. I was too busy resting in the fact that I belonged to someone else now. I could give up the fight I had been fighting, because I think I finally won.

CHAPTER 13

1:00 PM

My door wasn't made of bars. It was just a metal door. As I sat in my room, it opened and the police officer that arrested me walked in and leaned against the door frame. I looked at him, waiting for him to speak.

He said, "This morning 911 received a call saying a man on the third floor of the Johnston Terminal, at Technology Solutions, was waving a gun at people and making threatening remarks." I was tempted to say I hadn't actually pointed the gun at anyone, but I decided to remain silent.

He continued. "You matched the description, and you acted suspicious, so we arrested you. However, when we returned later, we found Technology Solutions completely abandoned except for a cell phone smashed and lying on the floor. One could guess that this was the cell phone used to call 911. And on top of that, we found no weapon on you." He paused for effect, or to wait for me to say something, then continued. "This means that not only do we have no evidence against you, we also have nobody accusing you. You're free to go."

I guess I should have been happy to get out of jail, but what he said disturbed me. Technology Solutions was abandoned? What did that mean? Did they get scared and take off? The peace I had been feeling was sort of going away. These people need to see justice and they just escaped. And what about my mom's money? I had to see this for myself.

The police offer said again, "I said you're free to go." He backed up and gestured for me to leave. I got up and walked out of my cell. After I picked up my stuff from their storage, and signed something, I left the building. On the outside, I paused and stood right where I was. It occurred to me that just an hour before I was staring down some serious jail time or something really bad. Now, I was free. I said to God, "Umm… thanks for that. Yeah, I'm yours. Tell me what you want me to do." It occurred to me that I should track down the guys, and the right way this time. But first, I wanted to see this abandoned office.

There was a bus stop near the station, so I hopped on the next ride and was soon back at the forks. As we drove past the parking lot, I spotted my car and it struck me again that I wasn't driving a Honda Civic. It was a Mercedes Benz. Here I was, driving a Mercedes. That was a nice car. And it was given to me by my father. Maybe, just maybe, this dad of mine wasn't quite as evil as I thought he was. After all, he did give me a sweet car. "Thanks… thanks, Dad." But maybe I should thank him in person.

I got off the bus closer to the Johnston Terminal and looked around, like I had so many times before. But this time was different. This time I didn't work there. I was unemployed. Because I had quit. I wondered if that was the right thing to do after all. Would a servant of God quit just because he didn't like his job? I don't know. Maybe not. As I walked to the Johnston Terminal, I considered the idea of working there again, but not for long. The thought didn't sit well with me at all. Except for…

Cheryl.

I stopped walking. I saw a bench and sat down, because this required some deep thought. I sighed. Cheryl. Was there something in my heart for her? Yes, I admitted to myself. Could our relationship get back together? I don't know. Then I thought some more. Nope, I didn't know. It was too complicated for me. I got up and continued walking. I had to see this Technology Solutions for myself.

I took the stairs up and turned left. There it was, Technology Solutions. The door was closed, but unlocked. I opened it and went inside. There wasn't a soul around. There were some desks still there, but all the computer equipment was gone. I wandered around, looking into the individual office rooms. There was nothing there. And it was quiet. I felt like I was invading someone's personal space, except that there wasn't anyone there to invade. It still made me nervous, though. I half expected someone to jump out at me. But that probably wouldn't happen, because these guys were gone.

I sat down in an abandoned chair and leaned back. Why would they take off? I think the answer is obvious. I was getting too close. They didn't want to get caught. I frowned. Maybe I had gone about this the wrong way. All I did was to scare them off. I'll have to remember that for next time. The next time I get close, if there will be a next time, I'll do it the right way. But what was the right way? Well, the police come to mind. I guess I should pay them a visit.

I started to get up off my chair when I heard the main door open. I was sitting in an office room, so I couldn't see the main door, but I guessed there was someone there. Who was it? A customer? The police? Someone from Technology Solutions coming back for something? Yash Nagi himself coming to finish me off? Probably not, but it might be. I hadn't looked around for security cameras, but I probably should have. They might still be hooked up to something. And I just showed my face all over the place. Maybe this wasn't the smartest thing to do.

I should have remained silent, but I was already getting up, and my chair thunked when it came forward. Then I heard footsteps. I sat as quiet as I could, but the footsteps came in my direction. I considered hiding behind a desk. Would that be a good idea? Umm... yes. I rolled the chair back, which made more noise. I was about to jump off onto the floor when a figure appeared in the doorway. It was my boss, Victor.

1:55 PM

My eyes darted to his hands, to see if he was carrying a gun. He was not. Then I glanced behind him to see if he had his posse with him. I didn't see any. That was good. I still had bad memories of when they beat me up. I relaxed a little.

We stared at each other for a second. I had nothing to say to him. If he wanted to say something, that was up to him.

He said, "I see they left."

"Yes," I replied.

"I think you scared them off."

I didn't say anything.

"I told you to leave them alone."

"You would have liked that, wouldn't you?"

"You're lucky to be alive."

"They did beat me up the other day."

Victor frowned. "You said you fell down the stairs."

"Yeah. Sorry."

Victor sighed. "I'm sorry too, Jeff. I'm sorry you got beaten up."

I laughed out loud. "You're sorry? Your guys beat me up and you're sorry?!"

Victor flashed angry. "They're not my guys! They don't work for me a... They don't work for me."

I paused. "What did you say?"

"I said they don't work for me."

"You were going to say 'They don't work for me anymore,'" weren't you?"

Victor looked around, nervously.

"Admit it," I pressed.

He sighed. "A few months ago I became a Christian, and when I did, I tried to turn my life around. I quit working here. I took a legitimate job. I also tried to convince these guys to go legit too. I thought they could run a real business, instead of scamming people."

"So you admit you're a scammer."

"Jeff! Will you stop accusing me of being a bad person? I left that life. I'm legit now."

"And you changed your name too?"

"What? What do you mean?"

"Yash Nagi?"

"I'm not Yash."

"No?"

"No. But I worked for him. And these guys worked for me."

I sat there, staring at this man, wondering if I should believe him. He didn't look his normal cocky self. He looked humble, almost timid, as if I just caught him in the shower or something. Yes, I would believe him. He wasn't Yash. He didn't give the order to beat me up. But that doesn't mean he's a nice guy. The silence between us almost grew uncomfortable, so I broke it by saying, "You know, for a Christian, you're awfully grumpy sometimes." I delivered the line with a hint of a smile.

He looked almost shocked I would say such a thing, but then he replied, "I haven't been a Christian for that long yet. I'm still working on it."

I smiled wider. "Keep working."

He threw his hands up and rolled his eyes. "Why am I even talking to you?" Then he turned back to me. "You were stubborn yourself too, you know?"

He had me there. I was. But I had good reason to be. I had a terrible boss. Except that he was still working on himself, so maybe I shouldn't be so quick to judge. I don't know. I didn't know what to think, so I shrugged. Was I stubborn? "Yes," I admitted.

Victor didn't respond right away. Then he nodded his head. "Goodbye, Jeff," he said, then walked away.

I scrambled to the doorway where he had been standing. I saw him walking back toward the door. "Wait!" I said.

He turned.

"That's it? Just 'Goodbye'? We need to find these guys."

"You want me to rat on my friends? Look around, Jeff. They're gone. And they didn't tell me where they went."

I didn't know what to say to that, so I didn't say anything. Victor walked out of the room, leaving me to myself again. And what was I going to do now? Victor might be giving up, but I'm not. There were bad guys out there who needed to be brought to justice, and that's what I was going to do, or at least help with. There was something I needed to do. I should have gone to the police days ago, but it's still not too late now. Maybe my old friend Detective Joseph Wakefield can do what I can't.

2:14 PM

I was almost to my car when I saw the tow truck. I couldn't see which car he was occupied with, through the sea of vehicles in the parking lot, so I ran the rest of the way. Yes, it was mine. I had driven forward into the parking stall, so the tow truck had lifted up the back. When I looked closer, the front wheels had wheel dollies on them. Since the C 300 4-matic is an all-wheel drive, nothing but the best for my dad, it needs all wheels off the ground.

The driver appeared to just be done. When he saw me, he jumped into the driver's seat and smashed his hand down on something, probably the door lock. I'll bet he's been accosted by owners before and didn't want anything to do with me.

When I got to his door, I mustered all my confrontational strength, which was not a lot, and said to him, "What are you doing?"

He rolled down his window a little, just to talk, and replied, "This is what happens when you don't make your payments."

"What payments?!" I said.

"That's between you and your loan company." He rolled up the window again.

"What loan company?! This isn't even my car."

He rolled down the window again. "If it's not your car, then don't worry about it." The tow truck started moving forward, and my car crept along with it.

"Well... it is my car. It was my dad's, but he gave it to me."

"Talk to your loan company."

"I don't even have a loan on this car."

The man shook his head. "Can't help ya."

"Yes you can. You can tell me who hired you."

"Hey, I just pick up the cars." He turned hard to his left and kept moving.

Not knowing what to do, I thought I should grab hold of my car and pull it away from this man stealing it, but my prefrontal cortex vetoed the idea. Instead, I jumped onto the hood and hung on underneath the windshield. The two vehicles kept on moving through the parking lot until reaching the road. The driver stopped the truck and opened his door. He probably coming around to talk me off my car. So instead I jumped off, unlocked the doors of my car with the remote key fob and climbed into the driver's seat, then locked the doors again.

Soon the man was at my window like I was just at his. I rolled the window down slightly, like he had done.

"You're not allowed to be in here," he said.

"Where are you taking my car?" I asked.

"To headquarters. 725 McCalmon Avenue."

"Why?"

"What do you mean 'Why'? Your car's being repossessed."

"Who are you repossessing it from?"

"What do you mean?"

"Who's the owner?"

"If I tell you, will you get out of the car?"

I shrugged. "If you don't tell me, I won't."

He sighed and looked around as if wondering what to do. There was another car behind us, which was right in front of me from my point of view, also wanting to leave the parking lot.

"They have all the stuff at headquarters," he said. "Tell you what. You can ride in the front with me, then examine the paperwork there all you like."

I thought about it briefly. We were at a stalemate as it was. At least I could have answers then. "OK," I agreed. I got out and closed and locked the door. I didn't want anybody getting into my car while it was sitting somewhere. It was one thing to steal a guy's car, but another to get on the inside. I went up to the truck's passenger side door. It was locked. I called out, "The door's locked."

He replied from the other side, "I'll unlock it." He got in, and to my relief, he leaned over to my door. But just before his hand landed on the lock, his left hand threw the vehicle into drive, and I heard the engine roar. He suckered me. I reached into my pocket to unlock my car again, but it was too late for that because the car was already moving. I would have to jump onto the hood again. But since my right hand was still holding the keys, and I didn't want to drop them, I only had my left hand to grab on with. I threw myself onto the hood when that end of the car was near me, but it was traveling faster this time.

I landed on the hood and reached for that nice place to hold onto underneath the windshield with my left hand. My left hand missed it, so I instinctively reached with my right hand. Three fingers found purchase, but when the truck took a hard right onto the road going too fast, my body lurched. I scrambled for a better grip, but the momentum threw me, and I was never an athlete by any stretch of the imagination. They never taught a course on How to Grab Onto a Moving Vehicle in the Computer Science department of University. I fell off and skidded to a stop in the middle of the road.

As I looked up, I saw my car disappear down the road. Then it went through a red light and kept on going. But considering how my dad likes to drive, I'm sure that wasn't the first time that car ran a red.

I stood up and brushed the dust from my clothes. When I did, I noticed my hands stung. My left one was red. I had gotten a touch of road rash from the fall. But considering breaking a finger and getting beaten up, it wasn't too bad.

I got off the road and reconsidered my options. First, I would have to tell my dad that his car got repossessed. I guess he isn't making payments in jail. Come to think of it, I was surprised he even got a loan for that thing in the first place. I assumed he would have paid cash or something, and under someone else's name. You don't run an organization called the Information Underground by putting your information out there for every loan company to see. Whatever. Maybe I could call that towing company and get to the bottom of this.

And second, I needed transportation, so I pulled out my phone and made a call. The female voice said, "J.W. McDonald Auto Service. Becky speaking."

I said, "This is Jeff Davis. I dropped off my Honda Civic a while ago. I was wondering how it's going."

"Let me see here..." she paused as if looking something up. "According to our records, we have done... nothing. We were waiting for you to get back to us."

"Oh. Oh yeah. Insurance. I thought you were just going to fix it."

"Nope. But we absolutely could if you want us to. But you probably want to make it an insurance job."

"Right. But I kind of need a car."

"Let me think. You drove it here, right?"

"Yes."

"But the tire was touching a broken panel and almost busted it. If you really need it, we could panel-bang it, throw on another tire, and you're good to go. But don't tell anyone we did that, because our motto is 'You break it. We fix it.' And we wouldn't be fixing it."

"Right. Yeah. OK. Let's do that. I need a car."

"OK, I'll get it going right now. It should be done in… oh half an hour. And we close at five today."

"OK. Thanks. I'll be there soon."

"See ya."

"Bye"

"Bye"

I hung up the phone. Then I sighed. Strange things were still happening. Then I walked to the bus stop.

CHAPTER 14

2:44 PM

Not that long ago I took a bus when I was running for my life, or so I thought. I had found a person who claimed that not only could he hear from God, he could teach others how to, too. Turns out he was right.

When I climbed on board the bus this time, on my way to the garage, I couldn't help but look around for any more crazy people. I didn't know what to look for, exactly–maybe an old unkempt man wearing a crumpled hat with dried bird poop on it or something. But I didn't see anyone that bad. Everyone looked mostly normal, whatever normal means.

I played it safe by picking a seat far away from everyone else. I picked an aisle seat with nobody sitting in the window seat. But when I sat down, I noticed something was there. It was a notepad and a pencil. I looked around me to see if anyone had dropped it. There was nobody close to me and everyone ignored me. So I ignored it too. It wasn't mine.

The bus took off and soon passed York Avenue.

Who uses a pencil nowadays anyway? A wanna-be artist drawing sketches? I glanced at the edge of the notebook and I could see thin blue lines. It wasn't a sketchbook. It was a notebook with lines. And none of the pages looked crumpled. It looked new. But it wasn't mine. I watched the scenery pass by. We turned left onto Pioneer Avenue.

I looked in the notebook to make sure it was new. I wouldn't want to look at someone else's writing. But it was blank. I wasn't intruding into anyone else's life. The pencil looked new too. It wasn't chewed on or anything. And it was still pointy. It was as if these things were left here for me.

I put them down, onto my lap, and looked around. Pioneer soon turned onto Main Street. I opened the notebook to the first page. The last time, the guy explained to me how to hear from God. Calm yourself down, look for vision, tune into spontaneous thoughts, and then write them down. He guided me through the first three, but we didn't have anything to write on. This time I had the notebook but nobody to guide me.

I would have to do it myself.

I closed my eyes and tried to picture myself somewhere calm. Hmmm… how about sitting on my sofa at home? That's a good place. Then I imagined God sitting next to me. He was dressed in white and shiny, with a smile on his face. He seemed very happy to see me. He seemed at peace. It made me feel better just sitting there next to him, as if his peace were radiating off of him and into me. I took several deep breaths and let them out.

Then I opened my eyes and wrote in the notebook. "God, you know where I am. You know what's happening to me. I need your help."

I closed my eyes again and imagined God sitting next to me. I relaxed and let go of the scene in my mind. It changed to me sitting on the bus, with God sitting next to me in the window seat. Some words came to mind, so I wrote them down.

"Jeff, my son, my loved one. My friend, my servant. I love you so very much. I love you with all my heart. It makes me so happy that you have given your life to me. I've been looking forward to this for a long time. Now you are finally mine. And I am yours."

His words filled me with warmth inside. I wrote down my response.

"I'm glad I did."

Then these words came to me, so I wrote them down. "You belong to me. You are mine. You are not perfect yet, but I am working on you. You are my project that I am working on, and it is my joy to do so. I love you."

A picture that came to my mind was of an old car in a garage, and someone was restoring it. He was taking his time and carefully fixing and repairing each part that was damaged. I continued writing. "You are my project, Jeff. You have given yourself to me, so now I can start working on you. You have some areas of your life that need tending to, but I am working on them, one at a time."

I asked, "What areas?"

The words "Your father" came to my mind, but I didn't write it down. Instead, I put the pencil down and stared out the window. I didn't know what to think about this. On one hand, I remembered all too clearly when he told one of his guys to kill me. How am I supposed to deal with that? Just sweep it under the rug and pretend it didn't happen? Of all the bad things in life that could happen to a guy, being killed by your own father must rank pretty high.

We were approaching Bannatyne Avenue, and I started reaching up to pull the cable that would tell the driver I wanted to stop. As I did, these words came to me: "Don't stop." I hesitated, and immediately began an analysis of all my previous attempts at hearing from God. How many were successful, and how many did I not hear correctly? I had to admit that most of the time it worked out. Then I multiplied that percentage by the probability that these words, "Don't stop," in my head were from God or not. That was a tougher one. I wasn't one hundred percent convinced, but it might have been. I sat there, with my arm up, about to pull the cable, looking outside. Then I watched Bannatyne Avenue come and go. I put my arm down and wrote some more.

"Well, I didn't stop."

God said, "Thank you, Jeff. I appreciate that. I was enjoying our time together. I didn't want it to end so soon."

I smiled to myself. Really? This is almighty God, and what he wants to do is spend time with me? Crazy. If I was God, and I found someone who could listen to me, I'd do something else. I would probably download plans for world domination. But this God? Nope. He just enjoys spending time with me, as if he cares about a heart-to-heart connection with his people more than solving the world's problems. Then it occurred to me that maybe a heart-to-heart connection with people itself might end up solving all the world's problems. Or maybe God cares and values my heart more than anything in the world. Huh.

I said, "You're welcome." Then I said, "You know, my dad did try to kill me."

He said, "I know. I was there. I saw the whole thing. I also saw that he couldn't do it himself. He had to tell Max to do it. Do you know why?"

I said, "Because he was weak?"

God said, "Because he loved his son. His love for you might not be as strong as my love for you. It might be weak, but it was there, and it is still there now, and it is growing. Love is not a weakness; it is a strength, and it is growing in your dad's heart. Are you going to acknowledge this?"

I stared at the notepad and the pencil in my hand. I knew what I was supposed to write next. It was the word "Yes," but it didn't come. I felt like a scientist who just discovered something with his own eyes and refuses to admit it. God's case was very strong. Why else would my dad have given the gun to Max? He could have done it himself. But he didn't. Why not? Weakness? No. Strength. A very very small amount of strength. You know, the 'L' word.

I found the courage to write, "He might have a very little bit in his heart toward me."

God said, "Good for you for opening your eyes to the truth. The truth is that your dad does love you, deep down. He is now working on bringing that love to the surface. But it is there. And you love him too."

I chuckled. "Do I really? You know that I did try doing something to him too."

"You did that because you let anger rise up to cloud out your love for him and your better judgment. But when your anger is gone, and your unforgiveness is gone, you will see that there is indeed love for your dad in your heart. I know it's there. I can see it. And it is beautiful."

"Maybe there is, a little, but not a lot."

"You can't see it, because it is covered by a layer of unforgiveness. You must tear down the wall of unforgiveness in order for the love to come up and grow. You need to forgive your dad, Jeff."

"He gave the order to have me killed."

"I know."

"He abandoned us when I was growing up. When I needed a father."

"I know."

"He became a drug dealer."

"I know."

"He did a lot of other bad things. He was a bad man."

"I know."

"And I'm supposed to just ignore all this?"

"No. Forgiveness is not ignoring the injustice done to you. It is acknowledging it, it is staring it in the face, then choosing to let it go. Yes, you have been treated unjustly by your father, Jeff. You have. It's true. But you must let it go. You must remove the weapon that is embedded in your body before you can heal. Pull it out and throw it away. Stop holding onto it."

I looked out the bus window at the buildings going past. I didn't exactly know where we were, and I didn't exactly know where forgiving my dad would take me either. But just like I was secure in this bus's route, I knew I was secure in God's direction. I closed my eyes and whispered out loud, "OK". It must have worked, because my heart left lighter. I breathed easier, and even smiled.

I wrote, "I feel better."

God responded. "I'm very proud of you, my son. You did good. Very good. Now there is something else you need to do. Don't pick up your car just yet. First, go back to work."

Great.

3:16 PM

I ripped off the pieces of paper I journaled on and stuffed them into my pockets. The notepad and artist pencil could stay there, because they weren't mine. I was grateful though.

The bus dropped me off near the Johnston Terminal. I didn't know what God wanted me to do here, so I just walked up the main stairs to the building, and took the elevator up. Before going into Omniscient Technologies, I looked right and saw Technology Solutions. The door was still open. I went and stood in the doorway, observing the emptiness. I thought to myself, "It's over," then another thought came to me saying, "No it's not. Keep going." I sighed.

Then I turned my head left and saw the place where I used to work. God wanted me to go back there, but I didn't want to. The thought of working for Victor still bothered me. I'd rather be unemployed. I hope, when God said to go back to work, he meant just stop by to visit, not become employed again. I groaned out loud. Yeah, that's probably what he meant, but he didn't explicitly use those words, so I'm off the hook for not disobeying. Technically I'm back here at the place I used to work, so technically I still obeyed. Well, I'm not exactly here, because I'm still in the doorway of Technology Solutions. But once I move my body closer to that side of this floor, then I will have obeyed.

I moved my body, using my feet, over to the big glass doors and paused for two seconds, to let the full impact of obedience be established. Then, feeling fine for having obeyed a direct command from God, I started back toward the elevator. I was interrupted on the way by someone yelling, "Jeff!"

I turned around. It was the new guy, Nigel. He ran up to me and said, "I've been meaning to talk to you."

I stood there, waiting for him to continue.

"I've heard that you quit," he said. "Is that true?"

"Yes."

"It's because I kicked you out of your job, didn't I?"

Things suddenly got awkward, and I didn't like it. I shrugged.

"I knew it. I could tell. You used to work in that corner room with the other developers. Then I moved in and you got kicked out. Isn't that right?"

That's not the only thing, but yeah, maybe, I thought to myself. I shrugged again.

Nigel nodded his head. "That's what I thought. I'm going to fix this."

He started to walk away, but my curiosity got the better of me. I called out, "What are you going to do?"

"I'm going to quit!" he called back.

"Umm..." I said, following after him, but I couldn't think of what else to say. I trailed behind this man all the way to Victor's office, where he went inside. I stayed back and lingered in the hall out of sight.

Nigel closed the door from the inside, so I couldn't even hear what was going on. But I did hear my name from down the hallway. I turned and saw Cheryl standing there at a distance. She was looking at me. She looked sad. I said, "Hi Cheryl."

She replied, "Hi," and kept looking at me, as if waiting for me to say or do something.

I suddenly felt like fidgeting with something, but I had nothing, so I thrust my hands into my pockets. "I... uh... should tell you something."

Her eyes opened wider and she took half a step closer to me.

"I... and...," I continued. "I mean God and I... had a talk the other day."

She took another step and bit her lip.

"I decided to..." I started. "I mean I decided... I mean I just..."

Her eyes drilled holes into me. "Yes?"

We were interrupted by Victor's voice yelling. I heard him say, "Jeff Davis!"

I said, "I have to go." I looked into his window.

He said, "Will you please come here?"

Nigel opened the door from the inside and moved over to the far chair. I sat in the closer one and closed the door. They both looked at me and said nothing. I returned their nothing.

Then Victor said, "Nigel here is threatening to quit."

I looked at Nigel, then back to Victor.

"He says he kicked you out of your position and doesn't feel right about that."

I looked at Nigel then back to Victor, who continued. "What he doesn't understand is that he didn't kick you out of your position. I kicked you out of your position, as is my right as boss. Do you disagree with this?"

I thought about it, then said, "I suppose the boss can do whatever he wants to, but that might not be the same thing as doing what's best."

Victor banged his fist on the table then pointed at me. "You don't even work here anymore. I won't take your backtalk."

Nigel interrupted. "He is agreeing with you, sir. He just said you can do whatever you want."

"He also said it wasn't the best thing."

"He just meant he might disagree with some methods, which is OK, because he's still willing to obey them. Isn't that the definition of a model employee? Even if he disagrees, he still obeys? You couldn't ask for a better employee than that."

Victor grunted a little, then said, "Getting back to it, Nigel here thinks I should reinstate you as a developer and make him the documentor. I was initially against it, because of his qualifications..."

I glanced at Nigel when it occurred to me that I had no idea what this guy's qualifications were, but Victor continued.

"But not only did he convince me that development efficiency would go up, but he threatened to quit if I didn't hire you back on."

I looked at Nigel and felt sorry for ever feeling anger toward this man. I had no idea he was willing to sacrifice his position as a developer for me. Why would he do this for me? He didn't even know me.

Nigel said to me, "I just reminded him that since I'm not familiar with the software, I won't be very productive, and the person who is explaining it to me won't be very productive, leaving only two productive developers. But if we switched positions, there would be four productive developers, which is twice as many."

"But you wouldn't be one of them."

He shrugged. "I'm OK with documentation, at least for now. I'm not the greatest coder in the world anyway."

"Um... thanks... Nigel."

"You're welcome, Jeff." Turning to Victor, he said, "And it's best for the team. It's a win-win for everyone."

Victor said to me. "Very well, Jeff, do you want to start right now, or wait until tomorrow morning?"

I took a deep breath, steadied my nerves, then said, "I haven't decided if I want to come back at all."

"What? After what Nigel is willing to sacrifice for you? Jeff, you are difficult to work with." He frowned.

"I'll come back on two conditions."

"I am the boss here! You have to listen to me, not me to you. I won't hear your conditions. Take the offer or leave it."

Nigel interrupted again. "They might be very easy things, or maybe I could help with them. It doesn't hurt to listen."

Victor sighed. "What are the conditions?"

"First," I began. "I don't want to check in my hours every day. It is an insult to my loyalty. We are salaried employees. We get paid by the month, not by the hour. I have often worked lots of overtime without extra pay. It's as if you don't trust us. It's a smack to the face twice a day."

Victor raised his arms in exasperation. "It is a boss's primary job to make sure his workers get their work done. That's why I'm here, to make sure you work."

Nigel responded. "Yes, that would be true for minimum wage or factory workers, but these are qualified professionals with University degrees. They can be treated better, and they have earned respect by making a great product so far. Jeff doesn't have a history of slacking off, does he?"

"Yes! The other day he took off in the afternoon without telling anyone."

"He was going to the hospital. A good boss should encourage his people to get better. You want him to keep all his typing fingers, right?"

"He should have told me."

Nigel raised his hands in concession. "You're absolutely right. He should have." They both looked at me.

I said, "OK, I'm sorry for not telling you. I'll tell you from now on if I have to go to the hospital."

"Or anything else."

"Or anything else."

Nigel continued. "And it's a small price to pay to have an experienced developer back at work. In fact, it's no price at all, because you're not actually losing anything. Another win-win."

"Fine," Victor pointed at me. "You, singular, Jeff, don't need to check in or out."

I said, "Thank you," and I meant it.

Victor continued. "If your second condition is that you don't have to follow Victor's Security Rules, the answer is No. No deal. You have proven yourself that when you don't follow them, we get hacked. If you don't want to follow the rules, you can't work here. End of sentence."

"I'm willing to follow the rules."

Nigel said to Victor, "See?"

Victor said to me, "Then what is your second condition?"

I took a breath, glanced at Nigel, then said to Victor, "Come talk to the police with me."

4:01 PM

"Police!" exclaimed Nigel. "Is there something I should know about?"

Victor said, "No!", and I said, "Victor used to work for Technology Solutions."

"The people across the stairs? You used to work there?"

"He was their boss."

"What's wrong with that?"

Victor said, "Nothing!"

I said, "It turns out they are a bunch of scammers, and scammed my mom out of thousands of dollars."

"Oh wow. Is that why you left?" Nigel asked Victor.

Victor was upset. "Nigel! This meeting is over. You're dismissed."

Nigel stood up and as he left the room, he said, "If you need to talk with the police, you need to talk with the police. You need to do the right thing." I smiled to myself. I think I like this guy.

When he closed the door, Victor said to me, "You didn't have to tell him."

I shrugged. "I thought you needed some encouragement."

"I don't appreciate my personal life broadcast to everyone."

"It was just previous work experience."

"You made me look like a criminal."

"Are you?"

"No! Not anymore. I left all that."

"You may have left it to the point of thinking it's no longer good, but are you at the point of thinking it's actually bad?"

"Of course it's bad. Wait." He pointed at me. "I know where you're going with this. You're going to say 'If you really think it's bad, what are you doing about it?'. I'll remind you, Jeff, that I'm not a snitch. It's called loyalty. You could learn something about that."

"So on one hand you claim to be on the side of good, but on the other hand, you claim to be loyal to bad people. Which one is it?"

"Can't you just leave this alone? Maybe the real world is more complicated than you think it is."

"Yeah, it might be. But even in the complexity of it all, we all have a choice. Are we going to side with the good or with the bad? We might not know everything out there, or see everything clearly, but there is one thing we can do. And that is to pick sides. We can pick our masters. We can pick our bosses. We can decide who it is we're going to serve. I've already decided who I'm serving. Maybe you need to do the same."

I got up and started toward the door when Victor said, rather loudly, "You are so annoying, Jeff!" He hit his desk for emphasis. "Agh! Especially when you're right. I hate that! Fine!" He calmed down a little. "Fine, I'll go talk to the police. I'm sure they'd love to hear from me." Then he paused, and almost had a hint of concern or fear cross his face, but then recovered. "Have you talked to them too? Have you reported your mom's scam?"

"Actually, no I haven't."
"Good. You're coming with me."

CHAPTER 15

4:43 PM

Victor drove a silver Lexus LS 500 with a red leather interior. It was a nice car, but maybe not better than my Mercedes. I mean my dad's Mercedes that got repossessed because he stopped making the payments. At one point, on the way to the police station, the sun was shining behind us, so Victor pressed a button and a sunblind shifted into place on the rear windshield. OK, my car didn't do that. That was pretty cool.

I noticed we weren't going to Gary Street, where I had spent some time this morning. That was fine with me. Instead, we went to the station on Pembina. That was where detective Joseph Wakefield worked.

Victor hadn't talked at all on the way there. He seemed almost nervous, in an angry sort of way. He was always angry, but now it was mixed with apprehension. That should have been a clue for me. I should have realized then who we were up against. Maybe these people were capable of more than just beating people up and abandoning their offices. Maybe I should have been concerned for more than just bruises on my body. Maybe my life was in danger. But I didn't care. We were doing the right thing. That's what mattered. I was a servant of God, and maybe my boss was too.

My eyes wandered to the time displayed on the car's console, and suddenly remembered that I hadn't picked up my car yet, and they were closing at five. I pulled out my phone and called them.

The voice on my phone said, "J.W. McDonald Auto Service. Becky speaking."

"Hi. This is Jeff Davis..."

"Yes! Your car is ready."

"But I won't make it there by five."

"Oh. And we're not open tomorrow. Monday morning, then?"

"Umm... is it possible for me to pay over the phone now and pick it up whenever I have time?"

"Absolutely. Just tell me your credit card number."

I pulled out my credit card and read off the digits to her, and the expiry date, and the security number on the back.

She said, "It didn't work," so I read all the numbers again, being extra careful this time.

"It still didn't work," she said. "It says the card is declined."

"Really? That's strange. It should work fine."

"Do you have another credit card?"

"No."

"I'm not sure I can help you then."

We pulled into a parking spot at the police station.

"I have to go," I said. "Bye."

"Bye."

I hung up the phone.

"Didn't your credit card go through?" Victor asked.

"No."

"Hmmm..."

"What does that mean?"

He opened his door and got out. "Let's go talk with the police."

5:01 PM

Victor started walking toward the building, and I followed along.

He opened the door, walked in and was greeted by a lady in uniform behind a glass wall who asked him, "How can I help you?"

He said, "We are here to report a crime."

"What kind of crime?"

"People getting scammed out of money."

"What kind of scam?"

"What do you mean what kind? People losing their money by being lied to."

"Was it a Ponzi scheme? Was it by false advertising or non-payment of a product? Was it by pretending to be interested in someone romantically? What kind of scam?"

Victor scowled. "It involved computers, usually by talking over the phone."

"Cybercrime," she stated, then turned around and yelled, "Joe! For you!"

The lady walked away and was replaced by a police officer, who looked more like a murder detective than a cybercrime nerd. He was somewhat round around the middle, his hair had mostly left him, and he looked old, probably over fifty.

"I'm detective Joseph Wakefield. How can I help you?"

"We want to report a scam."

"A cybercrime?"

"Yes."

"I'll get you the forms to fill out."

He turned to go, but Victor added, "It's more than just reporting a crime, it might also be… confessing to a crime."

The officer looked at Victor with those detective eyes that could see right through you. I was glad I wasn't on the receiving end. Then he nodded and said, "Please come with me." He opened a door next to us and invited us in. Seeing me, he said, "You're confessing a crime too, Jeff?"

"Ah. No. I'm just reporting one. Another one."

"You were just in here a few weeks ago, and now you're back. You caught another criminal, huh?"

"Well..."

"Is it this guy? You talked him into confessing?"

"Ah.. well.. yes, but no."

"I'll do my best. I know how to extract a confession."

Suddenly I was confused. Yes, I was trying to bring bad guys to justice, but I didn't mean Victor. Yeah, I couldn't stand him, but it's not like I wanted him to go to jail. At least I didn't think I did. But if he was guilty, then why not? Isn't the right thing for him to go to jail if he was guilty? I felt momentarily dazed and confused. I should have said something, but nothing came to me.

Joseph ushered us into a room that was equipped with a desk, a video camera, microphone, and lights. Joseph sat on one side and Victor on the other. I stood off to the side and I saw Joseph fiddle with his computer mouse on his side of the desk. He clicked some buttons that probably meant to start recording, and a small display of Victor's face appeared on his screen. I couldn't help noticing that the "Start Recording" button was way too small, and it was green. It should have been red with a circle icon, because a red circle is the universal icon for recording, not green. Green was for playing. Ugh. Bad software design was everywhere, even in police stations. It's a wonder how these cops got anything done.

The detective began. "We are being recorded. Do you understand this? And are you alright with it?"

Victor scowled. "Yes, to both questions."

"What do you want to confess?"

"Before I say anything, I want to know if you will deal with me in a more lenient way if I... give you information on other people."

"Plea bargaining is an option, but it's a matter for the prosecutor, not the arresting officer. And since we're being recorded, I should say that you should probably talk with a lawyer first."

Victor glanced at the camera, then said to Joseph, "Can I just give you information on other people without talking about myself?"

"You absolutely can. You're not under arrest here, so I don't have to remind you about your right to remain silent. You are free to talk. And I'm not coercing you in any way. Say or don't say whatever you want."

Victor took a breath, then said, "Some years ago, I was approached by a man to head up a group of people who would start a business by scamming people."

"You lead this group?"

"I'm not talking about me! I'm talking about them!"

"Who was this man who approached you?"

"His name is Yash Nagi."

"How do you spell that?" While Victor spelled, Joseph pulled out a small ringed notebook and took notes. For investigating cybercrimes, this guy was awfully old school. "What does this man look like?"

"He's about five foot six. He has a slight Indian accent."

"From India?"

"That's what I said."

"You said his accent. I'm asking if he is from India. Does he look like someone from India?"

"Yes. I believe he is from India, or maybe his parents or grandparents. I don't know. We never talked about it. His accent is only slight, so he's probably been here for a long time."

"Where are you from?"

"My parent immigrated from Russia before I was born. I was born here."

"How did you meet this Yash Nagi?"

"At a bar. As I said, he approached me."

"How did he hear about you?"

Victor scowled again. "We're not talking about me. We're talking about him!"

"Alright, so Nagi approaches you for an unknown reason and asks you to head up some new business."

"Yes."

"And you agree?" The police officer rested his detective eyes all over Victor.

Victor stared right back at him and said, "I knew two guys and he knew two guys, so I had four employees."

"And they did what you told them to do?"

"That's what a boss does, isn't it? A boss gives the orders, and his guys obey the orders. At least they should."

"They didn't always?"

Victor pointed his thumb at me. "This guy doesn't always obey orders. He's stubborn sometimes."

Joseph said to me, "Jeff, this is your boss?"

"Yeah," I replied. "But I'm not one of those guys he's talking about. I work at Omniscient."

Joseph continued his questions. "Did your business have a name?"

"No. We called it the business."

"What did your business do?"

"We sc... I mean they scammed people out of money."

"How?"

"By posing as computer consultants or help desk specialists."

"And then?"

"And then we would convince people to give us access to their bank accounts or credit cards. Or things like that. Gift cards worked well. Also identity theft."

"How did you accomplish these things."

"By gaining access to their computer over the Internet."

"How did you do that? Hack into their computers?"

Victor laughed. "No. We never hacked anybody. They all just handed over access to us willingly. They even thanked us for the help. Then we stole their identity and life savings."

"How did you steal their identities?"

"If you get a good one, they will scan in their driver's license and send you the file."

"Really?"

"This might hard for you to believe. You're a skeptical and cynical police officer, but let me assure you. There are many naive and gullible people out there. We preyed on them. And we were good, too. We made good money."

"So why'd you walk away?"

Victor looked off to the side, then finally said, "We're not talking about me."

"I'll need a list of everyone you've scammed."

Victor laughed. "You have to understand, officer. When I walked away, I left everything. I have no records. And there is no way I can remember them all."

"What are the names of the people who worked for you?"

"There was Nick, Dani, Sadu, and Sven. They worked for me."

"How can we get hold of these people?"

"You probably can't. These aren't family men who marry and settle down. If you settle down, you're vulnerable. They probably moved when they heard I left. They probably moved again when they abandoned their business at the Forks."

"They had a real storefront?"

"I managed to convince them to go legit, and they did for a while, or so I thought, until Jeff here scared them away."

"What did he do?"

He looked over at me, then answered with, "I'll let him tell you that himself."

"I would like to hear about it. But first, tell me about Nagi. How much was he involved, and can I find him?"

"I reported to him. When I left, he took over the business."

"Did he ever settle down?"

"I was once at his place. He lives in the bush just on the outside of the city."

"Could you find it again?"

"Yes."

When Joseph paused his questions, Victor asked, "So, what are you going to do?"

"First of all, I'm going to open a case, and I'm going to record your testimony in it. But if we have no hard evidence, and you can't think of any specific cases, and nobody to prosecute, there's not much I can do, is there?"

"You could go after Nagi. I know where he lives." Then he paused. "Maybe. If he's still there."

Joseph thought for a while, then said, "OK. We'll go after Nagi. And I have some ideas how we'll do it. But first, I want to talk to Jeff. Jeff, will you please take a seat?"

5:30 PM

I sat in the chair and immediately felt guilty. The camera and the light in my eyes made me feel like I was going to jail, and there was nothing I could do. I had been found out, all my sins were on display, and I couldn't hide them. But this wasn't the first time I was here. I sat in this chair once before, and it turned out fine that time. Bad guys went to jail. That was good. And I hoped that would happen again this time too.

"How are you involved in this, Jeff?" Detective Joseph Wakefield asked me.

"My mom got scammed by these people."

"Tell us about the scam. How did she get scammed?"

"She called them, and they convinced her that they overpaid her, which was not true, so she paid them back, but with her own money."

"Why would they pay her?"

"They said it was in exchange for user feedback."

"And she believed them?"

I shrugged. "I guess so."

"And how did they convince her that she got paid?"

"They transferred money in her bank account from her savings to her checking."

"How did they do that?"

"They took control of her computer."

"She let them?"

I nodded.

"So how did she send them the money?"

"She went to the bank and wired it to them."

"Thinking they overpaid but it was really her own money?"

"Yes."

"I will need the name of her bank, as well as her name, and the date and time."

"I don't have that all on me, but I'll get it to you."

"Go on."

"That's about it, really."

"What was that about you scaring them away?"

"I went to their place of business, Technology Solutions, in the Johnston Terminal at the forks, across the floor from Omniscient. I... th... I mean I... told them to give me my mom's money back."

"When was that?"

"Yesterday I think."

"And what was their reaction?"

"They..." I didn't want to say they called the cops on me, because I didn't want this police officer to know about that whole gun-waving thing, so I left out that part. "Their reaction was to abandon their office. When I went back, everything was gone. All their computers, everything." I met his piercing gaze, hoping to stash away this burning secret deep, deep in the recesses of my mind. I knew it was no use, because I was pretty sure he could see everything inside of me, but I tried anyway. There was no other way.

He stared at me for quite a while. It became uncomfortable. Finally he said, "OK. If that's your testimony."

I said, "It's true."

He continued. "How do you know it was these people who scammed your mom?"

"I…" Shoot. I couldn't say it was because I called the same number and hacked into their computer. That was probably illegal. "Because…" I think to think of something quick. Quick! Even if it might not be one hundred percent accurate. "Because the person on the helpline said their name was 'Technology Solutions.'"

"And from that you assumed it was the same people?"

"And I recognized their accent."

"You recognized their accent from what? When did you talk with them?"

"I called the same number my mom called."

"I'll need that number."

"I'll get it to you."

"You might be mistaken that these are the same people. It might not stand up in court. If we had records from your boss, that would be great. But as it is, our case is a little weak. However, I will do some digging. I'll look into phone records, the lease of their storefront, the owner of Nagi's property."

Victor added, "I'll get that to you."

Joseph clicked his mouse, probably to stop the video recording. Then he gave us both his card. "Get those pieces of information to me. If I don't get in touch with you, you can ask me how it's going."

"Thank you," I said.

Victor didn't say anything. We walked outside the building and back to his car.

Instead of starting the engine, he sat there. He looked less angry than he was before. "Thanks," he said.

"For what?"

"I've known for a long time that this is what I should have done. And I've been fighting it." He took a deep breath. "I don't know if they won't kill us both, but at least we did the right thing." Then he looked at the time. "I'm hungry."

6:15 PM

Victor and I sat in his car, eating fast food pizza. He said, "Where do you live, Jeff?"

"Um... well... I need to go pick up my car from the body shop."

"Where is it? I'll take you."

"J.W. McDonald on Bannatyne."

Soon we were driving again. After some minutes of silence, Victor said, "How's your dad doing?"

"He's in jail."

"I know. How's he doing in there?"

"Fine, I think. Do you... do you know him?"

He nodded. "Yash and Jade worked for the same guy. I bumped into Jade once or twice." Then he looked at me and said, "I recognized you when I started working at Omniscient. You look like him."

"I might look like him, but I'm not him."

"You're right there. Jade was easy to work with. You're not. And besides, for you to snitch on your own dad, you must not agree with him on something." He shrugged. "Or maybe you just hate him and want to get him in trouble. You succeeded there."

I didn't like that last comment. "I don't hate him."

"Really? You threw your own dad in jail. Now you're going to tell me you love him?"

I didn't like where this was going. "He was a thief and a bad man. I did the right thing."

Victor laughed out loud. "The right thing, huh?"

"Yes."

"This from the guy who went around waving a gun at people?"

"I... I threw that gun away."

"Why?"

"Because the pol... Do we have to talk about this?"

"Hey, you said you were doing the right thing. I'm giving you a chance to defend yourself."

I sighed in exasperation. "I shouldn't have threatened people with a gun, OK? I shouldn't have done that."

"So why did you?"

"I... I don't know. Because they were bad people. I wanted them to go to jail. I wanted my mom's money back. They stole forty thousand dollars of my mom's money."

"Yeah, that's something they would do. And they're good at it."

"And I was trying to get it back."

"You're not getting that money back, Jeff. They have it. They've probably already spent it."

"They can still go to jail. And you can help with that."

Victor kept his eyes ahead and didn't respond.

"Right?" I continued.

"I already made that decision."

"What do you mean?"

"I mean they probably already know we went to the police."

"Really?"

He shrugged. "Maybe not, but Nagi does have a lot of connections."

"Even with the police?"

"I don't know that for sure, but I do know this. From this point on, we have to catch him before he catches us. And to do that, we'll need all the help we can get."

"What are you referring to?"

"I'm referring to someone who has worked alongside of him, not just for him like I did. You don't have anywhere you need to be right now, do you? Because we need to go somewhere."

"Where?"

"Jail"

6:52 PM

Victor parked his Lexus at the Headingly Correctional Institute, and we walked in. I was getting used to security, and in a few minutes we were waiting in the same waiting room with the brown rug, old coffee machine, and drink machine from the 90's.

To be honest, I didn't know how I was feeling about seeing my dad again. I remember not that long ago shouting at him "I'll never be like you," when he said I should become a Christian like him. The fact was that I still didn't want to be like him. He was not my role model; he was still a bad person. But on the other hand, didn't I surrender my life to God since then? Didn't I commit to following him? Doesn't that, in fact, by definition, make me a Christian? I honestly didn't know. Does that mean I was now like my dad? I hoped not. Agh. It was confusing.

Did I still remember him being a bad father and abandoning us? Yes. Did I still remember him trying to kill me? Yes. Does God want me to forgive him? Yes. Have I? No. Does that mean I hate my father? I don't know. I'm not a psychologist. Life is complicated and confusing.

But when I saw him limp through that door, something in my heart felt a touch of warmth for this man. Somewhere inside,

I felt a feeling. What was it? It must have been compassion or something, because when I looked at his face, I saw deep bruises, damaged tissue, and a swollen eye. He had gotten beaten up, just like I had. I said, "Dad!"

He said, "Hi Jeff," then "Victor!"

"Jade," said Victor.

"What are you doing here?" my dad asked Victor. "And what are you doing with Jeff?" He seemed almost angry, as if he were trying to defend me."

"I work for him," I said.

My dad limped toward me. "You didn't join them, did you?! Jeff! I told you to stay away from these people!"

"You don't understand," I said.

"We don't work for Yash Nagi," Victor said. "We're trying to put him away."

My dad looked confused and looked between us. "But you work for him?"

Victor explained. "I quit working for Yash, and started working at Omniscient. I'm Jeff's new boss."

My dad dropped into a chair, and we also sat down.

"You got roughed up," Victor said.

My dad waved it off. "It's nothing."

"Was it Yash?"

He looked at Victor, then slowly nodded. "It turns out he has some muscle in here, or at least access to some."

"Did they tell you why they were doing it?"

He glanced briefly at me, then back at Victor and nodded again.

"It was a message for Jeff, wasn't it?"

"They said, 'Tell your son Jeff to back off, or something worse will happen... to both of you.'"

That hit me hard. It was my fault. It was because of me that my dad's face and body got broken. I remember the feeling of being pummeled with blows and not being able to do anything about it. It was a horrible, horrible feeling. If I looked in a mirror, I could still see evidence of that night.

I had to reconsider my actions. I thought of my mom getting cheated. And now my dad. I thought of my dad's warnings not to get involved, the last time I was here. And now I had to think of my dad's physical welfare. I might not love him like a son is supposed to love his father, but didn't I have some sort of small responsibility to make sure he didn't die? So I asked him, "Do you want me to back off?"

He took his time answering. "Jeff, when you got me arrested and thrown into jail, I thought you were a terrible person. But since I've been here, I think maybe God is using this somehow for my good."

Victor was surprised. "Jade! You're talking about God. You are a Christian?"

He nodded.

"Ha!" Victor shouted. "Me too!"

"Really? You?"

"Yes! That is why I left Yash."

"I respect that, Victor. I'll bet you took a big pay cut."

"Sheesh. You got that right. But I have some saved up, so I'll be OK."

"What about you, Jeff?" my dad asked me.

"I don't have that much saved up."

"I mean about becoming a Christian."

"I… I gave my life to God the other day."

"Jeff! My son! Is this true?"

I nodded.

My dad sat back and I thought he would start crying. "This might be the happiest day of life."

"Well don't go overboard," I said. "We still need to decide what to do about Yash."

"That is why we came here, Jade," said Victor. "You must help us. How can we get evidence on him? Would you testify?"

My dad shrugged. "I could testify, but I'm not sure it would do much good. If we had some hard evidence on him, like they got on me, it would make a big difference."

"I guess I did it once," I said.

"Be careful, Jeff. These people will kill you if they suspect something."

"I would prefer to not die just yet."

"But isn't that what we are asked to do?" Victor said. "As Christians, we must be willing to lay down our lives, right?"

Jade said, "Wow, Victor, you really got into this hardcore, didn't you?"

"I read my Bible."

"You're right," I said. "If we're going to follow God... we have to do it at all costs."

There was a moment's silence, then my dad held out his hand and said, "Good luck to you, Jeff." I shook it. Then he shook Victor's hand. "Good luck to you, Victor. I wish you both success."

"Thank you, Jade," Victor said.

We said our goodbyes and made our way out of the building. As soon as we had left, Victor got a phone call from Yash Nagi.

CHAPTER 16

7:35 PM

Victor answered his phone and said, "Yes... Yash! What can I do for you?... What's the time now?... That will only give me twenty-five minutes... I understand... Yes, I'll be there... bye." He hung up.

"Was that Yash Nagi?" I asked.

"Yes, and he wants to meet with me."

"When?"

"At eight."

"Just with you?"

"That's what he said."

"Are you going to drop me off somewhere first?"

"I don't have time."

"Why would he schedule such a fast meeting?"

"So I don't have time to plan anything myself, like something involving the police."

"He doesn't trust you."

Victor chuckled. "That's what makes him so successful."

"So what are we going to do?"

We got into his car. "We're going to meet him."

"We?"

"Maybe you should stay in the car when I meet with him."

"Are you going to try to record him on your phone?"

"I guess so."

"What app are you going to use?"

"Are you going to give me a suggestion?"

"If you use Sound Recorder, it will only record to your local phone, but if you use Omniscient, you can record and store the file on our servers automatically."

"I know that part. I'm the Director of Technology, remember?"

"Yeah. I just... I forgot last time. And I know of another app that lets you run things automatically. Like volume-down plus power button will start an Omniscient conversation with yourself."

Victor took out his phone and handed it to me. "Very well, install it for me."

I held up the phone so he could unlock it, and he did. When I looked at the home screen, I said, "On your home screen you have a Bible app."

"Yes. That's how I read the Bible. Aren't Christians supposed to read the Bible? I think it's a rule."

"Yeah, but you also have a porn app. I think there is a Christian rule about that too."

"That's none of your business!" Victor got mad. "Stop nosing into other people's business. Jeff, you are so annoying!"

I installed the app that connected the buttons to the Omniscient action. Then I configured it to do as I wanted. When I was done, I said, "It's done."

Victor responded with words I wasn't expecting.

"Uninstall the porn app."

"What?"

"I said to uninstall the porn app. Are you hard of hearing?"

"No. But why?"

"Why?! Because I'm trying to be a good Christian, that's why. I might be failing at it, but at least I'm trying. Now are you going to uninstall it or not?"

"Sure, OK." I did, then said, "It's done."

"Now give me the phone and let me practice."

I handed it to him, and he practiced pressing volume up and power with one hand. With the other one he drove. When he was confident it work working, he put the phone in his pocket. "Now we will have a conversation," he began.

"Uhhh... about what?"

"I'm testing the microphone to see if it can pick up our voices."

"Um. Yeah. Right. OK."

"Say something more."

"Uh. Hi. This is... Jeff Davis. I'm in the car with Victor A..." I caught myself just in time. I didn't get the full word "Adolf" out of my mouth, but I was left in an awkward situation because Victor's real last name had completely left my mind. I was frozen, not knowing what to do. Then he looked at me with furrowed eyebrows, as if disgusted that I wasn't saying his last name.

"Akulov!" he finished for me. "What have you been calling me up till now?"

"I guess just Victor," I lied.

Victor made another left turn. Over the last few miles, the city streets we had been driving on had become less and less crowded. Now we were near the edge of the city. He turned left again, and we were on what looked like a country road. He pulled over to the side. "This is his driveway," he said. Then he pulled out his phone and played the recording. It was very quiet. He adjusted the volume to the loudest position and held the phone to his ear. "Your voice is discernible. It will work." Then I heard the word "Akulov!" come out of his phone. It was very discernible.

"Do you want to hide in the trunk or the back seat?" he asked.

"Uh.. back seat."

"It'll be more dangerous. It's more likely they will find you there."

"But if something goes wrong with you in there, when would I ever get out of the trunk?"

He shrugged. "It's your choice."

I got out of the car and climbed in the back. I lay down on the back seat, then tried the floor to get lower. As I was trying to get comfortable, the car started moving, and I heard Victor say, "It's seven o'clock. Showtime. Stay down, Jeff. Make sure nobody sees you. And try to do as you're told this time."

7:00 PM

As we bumped along Yash Nagi's driveway, the evening light still clearly illuminated the tall evergreen trees visible out the windows. Soon the car made a sharp turn then came to a stop.

I whispered loudly, "Victor!"

"What?"

"We should have told Joseph what we're doing, so he can find the audio recording on our server if something goes wrong."

"Who's Joseph?"

"The detective we talked with."

"Then call him now."

"Victor!"

"What?!"

"Do you think they're going to kill you?"

He didn't immediately respond. Then after a while, he didn't respond at all. I heard the door open and then close, and then I was alone. I began to think maybe this wasn't a good idea. I probably should have gotten out at the end of the driveway and stayed there.

The ground outside must have been gravel, because I heard Victor's footsteps. Then I heard him say something to someone, and the someone responded. One set of footsteps walked away and the other stayed. Then they slowly approached the car I was hiding in. I had a bad feeling about this. I wish I had a blanket or something to hide under. I wish I had called the detective sooner.

I wish my heart wasn't beating so loudly. I tried closing my eyes, to hide, but it didn't work. I heard knocking, so I opened them and looked out the window to see a large man looking directly at me. His size may have been a lot of fat, but there also appeared enough muscle to know that this man would win any fight he was in. His hair, what was left of it, was black, and only showed up on the edges and back of his round head.

"Open the door," he said.

I didn't move. So much for hiding. I didn't even call Joseph. Stupid. How many more things could go wrong?

He reached behind him and held up a handgun to the window. "Open the door, please," he repeated.

I imagined a bullet cracking up the glass, then cracking up several of my body parts. I concluded that I didn't want that to happen, and the best way would be to make this man happy instead of grumpy. I sat up and opened the door a crack. He grabbed it and opened it the rest of the way. When he saw my less-than-muscular, computer programmer build of a body, he relaxed and holstered his weapon. "Please join us inside. It will be much more comfortable for you."

I didn't know if that was a threat. It probably was, of course, so I complied. It wasn't just his weapon that was intimidating. It was the rest of him too, except for his bald head.

When I got out, I looked at the house we were parked in front of. It was a large, one-story house. The roof was made of cedar shakes. The walls were made of slabs of some kind of rock. The garage had no less than four garage doors to it. I could only imagine what kinds of vehicles were inside.

"This way," the man directed me. I walked.

The inside of the house was all open, and it echoed because of the hardwood floor and walls made of something else smooth. I had no idea what they were made of, something rich was all I could guess.

The man closed the door behind us and said, "I'm going to pat you down. Could you raise your arms please?"

I had never been pat down before, so this was new to me. I raised my arms and watched what he would do.

He patted me under my armpits, then on my back, then on my front with the back of his arm. He patted down each of my legs, then my pockets, where he clearly felt things. He reached into a nearby closet and pulled out a small basket. "Please empty your pockets into here."

I didn't like the idea of someone taking my phone away, because it was my personal possession, and because I might want to record something with it. I said, "Why?"

"Security reasons."

"I'm not carrying a gun."

"I know, but keys can be used as weapons, if you know what you're doing."

I hesitated, so he said, "You will receive everything back when you leave. This is strictly for security reasons. It's what I'm paid to do."

I reluctantly put my keys into the basket.

"And your phone."

"I like my phone."

"These are the policies Mr. Nagi has put in place. I'm just doing my job."

"What if he asks me to schedule something? I'll need my calendar."

"I'll be more than happy to retrieve your phone if he asks me to."

"Maybe I should just wait in the car."

He took half a step toward me and said directly to my face, "I think you should comply."

I evaluated my options. There were none. So I reluctantly placed my phone in the basket. Then he lifted the leather seat of a nearby bench and placed the basket into it. While the lid was up,

I caught a glimpse of another basket in there holding another phone I just had my hands on. It was Victor's. There was no way any sound could get recorded there. I groaned to myself. This was not going well. All our plans were officially out the window. We were now at the mercy of Yash Nagi's plans. I had no idea what those plans were, but I was about to find out.

7:14 PM

Our footsteps echoed off the hardwood floor and the walls that were made of something I didn't recognize–certainly not painted drywall–maybe marble. Even though it all looked very expensive, I didn't even like it. Give me some soft carpet any day.

My guide opened a door for me and ushered me into a room that must have been an office. It was bigger than my living room. There was a large desk on the far side. In front of the desk sat Victor, who turned around to look. On the far side sat another man with slightly darker skin, thinning black hair, and noticeably slimmer and shorter.

My guide said, "Sir, I found his gentleman hiding in the back of your guest's car."

Yash looked up and replied, "Thank you." Then he gestured me to come forward. "Please join us, Jeffrey Davis."

I started walking forward as the door closed behind me. Off to my right I noticed another man standing there. Another bodyguard. I looked at Victor, then sat on the other chair next to him.

"I'm so glad to see you, Jeff," said Yash.

I waited for him to continue.

He did. "You see, I was just discussing with your boss here, the question of if we could still trust him. When he left our organization, I feared he would tell the authorities all our little secrets. He persuaded me at the time that he would not. But since he was just seen at a police station, I started to doubt his commitment."

Victor interrupted, "I told you, they just wanted to talk to me about Jeff waving a gun around."

Yash held a hand up. "Please don't interrupt, Victor. I was talking with the boy. Now Jeff, up until this very minute, I was inclined to believe him. After all, he has been a very good employee of mine for many years. But you. You just changed all that, didn't you?"

"How?"

"Your very presence. I know who you are. Victor here is associating with Jade's son, the very one who got him arrested. Normally, I would quote the proverb 'Like father, like son,' but not in your case. No, you don't share your father's... ambitions, do you?"

Now I had to think. If I told the truth and said my dad was so evil I tried to kill him, I would be positioning myself as an enemy of this man, thus endangering my life and Victor's too. But if I lied and said I wanted to be as corrupt as him, I would not be honoring God whom I'm trying to obey, since I think he doesn't like lying. But maybe I'm allowed to lie in cases such as this. Then suddenly I thought of a way out of my predicament. My dad said he became a Christian, didn't he? Yes he did. And then I said I would never be like him. Well, maybe I was wrong.

I finally replied, "I once said to my dad that I would never be like him. This was after he asked me to join him. Since then I think I have changed my mind. I think I should actually be more like my dad. I think there are some good points in him that I should... respect and admire." Even while those words were still in my mouth, I felt something shift in my heart. Somehow my words were pushing the hatred away. My own mouth was convincing me to start loving this man I hated. Or did I only used to hate him now? I thought about him sitting in jail and then deciding to become a Christian after all he's been through. That was probably a very hard decision, to stand up for God like that. That's more than I've ever done. That's a respectable thing to do. I've only been a coward, but my dad has shown courage.

My emotions must have shown, because Yash said to me, "Really?"

I nodded. "I wish I were more like my dad."

He continued. "I would not have thought this was possible. Please tell us how did this come about?"

I shrugged. "I visited him in jail a few times."

"And that was enough to change your mind about what you did to him?"

"I should have treated him differently all along."

Yash turned to Victor. "Victor, do you see this? Jade's son is changing his mind about his actions. Maybe you want to too. Maybe you want to come work for me again."

I also turned to him, wondering what he might say. I saw his hard angry eyes think for a minute, then he said, "Honestly, the pay isn't nearly as good in the private sector."

"Of course not. I pay very well. You missed buying new cars all the time, didn't you? This thing you're driving, it's a few years old already. I don't know how you stand it."

"Thank you for your offer, sir. Can I think about it and get back to you?"

"No, Victor, you cannot. Since Jeff's gun incident this morning, I've had to make some changes to our operations. We've already left that building, and now more decisions need to be made urgently. If you want your job back, say so now."

"OK, I'll take it." I looked at him to see if he was serious. For a moment, I thought I may have convinced even him that I wanted to be a part of this organization. And now he was agreeing. I started getting nervous.

Yash smiled. "Good."

"What about Jeff?" Victor asked.

Yash turned to me, "Jeff, if you are serious about regretting your actions regarding your father, would accept a job offer to work for me, his former associate?"

I looked at Victor, hoping for a clue on what I should say. He only said, "You should accept the offer, Jeff."

So I said, "OK, I accept."

7:28 PM

"Excellent, Jeffrey. I would much rather have someone as an employee than an enemy. Up until now, you have been acting the part of the enemy, so I had to treat you as such."

"You had me beaten up."

"Only to send a message to you father, understand. And when that didn't work, I put pressure on you financially."

"How?"

"How?! Didn't you notice your car got repossessed? And your credit card stopped working?"

I paused and wondered how this man could know that, but then I was forced to answer, "Yes."

"That's because your credit rating suddenly took a dive."

"How?"

The man laughed. "That's the simplest thing. You will learn that on day one. You simply steal someone's identity and take out loans in their name."

"You can't do that."

He laughed again. "If I gain access to your email, I can take whatever I choose. I can tell your bank I forgot my password, so it sends me a new one to your email address. Simple."

"You can't get access to my email address."

"Oh no? What if I say I forgot my password?"

"It will ask you security questions."

More laughter. "Like your mother's maiden name? Stevens. Your mother posted to social media about her father, Dennis Stevens. Easy. The make and model of your first car? Your mother posted that too. Nice woman."

I was stunned. He continued. "And your phone number and address? You included that in your resume you posted online. Thanks for that."

I sat there, too shocked to reply, until I finally said, "I assumed my dad's credit was bad, so they were repossessing his car."

"Ha. Ha. I'm sure Jade would have paid cash for it. But not to worry. If you want to join our team, all this will be given back to you and more."

I knew now more than ever that these people needed to be taken down. If they could do this to me, they could probably do it to anyone. Enjoy this laughing while you can, Yash Nagi. You're going down, and I'm going to be the one taking you down. I nodded. "I'm in."

"Good, Jeff. Then I shall treat you accordingly. But just so you understand, if you should change your mind and work against me, I will treat you according to those actions as well."

"I understand." Yes, I understood the threat. My plan was that we would never get to that point. Once we left this building, I didn't ever want to return, except maybe with a police escort.

7:39 PM

Yash Nagi smiled at us both. "Good. Very good. It will be good to have you back, Victor. I didn't have the time to run the crew myself anyway. But you will, as of right now."

"I understand," Victor nodded.

"If you have any questions," Yash said to me, "you can ask Victor. You report to him."

I looked at Victor and he scowled. I don't think he liked me that much.

"Very well, good evening gentlemen. You are dismissed."

Victor and I stood and made our way out of the room and down the hall. As we were retrieving our things, Yash came down the hall and said, "Victor! Before you sever ties with Omniscient, you should save a copy of all email messages. This would normally be Jade's domain, but seeing as he is not available right now, maybe we can expand our business."

Victor nodded. "OK."

I said to Yash, "Sir, I have a question."

"What is it?"

"My mom got scammed out of a lot of money by your crew. Do you think I can have it back?"

"We scammed your mom?! Jade's wife?" He looked to Victor for confirmation, who just shrugged.

"They divorced a long time ago," I said.

"Oh, in that case, Jade might appreciate it. We did him a favor. No, Jeff, your mom won't be getting her money back. But cheer up. We scam a lot of people, so you'll probably make that money back soon."

"Sounds good," I said, and I meant it. I even had to hide a smile coming to my face.

"Oh, one more thing, Victor," Yash said. "There is no leaving this time. From now on, there is only one way out of this organization. You know I clean up loose ends."

"I understand," Victor said.

Yash also looked at me, but I didn't say anything.

We went to our car and started driving.

Once we were away, I finally let the smile onto my face.

"What?" Victor asked gruffly.

"What?! We got him! He admitted to scamming people, and we got it recorded on your phone. Right? Give it to me. Let me check."

Victor didn't move.

"Victor! Give me your phone. Let me check to see how the recording went."

He just said, "These people are dangerous."

"You're kidding me! We have hard evidence on Yash, and you're not going to hand it in?"

"He has killed other people before me. I know. I've seen it."

"He can't kill anyone if he's in jail."

"He's not in jail, is he? He's in his castle, and he is king. To disobey is to be killed. It's as simple as that."

"Didn't you just visit the police and confess to them?"

Victor scowled.

"Didn't you just tell me you read your Bible? Aren't you trying to follow God's rules?"

He scowled some more.

"Didn't I just delete your porn app because you are trying to follow God?"

"Shut up, Jeff! You are so irritating! Just shut up. I'm going to drop you off wherever you want to be dropped off. Then leave me alone."

We sat in silence for a minute, before I said, "You want me to install your porn app again?"

"Agh!" Victor yelled, then reached out, and punched me in the leg. It hurt. That's what I get for being so irritating, I suppose. "Agh!" he yelled again. Then he took out his phone and almost threw it at me. "Fine! Take this phone and email the recording to the police."

As I surfed through his phone looking for the recording, I made a conscious effort to not rub my leg where it got punched. Soon I said, "I found the recording." I started playing it and repositioned it a few times to find the place where Yash Nagi confesses to scamming people. I found it and played it. It was good. It was clear. He clearly said, "We did him a favor," and "We scam a lot of people." I wasn't a lawyer, but I thought this was good enough.

I sent the audio recording in an email to Detective Joseph Wakefield.

From: victora@omniscient.software
Subject: Evidence on Yash Nagi
Attachment: audio0153.mp3
Hi detective. This is Jeff Davis sending you an email from Victor Akulov's phone. We caught Yash on a sound recording confessing to scamming people. Here it is.

—

Jeff Davis
jeffd@omniscient.software

When I pressed Send, it took a while to send over Victor's cell phone signal. When it finally did, he got an instant reply, which I read, then exclaimed, "Oh! We got a 552!"

"What's that?"

"SMTP error 552 is 'Message size exceeds maximum message size'. Joseph's email server can't handle large files. If they are using Postfix to handle their mail, it defaults to about ten megabytes, which is way too small in my opinion. You can change it in Postfix's config file, which I believe is located at /etc/postfix/main.cf"

"I don't care how smart you are with email, Jeff. Can you fix it?"

"We could chop up the file on a computer or laptop."

"Fine. We'll stop by my house. You can do it there."

I sent Joseph another email with no attachment, telling him what we got and saying we'll send the sound file soon.

We drove in silence for a few minutes. At one point I said, "We're doing the right thing."

"It's not over yet."

"It soon will be."

"You don't know who you're up against."

"You're just being pessimistic."

"How did he know we were at the police station?"

"Ummm…"

"Exactly! He has spies, or has hacked their computers, or something."

"I wonder if he has access to Joseph's email account." I said that because I just sent an email to it.

Victor groaned.

Chapter 17

8:03 PM

Victor's house was large and beautiful. But unlike Yash Nagi's house, it wasn't expensive for the sake of being expensive. It was just beautiful. We parked in his double car garage. The other spot was taken up with a red Porsche. I assumed it was a 911, but I saw the number 718 on the back. I suppose that was his weekend car, and this Lexus was his daily driver.

We walked through the house turning on lights. I never stopped to wonder if Victor was married or anything, but his house looked empty. I guessed he was single—single with maid service.

He led me to his office where he had a laptop. He put his phone on the desk as well as a phone cord he grabbed from a drawer. "There. Chop up the audio file and send it. The sooner the better."

I sat in the chair and said, "I don't need the cable and the phone. You can log in online and I can download that file."

He rolled his eyes. "Fine, have it your way." He logged in, and soon the large file was downloading.

"It would still be faster to just plug in the phone," he said.

I wasn't planning on replying, but my non-reply was interrupted by his phone. He answered it, and since the volume was still set so high and he was so close, I could hear both sides of the conversation.

Victor said, "Hello."

"Victor, this is Yash Nagi."

"Yash. What can I do for you?"

"I am disappointed, Victor."

"What about?"

"You were so eager to work for me again."

"Yes, I still am."

"Then why did you send an email to the police?"

Victor froze.

Yash continued. "Remember I said you would not be leaving again? There there was only one way out of this organization? You just made your choice. Goodbye, Victor."

The line went dead.

Then Victor started to sweat, and his breathing increased. He started walking in small circles. Then he stopped, held his head, and said, "Think. Stop and think. No. There is no time to think." He reached out and slapped the laptop closed, then ran out of the room with it.

I followed.

He went upstairs to his bedroom, to a closet and hauled out a backpack. It looked heavy. He put it on. That's when we heard the doorbell. He ran some more. I followed him down the hall, down the stairs, not to the door, but back to the garage. That's when we heard gunshots, and the door being kicked in.

In the garage, Victor simply said, "We'll take the Porsche." I skirted around to the passenger side and got in. He also got in and threw his stuff behind him. Yes, there were seats back there, but they were very small.

We belted up and Victor inserted the key and just sat there with his hand on the key, without turning it, in the ignition.

"What are you waiting for?" I asked.

He rolled his eyes. "For a developer, you're not that smart are you?" Then he said, "As soon as we open the garage door, they will know we're here, so I'm waiting until they are as far away from this point as possible."

"How will you know?"

"I'm estimating." Then he pressed the garage door opener button on his visor and started the engine which roared to life. While the garage door opened, Victor crouched down as much as he could, which inspired me to do the same.

"There might be a vehicle behind us. If there is, I will try to go around it. If we can't, we should get out and run for it."

"OK."

Just then the door to the house opened and a man stood there holding a gun. He raised it and fired, but we were already moving. The roof bumped a little as we just barely fit under the garage door, but we were moving, and the shot missed. I was thrown to the right as the car swerved to the left. We were going quite fast by the time we hit the front lawn. Then Victor swung the car around, destroying the grass, and shifted from reverse to first gear in the middle of the slide.

I glanced backwards and could see two black cars in the driveway that weren't there when we arrived. One of them was already moving.

"They're following us," I said.

"You're not helping, Jeff."

"Well what do you want me to say?" I could feel myself getting angry.

"You could start by apologizing for getting me involved in this."

"What?!"

"I was happily working a legitimate job until you came along."

"Don't blame this on me. It's not my fault Yash is trying to kill us."

"Actually, yes it is, Jeff. It is your fault Yash is trying to kill us."

I sat back in my seat. I couldn't believe this guy's attitude.

"There is one thing you could do to make yourself useful," Victor said.

"What?"

"You could plot us a course to the nearest police station."

I pulled out my phone and my map app was soon showing us a route. "If we were going the speed limit, the nearest one is seven minutes away. But at the speed we're going, we'll be there sooner. Then we'll be safe, if we can get inside."

"Not 'we'. You."

"What?"

"I'm dropping you off."

"And what about you?"

"I'm leaving town. Permanently."

"The police can protect you."

He laughed. "The same police that can't even keep their email safe? They're going to keep me safe? No. I'm better off running."

"We still need that audio recording of yours."

"I'll send it to you." Then he added, "Did it finish downloading onto the laptop?"

"No. About half."

"That's not enough."

"But it's still on our server."

"I know it's on our server. I know how our software works. I'm the Director of Technology."

"Are you?"

"Yes! Or, no. Stop asking hard questions. You can always find the file on our server yourself."

"Unless you delete it."

"Why would I delete it?"

"I don't know. I'm just saying that if you delete it, we won't have any other copies. That's all."

"I won't delete it."

"OK."

That's when we hit a construction zone and we came to a stop.

8:32 PM

When our car stopped, I looked behind us. I couldn't see any of those black cars, so I got out and stood. It was getting dark, but I could still see a little.

"Any sign of the BMWs?" Victor asked me.

"No. Is that what they are?"

"Yes."

"Why are BMWs always the bad guy's car?" I asked.

"It's because they are German."

I got back in the car. "What?! That's not true. German engineering is… legendary. You can't say that about a whole country."

"No? What if I said they were Russian? You could easily believe all Russians are bad guys, right?"

"Well…"

"See? You think Russia is bad and Germany is good. But if Germany and Russia fought, like they did in World War Two, I would cheer for the Russians, what about you?"

"I don't know."

"If you don't know, I'll tell you. Russia, Britain, and the United States were all allies in the war. You would have cheered for Russia, like me. This makes Germany the bad guys."

"They still make good cars. And I still don't think that's true."

We crept forward a car's length, then I said, "Hey, isn't Porsche German too?"

Victor said, "I like to think of it more as an Italian vehicle."

"What side was Italy on, in World Word Two?"

"They switched sides."

"Like you?"

"I'm not..." But Victor didn't finish the sentence, and when I looked at him, I saw why. He had his hands up and was looking at a man outside the car who was pointing a gun at him. Then I heard a tap on my window and saw another man pointing a gun at me. Instinctively, I raised my hands too.

I recognized the man outside my window, as well as the man outside Victor's. They were the people from Technology Solutions, the same people who beat me up. Yash's men. Victor's guy said, "Get out," but Victor didn't move. He glanced ahead, to see if the traffic would let him drive soon, but it didn't look like it.

Then a boom filled the car. Someone must have fired a weapon. Victor's window was all cracked. Mine wasn't. Victor slowly opened his door and got out. I guess he didn't get hit. Good. I didn't feel pain anywhere, so I must not have got hit. I didn't have time to guess where the bullet landed. It was a warning shot. I got out too.

Victor addressed his man. "What's going on, Sadu?"

"Nagi wants to see you. Let's go." We started walking away from our car, presumably back to theirs.

"Don't do this. Let us go," Victor replied.

"I don't work for you anymore, Victor. I work for Yash Nagi. He pays better, and he's not a jerk like you are."

As we kept on walking, I wondered why nobody was doing anything. Even though traffic seemed to be moving now, we were still walking right past cars with people in them who were just staring at us. If this was Texas, somebody would probably be doing something. Why don't I live in Texas?

"Well good help is hard to find," said Victor. "I obviously did a bad job hiring you two."

Sadu then shifted his gun from his right hand to his left, then reached back with his free right hand and struck Victor in the side of his head. Victor immediately struck back, and the fight was on. My guy went to join in. As Victor got struck to the ground by two men, he turned to me and scowled. "Run, you fool!"

I took off as fast as I could, dodging cars that were now moving. As I ran past the Porsche, I stole a quick glance inside to see if, per chance, in the confusion of being fired upon, Victor had left the keys in the ignition. He had. I jumped in and started driving. In my haste, I stalled the engine once, but started it again. This time when I took off, I heard a loud screech as I left long black marks on the road. I wasn't used to this transmission. Then I heard another gunshot and my heart almost stopped. The shot missed me, but it did hit the windshield, because it spidered into a hundred crack lines. Both me and the windshield held together, so I kept on driving.

Soon I was at an intersection, and I wished I had my map to show me the way to the police station. Then it occurred to me that Victor was back there, and there was a good chance they were going to kill him. Did I want that on my conscience? No, I didn't. Did I want to turn around and confront those killers again? No, I didn't. Did I have enough time to call 911 and then turn around? No.

I quickly considered what a servant of God would do in this situation. He would probably go rescue his friend. But Victor wasn't really my friend, so what would a servant of God do? He would probably go rescue someone who wasn't his friend. With an audible groan, I made a U-turn and headed back to find those black BMWs.

8:49 PM

I didn't exactly know what I was planning to do once I found them, but I knew I had to do something. And I wasn't comforted by the thought that black BMWs can hide a lot better than a red Porsche can. I probably stuck out in traffic.

Pretty soon I found them, and they probably saw me too. We were on opposite sides of the median. I cranked up the speed, intending to fly past them. Maybe if I could get around from the back I could follow them and keep an eye on them. As I went past, I ducked down in my seat, and it was a good thing, because the B pillar right behind my head banged just like a bullet hit it. I didn't have time to conclude what I thought about that, because my heart was beating so fast, that it was hard to think. Maybe I need to call 911. Yeah. Yeah, I definitely do. Too bad I don't have time.

When I was at the next intersection, I swerved the car around and gunned it back, hoping to catch up to them and follow. Instead, they must have done the same thing, because I saw a black BMW coming up from the other lane, where I had just been. Not wanting to be shot again, I darted off the road to the right, onto a parking lot. There was a Tim Horton's sitting there, so I drove around the coffee shop, hoping to get out of their sight, and hoping to see them from the other side. On the other side, I didn't see anything, so I got out and stood, hoping to see farther. It worked. Out in the distance, to the left, I could see their vehicle. I got back in and took off in that direction, cutting across traffic for a while. I yelled "Sorry" as I cut off some car coming at me. Maybe if I got lucky a police car would start following me with his lights on. That would be great.

I could see the black car in the distance, driving fast and cutting in and out around cars. So I drove even faster. Soon I found myself at a good distance behind them so that I could keep my eye on them and hopefully they couldn't see me. That's when

I considered calling 911, so I pulled out my phone and started opening the dialer app, but then I almost hit another car, and I lost sight of them. I put the phone in my lap and stepped on the gas again. Once I could concentrate on driving, I found them again.

Just as they turned sharp left onto another wide road, the lights turned red. By the time I got to the intersection, I decided to go for it. It takes some nerve to drive into oncoming traffic, but I hoped any car coming at me would see me and avoid me. They did, and honked loudly, but I survived. However, that manoeuvre may have given away my position, because as soon I was through the intersection, the black car pulled over onto the shoulder. There was no way I was going to drive past them, because the chances of surviving that were slim, so I pulled over too. Of course, I could see them directly ahead of me, and I was sure they could see me too. Suddenly I felt very nervous. I felt even worse when their car did a reverse turn onto the road, then started driving down the shoulder straight at me. The hunter had just become the hunted.

I panicked and threw the Porshe into reverse and gunned the engine, sending me streaking backwards at speeds I've never experienced before. The car tended to fish-tale, and they were gaining on me, so I knew I had to turn around. When there was a little break in traffic, I cranked the steering wheel around, causing my front end to swerve around, leaving black streaks on the road. Due to my complete inexperience at driving like this, the 180 I was hoping for was off by a few percent, and I found myself driving beside the road in a shallow ditch. Looking back, I saw the car looming down on me. I had to make some distance somehow, so I cut across the ditch and found myself in a parking lot of some big box store. They followed.

There were a few cars in the parking lot, so I had to be careful not to hit any. I roared through the parking lot, trying to get away from the bad guys right behind me. I took corners fast.

So did they. I drove fast, I accelerated hard and braked harder. So did they. I didn't want to die, so I started taking corners even faster. At one point I slid sideways and hit the back of a pick-up truck with the side of my car. It made a nice crunching sound. Sorry about your car, Victor. I'm just trying to save my life.

Once or twice I thought I heard gunshots, but nothing seemed to hit my car. When I looked back, I understood why. The two men in the back seat were fighting. Victor was distracting the gunman in the back so I could escape. Too bad the driver was still keeping up with me. Maybe there was something I could do.

Without warning, I slammed on the brakes. The BMW was so close he couldn't stop in time, but swerved to the right to try to avoid me. While I was still slowing down, I quickly shifted into reverse and gunned it. I impacted the middle of the car on the driver's side, right where I intended to. I got lucky. I was shoved into my seat, and the driver's airbags went off. While he was distracted, I grabbed something to go fight him with. The thing I grabbed was Victor's backpack. It was heavy. Good.

By the time I got out there, the driver was just extracting himself from the car, and I hit him full force with the backpack to the head. He collapsed to the ground.

Then Victor got out. He looked bad, but the other guy laid out in the back seat looked worse. I had no idea the VP of Technology could fight so well.

I said, "What do you have in this bag? Lead weights?"

"Close. I'll take that." As I handed him the bag, he said, "It took you long enough."

"I was trying not to get killed!"

"I told you these guys were dangerous. Do you believe me now?"

"Yes"

"And you wrecked my car."

"Well I... " And then I remembered something. "Hey, weren't there two cars following us?"

Then the second BMW pulled up and two more men got out, weapons drawn.

9:20 PM

"Victor, the boss wants to talk to you," the man on the left said.

"Dani, you don't have to do this," Victor replied.

"Oh, I do have to, because Yash says I have to. He's the boss, so I have to do as he says. You know how it works."

"You used to work for me."

"But I don't anymore, do I? I've moved up in the world. Now let's do this the easy way, OK? Boss says to bring you in alive or dead, preferably alive, so will you please get in the car? Otherwise, we'll do it the other way."

I looked around for our options. We had none, so we got in the back seat. As Dani got in the driver's seat, the other man walked around and said, "Are we just going to leave Sadu and Nick here?"

"Yes we are."

We all got in and started driving. The man on the right faced backwards, toward us, and kept his gun on us.

After a few minutes of silence, it occurred to me that I could talk to God about this. Maybe he had some good advice for me. Maybe if he was my boss he might tell me what to do. I closed my eyes and imagined him here in the back seat of this vehicle. He was at peace and smiling. In fact, he looked like he was in a carload of his friends having a good time together. Then he turned to me and said, "Why don't you ask these guys how they met?"

I was never really good at making conversation, and so I didn't enjoy it, but if my boss says to do something, you have to do it, because that's how it works. It's true that it was awkward because one of the guys was pointing a gun at me, but I usually found social situations awkward anyway. I didn't know his name, so at one point when we had eye contact, I said, "So, how did you meet Victor?"

He said, "Shut up."

I said, "OK"

Then Victor said, "I met Sven outside a bar one night. There was a fight and I broke it up."

"Why?" I asked.

"Because Sven was losing and he owed me money. Then he paid back his debt by working for me. This was before we met Yash."

I looked from Victor to Sven. Sven didn't reply.

"You know, of all the incompetent, disobedient, lazy employees I've ever had," Victor continued, "Sven here was none of those. He was actually a good guy. Maybe the only one I've ever met."

Sven didn't answer, but Dani did. "Hey shut up back there! Don't talk. Don't let them talk, Sven. They'll get into your head. Do you know what they were going to do? They were going to turn us in to the police. Then we'd all be in jail. Do you want that?"

"Of course not," Sven replied.

"Then don't let them talk."

"You could join us, Sven," Victor said.

"Shut up! Shut up!" Dani yelled. He waved his own gun at us. "If any of you say even one more word, I will personally put a bullet into your head. Do you understand?"

We nodded.

It was a quiet journey the rest of the way back to Yash Nagi's house. I thought of trying to pull out my phone and call 911, but Sven was too vigilant. He would have noticed. When we finally arrived, I thought of opening the door and making a run for it, but Sven had his eye on both of us. I ran simulations in my head of me trying to bolt out the door and of Sven pointing the gun and pressing the trigger. Sven won every time. Since I trusted that my mental simulations were probably accurate enough, I didn't even try.

We were met by the same man who caught me in the back of Victor's Lexus not that long ago. He said, "Yash is expecting you. He wants to see everyone in his office."

Victor and I were escorted inside the house and searched. The man took our phones and everything like last time. Then the four of us went down the hall to see Yash Nagi again. This time I didn't think we'd be able to talk our way out. I had to be honest. I saw no way of escape this time.

CHAPTER 18

9:58 PM

Yash sat behind his very expensive teak desk and regarded Victor and me with displeasure. Our escorts, standing behind us, made us sit in chairs facing him.

Finally, Yash spoke. "Victor and Jeff. I do not consider myself a stupid man. And yet you have forced me to regard myself in such light. Just imagine that I trusted you two after you had already demonstrated by your actions that you could not be trusted. I must be utterly foolish. And I don't like looking foolish. Let me assure you, this will not happen again. Do you two have anything to say? Any last words, before you meet your end?"

Victor looked as nervous as I did. In fact, he only looked nervous. I was downright scared. He said, "Yes sir. I'm sorry sir. It was wrong of me. I should have never done it. I should have stayed loyal to you, Mr. Nagi. I understand that now."

"Oh do you?"

"Yes sir." Victor was breathing hard, and his face was looking damp with sweat.

"So if I offered you a position back on the team, you would take it?"

"I would do whatever you asked me to, sir. I would be yours to command."

"Anything?"

"Yes sir."

"Prove it. Show me this recording you tried to send to the police."

He started to reach for his pocket, then said, "I don't have my phone."

"Yes..."

For a moment I thought Victor was thinking strategically, trying to get his phone, and for a moment I thought it was going to work. But Yash spoke to the man guarding Victor. "Dani, go get me a laptop." So much for the phone. Dani walked out.

"If you really say you will do whatever I ask, Victor, I'm going to ask you to show me the recording you made, and I'm going to ask you to delete it."

Victor was still sweating. He nodded. "I'll do it. As I said, Mr. Nagi, I've always respected your power. It was a terrible mistake to go against you."

I didn't know what he was up to. I didn't know his plan. If I did, I could help him somehow.

"Perhaps this young man here has led you astray?" Yash asked.

Victor nodded, without looking at me. "Maybe he has. It's hard to find good help."

I was getting tired of Victor's remarks like this. It wasn't helping.

Then Dani came in with a laptop. He placed it in front of his boss and resumed his place behind Victor.

Yash opened the lid and logged in. Then he opened a web browser and turned the computer so that we could all see, and said to Victor, "Please log in to Omniscient and show me this recording."

I thought Victor might fake his password three times to get locked out, but to my surprise, he logged in correctly the first time. Then he found his list of audio recordings. Sure enough, he pointed to the right one.

"Delete it," Yash said.

Without looking back at me, Victor clicked the garbage can icon.

I shouted, "Victor!" as a confirmation dialogue box popped up saying, "Are you sure? This cannot be undone."

Without hesitating, Victor confirmed the delete. The confirmation message, "Your recording has been deleted," showed on the screen. It was done. The recording was gone. Our only evidence against this man just went poof into a cloud of smoke. Not only were we going to die, but our deaths would not even help anything. I was hoping that someone might look through the server for evidence, but now even that was gone.

I said, "What are you doing?"

Victor now turned to me. "I shouldn't have listened to you, Jeff. I should have never listened to you. You've been nothing but bad news since I met you." To Yash, he said, "It's done. The recording is deleted. Again, I'm sorry for all this."

"You didn't download this file anywhere else?"

"No. We started to, but didn't finish. We canceled it before we got to the important part."

"There are no backups on the server or anything?"

"No. Nothing. We do daily backups at 3:00 AM, so it wouldn't have made it."

"There is no evidence against me at all, anywhere, that you know of?"

Victor shook his head. "Nothing, sir."

Turning to me, Yash said, "Can you confirm this, Jeff?"

I thought of Victor's phone, being held in that box in the entrance. It must have a local copy. Wait, let me think. When Victor deleted the recording from the web browser, it would tell all clients, including the one on his phone to do the same, so everything stays in sync. So his phone would delete its local copy as soon as it would get the message. The box it's in might shield it from any connection, so there might be a chance of saving the local copy, if we are careful. Or maybe the deleted file could be recovered.

When I didn't answer right away, Yash smiled. "Good," he said. That makes me feel a little better. "Oh, one more thing." To Dani, he said, "Dani, go tell Conrad to take these gentlemen's phones and smash them with a hammer and throw the remains into the river."

Oh no. There goes my last hope.

Dani nodded and left the room.

Victor looked at Yash and said, "I'll need my phone to work for you, sir."

Yash drew in a long breath and said, "Victor, you won't need that phone anymore. You won't need anything anymore."

Victor stood up. "Sir! I've proven my loyalty to you."

Sven moved around to the side, gun raised, protecting Yash.

Yash remained seated and said, "No, you've proven that you say what I want to hear when you're in my office, then go out and disobey. As you yourself said, not that long ago, good help is hard to find."

Victor looked at Sven, then back to Yash. He was cornered and looking for a way out. He was getting desperate, and desperate people do desperate things. Still, Sven's gun was pointed straight at him, and it's hard to do anything in that position.

I almost thought Victor was going to make a move when Dani came back and saw Victor. He also moved around, his gun drawn.

Then Yash said the words. "Dani and Sven, dispose of these men."

10:20 PM

Sven moved his gun to me, and I suddenly became very nervous. My brain almost shut off. I didn't know what to do. What was I supposed to do?!

I heard Yash say, "Not here! Go shoot them down by the river, and dispose of their bodies the usual way."

Dani waved his gun and said, "Move!" I got up and started walking, thinking that I should be doing something different. I should have a plan or something, not just voluntarily submitting to my own death. But I couldn't think of anything.

Outside the office, in the hallway, I thought maybe I should run for it, but even through the fog of my panic, I knew that if I ran, I would get shot on the spot. Better to go along with it and die two minutes from now than die right here right now.

When we were out of the house, I saw Conrad, the man who first spotted me in Victor's car, smashing our phones with a hammer. Victor's was already in a million pieces, and mine was already broken. Dani and Sven marched us across the driveway. The ground sloped down here. Presumably there was a river at the bottom.

I had about a minute to live, or less if I ran for it.

The sun had set. It was very dark. It reminded me of a few days ago when it got dark because of thick clouds during the day. That's the day I got beaten up. I had cried out to God to save me, and I thought he ignored me. I wonder if he was going to ignore me this time too. He might, but he might not. Then I caught myself actually looking around for any bushes that might be hiding a gun I could use. Of course there wasn't any. I did the only thing I could think of. I tried to listen.

If it was possible to calm down while being lead away to your execution, I tried to calm down. I imagined God next to me. I said to him, in my mind, "Will you please help us?" and tried to be open to any thoughts that came to me. I imagined God's peaceful, smiling face, and the words "Make conversation" came to my mind.

I didn't have time to argue. I was God's servant, and whatever he said I did. So I said to Victor, "What made Sven such a better employee than me?"

Dani said, "Shut up! Don't talk!"

Victor replied, "Because he listened when I told him to do something. No backtalk. No complaining. He was a joy to work with."

That was high praise coming from Victor. I didn't think he liked anyone, ever. And I couldn't imagine anyone working for him who would obey so well. This Sven must be a good employee if he could make Victor think highly of him. I stole a glance back at Sven, who was directly behind me. He seemed troubled. I suppose that's how you look when you're about to kill someone.

Then we were at the river. It was not as wide as the Red River or the Assiniboine, but still I could barely see to the other side, since it was late and almost dark. There were a few trees down here, which you could mostly make out from the stray light coming down from the house up there.

"OK, boys, this is it," Dani said.

Victor and I turned around to face our executioners.

Dani wasted no time. "On three," he said, holding out his weapon at Victor. Sven pointed his at me.

"One!"

I thought about running. I thought about making more conversation, but no words came to me. I thought about praying.

"Two!"

It turns out that in the heat of the moment, my true self emerged. When everything else was stripped away, the inner me came to the surface, and what I found surprised me. It turned out that I still had a lot of fear hiding down in there, because when it came to the surface, the only thing I did was to clamp my eyes shut, knowing that I was about to die. Then a gun shot echoed in my ears. I breathed a few more times and was forced to acknowledge that I was still alive.

I opened my eyes and what I saw surprised me. Sven had his weapon pointed not at me, but at Dani. And Dani had fallen to the ground. He lay there, arms out, not moving. I could see a lot of dark red liquid coming from his head. He was shot! Sven killed him!

For a moment, we all stood there, then Victor said, "Sven! Thank you. I knew you were a good man."

Sven said, "You were the first person to ever believe in me. I couldn't let you be killed."

"But what about Yash?"

"I will tell him that you and Dani fought and that you killed him and ran off."

"Thank you, Sven."

"Now run off."

"What about Jeff?"

Yeah. What about me?

Victor moved closer to me while Sven explained. "I never did like this one. He betrayed his own father. How evil is that? Do you know what I would have given to work with my father?" Turning to me he continued. "Victor here was the closest thing to a dad I've ever had. And you betrayed your dad and sent him to jail! I should have driven a little faster when I drove into you in the parking lot on Tuesday. I should have kicked you a little harder in the head when we beat you up on Wednesday. But now Yashi wants you dead, so I have to obey." He lifted up his gun at me again.

Victor stepped in front of me with his hands out. "Sven, let's..." But he didn't finish because another gun shot rang out. I looked around for anyone else, but the three of us were alone, and I still wasn't injured. I was just about to conclude it must have been a warning shot when Victor crumpled to the ground in front of me. He lay on his back, blood staining the shirt on his chest.

10:24 PM

I gasped. Victor!

Sven shouted "Victor!" and ran over.

At this point, something in my head shouted at me. Now is your chance! Run! Run! Run! I considered this advice briefly and concluded very quickly that it was good advice, or at least as good as you could get considering the circumstances. I took off running as fast as I could. Another gunshot. I dodged and weaved. Another shot. I ran behind trees and bushes, anywhere I could go to get away. Another gunshot. It was closer. He was following me. So far all shots had missed, at least that's what I thought in my panicked state.

Along the river, away from the house, which was the direction I was going, the trees got thicker, and the light got dimmer. I could almost hide here behind one of these big trees. I kept on running. At some point I would have to hide, because I was getting tired. I never was in great shape. Hopefully neither was Sven.

Then I stopped. My breathing was so hard, Sven could probably shoot me just by firing in the direction of the sound. I picked up a stone near the river, and brought it up the bank some distance. Then I found a big tree to hide behind, and threw the rock into the river. I didn't have a strong arm either, so it barely made a splash in the shallows. But hopefully it was enough to throw off my hunter.

I breathed through my wide-open mouth to try to stay quiet, and I stayed there for some time. Finally, I saw the silhouette of a man walking along the river. Sven. I was peeking around the tree, because I couldn't bring myself to just hide there, not knowing if he might walk right up to me. Then I saw him turn toward me. I froze. I was pretty sure he wouldn't be able to see me from this distance. I thought of running again, but I willed my feet to stay put. It was dark for crying out loud! He can't see me! I can barely see him and I'm behind a tree!

Finally, after what seemed like an hour, he turned back forward and kept going along the river. When he was out of sight, I dared to move. I walked slowly to the next tree, then the next, making my way back to the house and back to Victor. It took some time, but I finally made it, and I did it without running into Sven. He must have gone farther down the river.

I found my boss, sitting on the ground, leaning against a tree. I slowly approached him. The light from the house was enough to see him. His face was pale, and he wasn't moving. No, he still was moving—I just saw him take a breath. "Victor?"

He moved his head toward me. Good. He wasn't dead.

Not knowing what to say in this awkward situation, I asked, "How are you?"

He took a labored breath. "I'm dying..." He inhaled another lung-full. "No thanks to you."

I still didn't know what to say. "Yeah... uh... I guess I should say 'Thank-you' for that."

He didn't answer.

I said, "Victor, you took a bullet for me. I... I'm sorry."

He didn't answer. Instead, he closed his eyes.

"Victor!" I smacked his cheek. "Victor!"

He opened his eyes.

"You're not going to die! We're going to get you to a hospital." My mind started planning. We don't have our phones, so I can't call 911. Maybe I could get a vehicle down here. But we don't have the Lexus or the Porsche. Getting keys to one of those BMWs would be hard. Victor interrupted my plans. He was shaking his head. I said, "What?"

He managed one word. "Ambulance."

"OK, then I'll call an ambulance."

He shook his head again. Then he looked past me at something. I turned around, hoping it wasn't who I thought it was. But it was.

11:02 PM

The wind was gently blowing, just enough to rustle the leaves in the trees, just enough to hide the sound of Sven walking up behind me. I turned around to see him standing there, gun extended.

"I hate you," he growled.

And before he pulled the trigger, the wind suddenly stopped. It all became calm, and in the calmness we could hear something. It was the sound of sirens coming toward us. And they sounded close. Were they on the driveway?

Sven obviously heard them too. I could see on his face the rage as it turned to fear. Killing someone he hated was one thing, but shooting someone when the police were so close was another. He lowered his weapon, then turned and fled.

In surprise, I turned to Victor. "How did they…?"

Victor held up his hand, and for the first time I noticed he was holding a phone.

"Where did you get that?"

I followed his gaze as he looked over at the lifeless body of Dani. I could just barely make out traces of blood leading from Dani's body to where Victor sat propped up against a tree. He wasn't breathing very much anymore.

"How could you use it? It must have been locked."

"You can always call 911. You should know that." He coughed, and blood came out his mouth. "I can't believe I gave my life for… someone so stupid."

I was sorry this guy was dying, but did he have to be such a jerk? Then he did something I didn't expect. He started laughing. More blood sputtered out of his mouth as he laughed. Or was it crying? It was hard to tell. Finally I said, "What?"

His eyes found mine. "It seems I finally got it right."

"Got what right?"

"For a while now I've been trying to follow Jesus. I finally got it right."

"How?"

"Didn't Jesus die for sinners? It seems... I did the same." Then he closed his eyes.

I slapped him again. "Victor!" He opened his lids half way. By then the lights from the ambulance were shining on us. I ran up the hill, waving my arms. I found the vehicle, bathed in red lights, with emergency responders ready for action. When they looked at me I said, "He's down there. I mean they are down there." Then I added, "You'll need a stretcher."

Two women ran with me toward Victor. When we got to him, one went to work slapping him and telling him to "Stay with me."

I stood back, not knowing what to do. I said, "His name's Victor." Then I pointed off to the side. "And that's Dani."

Then the stretcher arrived and I helped them load Victor onto it. He slowly opened his eyes and looked for me. "Jeff...," he sputtered.

"I'm here, Victor."

"Jeff, you can have my backpack. I'm sorry about your mother."

I was going to say, "What does your backpack have to do with my mother?" but he closed his eyes again. The Emergency Medical Technician smacked him around again and told him to stay here. She seemed to know what she was doing. I wondered if she was a doctor. I looked at her name tag, which said "Kayembe" So I just said to her, "Is he going to be OK?"

"We'll do everything we can," she replied, then added, "but it doesn't look good."

Then we were at the ambulance. They rolled him into the back and drove away in a rush, lights and sirens flashing.

I would have liked to stop and rest, but things were still happening. A second ambulance just arrived and the people were rushing out. They must have been told about Dani, because they headed straight down the hill.

A police car just arrived and the officers started questioning me about what happened. When I got to the part about Sven running away down the river, they decided to pursue him together. They left me in the care of an officer in a second police car that just showed up. He was a slightly large man and he had a hard complexion, as if he'd seen so many murders that one more didn't bother him. He came straight up to me and said, "Jeff Davis. What made me think you would be involved in this?"

I replied, "Hello Detective Wakefield."

"I heard the call go out to this address, and I remembered it belonged to Yash Nagi. I had a hunch you might be here."

More police cars started showing up. I guess if there's a shooting and someone dies, and there's a shooter on the run, the law gets involved. Probably a good thing.

"You'll have to give a formal statement at some point, but first, did you get any evidence on Nagi? I got your email, but no file with it."

I sighed and lowered my head. "No. It got deleted."

"What about your server?"

I looked up. "What?"

"Your server. Last time you had something on your server, not just on your phone."

"Right. No. It got deleted from Omniscient's server too." I paused and looked off into the distance.

"I can see you thinking. What are you thinking about?"

"My server."

"You just said it was deleted from your server."

"No. It was deleted from Omniscient's server."

"Yeah?"

"I have another server."

"Do you?"

"Yeah I..." I was going to say it's the server I spy on people from, but this lawman might not appreciate that terminology. So I said, "I store information there." Turning back to him I said, "Detective, can I borrow your phone please?"

He eyed me like only an experienced detective could, which meant he was looking right through me to the very intentions of my heart. I must have been clean, because he unlocked it and handed it to me. "I'll trust you, kid," he said. "It's police property, so don't do anything bad with it."

I opened a web browser and browsed to the web interface of my server. The last time I was here I set it to record everything. I had a hunch, to borrow the term, that there might be something here.

My mind was thinking. The virus I constructed to infect their computers worked, because I saw them through their webcam. Then when they abandoned their retail shop, what did they do with their computers? They must still be using them. Yash himself might be using one of the infected ones. He may have used it himself when we were meeting with him in his office. I looked around on my server for audio recordings. It took a minute or two of hunting, during which time Wakefield didn't look very patient, but I finally found what I was looking for. At about 10:20 PM, there was the crisp and clear recording of Yash Nagi's voice saying, "Not here! Go shoot them down by the river, and dispose of their bodies the usual way."

When I heard those words, I smiled, and the detective almost got excited. He said, "That's it. That will do it. Let's go take him in for questioning." Then he added, "That won't get deleted, will it?"

"Nope." I checked to see if his laptop was still connected to my server, I mean God's server. It was. On a hunch, I set the setting on his laptop to stay powered on, even when the lid was closed, because at this point I didn't want to take any more chances.

Then Detective Wakefield strode out to the front door of this very expensive house. I tagged along, because I was sure something interesting was going to happen.

CHAPTER 19

11:44 PM

Wakefield knocked loudly on the solid oak door, and said the words every criminal dreads, "Open up! Police!"

Nothing happened.

He knocked again, louder. He knocked and called out several more times, until finally the door was opened by the same man I'd seen here several times. He said, "May I help you?"

"We would like to talk with Yash Nagi," the police officer said.

"Do you have a warrant?"

"I could get one."

"If you're going to arrest Mr. Nagi, you need an arrest warrant."

"We're just here to talk. Can we come in please?"

I noticed through the open door that Victor's backpack was sitting there, against a wall. I pointed to it and said, "That's my backpack," and walked toward it. The man must have been taken off guard, because he let me in, probably by reflex. "You're not allowed in here," he said.

I hefted the pack onto my shoulders, and started back to the door, but Joseph stepped inside in front of me. "Could you get him please?" he asked the man. "We'll wait here."

"He's not here."

Then we all heard it. It sounded like a garage door opening.

"What's that?" Joseph asked.

"Nothing. It's the garbage disposal."

Joseph bolted outside, with me right behind. I think the door got slammed shut again. He ran around to where the garage doors were. There were four of them there, but they were all shut.

Joseph was upset. "I was sure that was a garage door."

"I don't hear a car engine running," I offered. "Besides the emergency vehicles."

Then we heard a faint sound coming from the other side of the garage. Curious, we ran to the other side to see a car fleeing the scene. This garage had another garage door on the far side, and there appeared to be some sort of driveway or path on this far side. The car was speeding down it, silently.

"An electric car," I said. "That's why we didn't hear it."

He grabbed his radio and said, "Suspect is escaping on the back side of the garage, in a black Tesla." He ran to his own police car, and I followed, hoping to be allowed to go along. By the time we got there, three other police cars had already passed us, in pursuit. We got in anyway and started driving, but then someone on the radio said, "There is a heavy gate here, which is closed. And the black Tesla is nowhere to be seen."

Wakefield hit his steering wheel and swore.

"What about a helicopter?" I asked.

"It's pitch black. He'll never find anything."

"What about... It's a Tesla. Maybe you could track it with its GPS."

"And how would I do that?"

"I don't know. You can with the Tesla app."

"Do you have this guy's phone?"

"No."

But Nagi probably did. And I wondered if he took his laptop with him too. I was still holding the detective's phone, so I checked my server to see if Yash's laptop was still connected. It was. On a hunch, I checked to see if it had a GPS sensor built into it. It didn't. Then I checked to see what the nearby Wi-Fi access points were. I found one named "tim_hortons."

I said, "He's near a Tim Horton's."

"How do you know that?"

"Because his laptop can see a Wi-Fi AP named that. I think he took his laptop with him."

He looked at me suspiciously. "How do you know what his laptop can see?"

I said, "Ummm... maybe we should discuss this afterwards."

He pointed his finger at me and was about to say something, but must have changed his mind. "Keep your eyes on that thing." He turned on his lights and siren, and barreled down the driveway, the real driveway. Soon we were in pursuit of a vehicle I didn't know if we would be able to find.

11:58 PM

"Do you know how many Tim Horton's restaurants there are in the city?" Joseph Wakefield asked me, as we headed toward town, presumably where Yash was going.

"No."

"About eighty."

"Well, if he's moving, we'll be able to see something else soon."

"Maybe he can see more than one Wi-Fi."

"Oh, sure, he can see lots. Let's see, there's one called GetOffMyLawn, and one called nacho_wifi, and one called use-this-one-mom, OccamsRouter, john316, and my personal favorite, TellMyWiFiLoveHer."

"'Tell my wife I love her' is your favorite?"

"No, Tell my *Wi-Fi* love her."

"Oh. Yeah. Cute. See anything else yet?"

"I'm refreshing the list, and the radio strength changes each time, so he's still moving. Oh! I thought I saw a Canadian Tire in there, but it was faint."

"There are a few of those around, but I think I know the closest one." The siren and lights were still going, but he seemed to step on the gas, getting us there even sooner.

"Wow, we'll be there soon at this rate."

"That's the idea, kid."

"OK, Canadian Tire is gone now. But I'm seeing something with Grace Hospital in it."

"Good. We're going in the right direction. We'll be there soon. I think this is working."

There weren't that many cars on the roads at midnight, but there were a few, and they seemed to know to get out of our way. There was one guy driving along in the left lane who swerved into the right lane when he saw us. Good thing Joseph didn't try to pass him on the right. I guess he knows what he's doing. He passed him on the left and kept going.

"Grace Hospital is getting strong."

"Good. We're soon there. We can start looking for him soon."

"Black Tesla."

"Black Tesla."

I continued to monitor Yash's laptop's Wi-Fi signals. "I see something called Underdogs. Is that a thing?"

"There's a sports bar near here called that."

"Yash might be hiding there."

"If it is Yash."

"What do you mean?"

"I mean it's the oldest trick in the book. If your house is surrounded by cops, you send a young punk with a fast car out on a car chase, and meanwhile the real perpetrator sits at home, waiting for the cops to leave."

"You mean, Yash might not even be here? This could be someone else?"

"Yup."

I didn't like that idea at all. I wanted this guy caught, if for no other reason than so that I could sleep at night. If Yash got away, I didn't know what I would do. Change my identity? Leave the city? Buy a gun? No, no that was probably a bad idea. I should probably stay away from guns. I glanced down to see if the detective was carrying a weapon. He was. Good.

I checked the radio signals again. "The radio strengths aren't changing anymore. I think he's not moving."

"What's the strongest?"

"Underdogs."

"We're just pulling into Underdogs now. Let's check it out."

He pulled into the parking lot, not from the parking lot entrance, but from the exit, and parked the car right there, so nobody could escape. Then he radioed for backup.

I pointed to the far end of the parking lot. There, in the relative dark, sat a black Tesla Model S.

"I can't ask you to come with me," he said, as he got out of the car.

I placed my hand on my door handle as the other door closed. My hand didn't move. For some reason, I couldn't open the door. For some reason, I didn't want to go out there. For the first time in a long time, I felt safe. I was safe inside this car and I didn't want to leave it. I couldn't. I had been too close to death already this evening, and I couldn't bring myself to face it again.

I watched Joseph walk out to the Tesla and look inside it. He must have considered it empty, because he now walked back toward the sports bar and went inside.

I sat in the police car, not seeing, not knowing what was going on inside.

Now that I found a moment of relative calm, I thought I should probably ask God what to do. In my mind I said, "Well, now what?"

I didn't hear any voices in my head. I didn't receive an email, or anything at all. But for some reason, the words "Finish it" came to my mind, and also "Go all the way." I sighed. I was tired of the fight. I wanted to rest. For a while I still sat there, but soon I realized I was not obeying. By my inaction I was disobeying. Didn't I claim to be God's servant? And doesn't a servant do what he's asked? I sighed an even bigger sigh, then with what felt like all my might, I pried the door open and stood up outside the protective walls of the police car. I was now out in the open, ready to be shot.

I didn't know what I was supposed to do, so I started walking toward the building, but before I got there, a light blue Ford F150 pulled up to the police car. I didn't recognize the driver, but I saw he was angry at the blockage. He had no choice but to back up and try the other exit. As he was backing up past me, I saw someone else in the vehicle. He was crouching on the passenger seat, but looked up just in time to meet my eyes, and I met his. It was Yash Nagi.

12:16 AM

The half-ton reversed to the back of the parking lot, then turned around so that he was going forward again and drove around the back of the building.

Meanwhile, I ran toward the building to get Joseph's attention. I threw the door open, but couldn't see him anywhere. I yelled "Joseph!", then came outside the building again. I ran around to the front. I banged on the windows with my hands, yelling "Joseph!" Then I ran to the parking lot entrance, and stood there.

The truck was around the back of the building by now, and was facing me down. I stood my ground in the middle of the entrance. He would have to get past me to escape.

Then the truck took off toward me and at higher-than-recommended speed. I didn't exactly know what I was going to do when he got this far, but I stood there. I placed one foot forward and held out my hands, as if by pushing I could keep the truck from running me over. He was halfway toward me by now, and I was still there.

It was at that point I realized that there was no way this truck was going to stop, so I panicked and held my arms over my head. My feet, however, didn't have the brains to move, so they stayed right there, in the path of the oncoming vehicle.

It was at that moment that I heard an explosion. I looked up in time to see the truck swerve off to the side, narrowly missing me, and crash into a small concrete fence. I also saw that a window in the sports bar was mostly missing, with glass sprayed around on the ground.

Detective Joseph Wakefield stood on the other side of the glass, gun extended. Then I put it together. He had just shot the tire of the moving truck from inside the building. Yeah, he may have just saved my life. As my heartbeat was trying to return to normal, he ran over and made sure the two occupants of the truck weren't going anywhere.

I finally moved out of the way as another police car pulled into the entrance. That was Joseph's backup.

I sat down on a chair at an outdoor table and tried to catch my breath as I watched the two men in the truck get handcuffed and led away.

Then it hit me. It was finally over. No more getting shot at. No more getting beaten up. No more running from bad guys with guns. They were all going to jail, and I could finally relax. Life could start getting back to normal, if I knew what normal was.

I thought about working at Omniscient again. I would like that. I thought about programming again with the guys, reading Garth's joke of the day. That would be nice. Come to think of it, I think I missed today's joke. I'll have to ask him what it was. Then

I thought about Cheryl, and my heart felt something else, something more. When I looked around at where I was, and saw police doing their thing, and saw the people in the sports bar hanging out and having a good with each other, and staring at the scene outside, I felt... I felt... alone. I felt lonely, like I was all by myself.

I wandered into the building, just to look around and see the people. Maybe just being in that atmosphere would make me feel better.

There were lots of screens and noise and people talking, but for some reason you can always hear your name above the crowd. I heard someone say, "Jeff Davis! I have a phone call for Jeff Davis!"

That was surprising. There must be another Jeff Davis in town that comes here. It was someone behind the counter that was shouting my name. But out of curiosity, I approached him and said, "I'm Jeff Davis."

He handed me a cordless phone. I held it to my ear and said, "Hello?"

The voice said, "Jeff?"

I recognized that voice, so I said, "Cheryl?"

"Hi Jeff. How are you?"

"Me? I'm... fine. How are you? And why are you calling me so late... and... here?"

"It's a long story I guess. Did you want to talk about something?"

"Do I want to talk? Um... maybe. Maybe I do. I was just feeling... but how did you know I was here?"

"I could explain it. Should we get together?"

"Now?"

"Sure. I couldn't sleep. I was thinking about you, and praying for you. How are you, Jeff?"

How was I? Now that was a question. After all I had just been through in the past few days, it would take a while to even say how I was. Where did I even start? And how can I even describe it? Maybe this woman Cheryl would be able to understand. Maybe I could talk to her about things, about everything. Maybe I might even enjoy it. "I would love to get together with you, Cheryl. Do you want to come here right now?"

"I would like that. Where are you?"

"You called here and you don't know where this is?

"I'll explain when I get there."

"OK. Underdogs Sports Bar. On Portage."

"OK. I'll be there soon. See you soon, Jeff."

"Bye"

"Bye"

12:45 AM

I was relaxing in a booth when I saw Cheryl come in the room. She looked good. It's as if she was glowing, but it was more than her smile. I should ask her about that. I waved at her, and when she saw me, she came over and joined me.

"Hi," I said.

"Hi," she replied.

And with those two words, our conversation began. It was mostly me talking. I talked about Yash Nagi and his guys and what they did. I talked about hacking into their computers and recording stuff. I talked about Victor, a lot about Victor. I talked about how I almost went insane waving a gun around and ended up throwing it in the river and getting arrested. And I shared what happened to me in jail, how I finally broke down and came back to God, or maybe for the first time.

She took it all in, listening to every word, as if she cared, not just about what happened to me, but about me. I got the impression that she was hoping my story would be her story, as if she wanted to be a part of my life.

I said, "You know that email you sent me that said you can't see me because I'm not a Christian?"

She nodded her head, while holding her hands over her heart.

"Well, I think I am now."

She smiled. "Good. I was hoping that would happen."

I reached for her hands and she gave them to me. "Cheryl," I began, "Let's make this official. Will you be my girlfriend?"

She smiled so hard she burst into laughter. "Yes, Jeff! I would love to be your girlfriend."

I lifted up her hands to my mouth and was about to kiss them when we were interrupted by a large object dropped onto our table in front of us. It was put there by a large police officer. He said, "I had a hunch you'd still be here. You left this in my car." And with that, Detective Wakefield turned and left as abruptly as he had arrived.

I called out "Thank you!" after him.

"What's this?" Cheryl asked.

"Oh right. This is Victor's backpack. He said he was giving it to me, and something about my mother, but I don't know what that has to do with it. He was probably delirious."

"What's in it?"

"I don't know. I assumed it was an overnight bag, with a change of clothes and things."

"If it's yours now, you can look."

"I guess so."

"So look."

"What, you're curious?"

"Yes!"

I said, "Oh, fine!" I put the backpack beside me on the bench, and started bringing things out. I pulled out some clothes and said, "These are clothes." Then I pulled out a small bag and said, "These are toiletries." Then I pulled out a thick envelope.

"Open it!" she said.

I opened it and we both stared. It was a wad of hundred dollar bills.

"This is what Victor meant!" Cheryl said. "He wanted to pay back your mom for the money she lost."

"I guess so." I quickly counted them. There were thirty-two hundred dollar bills. "That's only three thousand two hundred dollars, but it's better than nothing."

"Turns out Victor was a nice guy in the end."

"Yeah," I said, and I still didn't know how to feel about it.

"What else is in there?" she asked.

I reached into the bag and pulled out something else. It was a smart phone. The model was no longer new, but it appeared to be in good condition. And it even had some battery left. And it was unlocked. "Huh! It's a phone."

"Now you have a phone again."

"Yeah, I guess so."

"This is like Christmas! Is there anything else?"

Before I reached into the backpack again, my new phone made a noise. When I checked it, it looked like an email message had just arrived.

"What is it?" Cheryl asked.

"I think this phone just received an email."

"Read it."

"Why? It's obviously not for me."

"You should at least check."

So I checked, and I found an email from God. I read it out loud.

From: god@heaven
To: Jeff and Cheryl
Subject: My children
Jeff and Cheryl, my dear children, my friends, my servants, the ones I love. I love you two very much, very deeply. I am so proud of you. I have seen what you have done for me. I have seen

your actions. And I receive them. They are recorded in my book as good works done for me. Well done, faithful servants.

Cheryl, my beautiful daughter, thank you so much for making the right choice, for choosing me above all. The thing that you gave to me, that you laid at my feet, I'm now giving back to you. I love you Cheryl. I want you to be blessed more than you want it for yourself. Your papa is taking good care of you.

Jeff, my son, my servant, my friend, you have once again accomplished the task I set before you. You are accomplishing your assignment. You are doing well, son. I'm very proud of you. I especially like that you gave me your whole heart. Thank you for that. Your heart, Jeff Davis, is one the most valuable things I have ever created. It touches me deeply for you to give it to me. Thank you. It means a lot.

I love you both.

I looked around without saying anything, just to give my heart some time to breathe. It was feeling… I don't know… full or something.

"It feels good, doesn't it?" Cheryl asked.

"What?"

"To hear from God."

"Yeah. Yeah it does. There is more to the email. Let me finish. It also says, 'Jeff, I just gave you a new phone, because I always take care of all your needs. You also have other needs that are coming up that I'm also taking care of.'" Looking at Cheryl again, I asked, "What do you think that means?"

Then she leaned forward toward me with a twinkle in her eye. "I think I know. I think I know what else is in the backpack."

"What? How can you say that?"

"Same reason I knew how to call this place."

"Which is what?"

"I'll tell you, but first bring out what else is in there."

I reached into the backpack beside me and pulled out a very heavy black velvet bag tied shut with a string. It jingled. When I untied it and opened it up, we stared at a very large pile of coins. Some said, "Liberty" on them. Some had maple leaves. Some had a picture of what looked like a deer and said, "Krugerrand" on them. They were all pure gold.

My eyes went wide. "Wha...?"

"There's enough to pay off your mom completely there."

"Yeah, and a lot left over."

"Be careful what you do with it."

"Why do you say that?"

And then Cheryl told me her story. I had no idea that behind the scenes, God was doing things with her, too. I was fascinated by what I heard.

We talked late into the night, and finally she drove me home, because I didn't have a car. I didn't know exactly what God had planned next, but I was pretty sure it was going to be interesting.

CHAPTER 20

Monday 8:01 AM

I pulled open the large glass doors to Omniscient Technologies and hurried inside. I said a quick "Good morning" to Luanna, and she replied, "Hi Jeff!"

I enjoyed the freedom of not having to sign in, but I was still trying to do the responsible thing by being there on time.

Instead of turning right to go down that hallway, I went straight, so I could walk past my girlfriend's cubicle. I turned the corner, and smiled at her on my way by. "Hi Cheryl."

"Hi Jeff!" she smiled back.

Before I made it to my desk in the corner office, I was interrupted by the big boss himself, who said to me, "Jeffrey, we're having a meeting in the board room. Please join us."

"OK," I replied, and turned around. We both walked out there and went in. Around the table were the whole team, well, minus one of course. I sat down in one of the comfy board room chairs and Peter went and sat at the head of the table.

"It is a sad day here at Omniscient Technologies. In all my years, I've had to say goodbye to a number of people I've worked with, both above me and below me in the structure of the company. Some people have left for good reasons, and some left for very poor reasons. But I've never had to say goodbye to someone who was taken from us so violently. It is... a tragedy. The details of Victor's funeral will be forthcoming." Peter Steele paused briefly and took a deep breath. "However," he continued, "life and work must go on. And as CEO, it is my job to make sure work does go on. That brings us to the position of VP of Technology.

"A good manager should be someone who is looked up to and respected by every member of the team. With all due respect to the previous holder of this position, Victor may not have been all that. Now nobody formally complained to me about Victor, but I've lived in an office environment long enough that I can sense the general atmosphere. So the next VP of technology will be someone who is already respected by all."

When he said that, I looked around the table, and noticed that everyone was also looking around the table, glancing here and there, probably doing the same thing I was. Was it Garth? Probably not. Scott? Maybe. Doug? Maybe. Oh dear! I seriously hope he doesn't mean me!

"When we hired Nigel Merrywether...

I thought to myself 'Merrywether'? His name is 'Merrywether'?

"... he didn't have as much development experience as some of you, but he did have several years of being a team leader. I told him he was overqualified for the position, but he said he was willing to take on the position of developer, because he enjoys working with people. From what I've seen around the office, people also enjoy working with him. Therefore, I convinced him to take the position of VP of Technology, and he has agreed."

I looked at Nigel, wondering what kind of boss he would make. Wasn't he kind to me this whole time? Didn't he even bend over backwards to get me back into a developer role? Is that what a boss is supposed to do? If that's his idea of a boss, I'm all for it. If he continues to be nice to people and get us what we want, what more could you ask for in a boss, really? That's sure better than Victor. Then I caught myself and remembered that Victor had actually given his life for me, so maybe I shouldn't think so badly of him. Come to think of it, maybe I should even review his list of rules. I suppose reading over someone's rules is the least one could do when that person gives his life for you. Another thought came to me about someone giving his life for me, but Nigel cut me off.

"It has been a lot of fun working with you guys," he began, "and I think we're going to have a lot more fun making Omniscient together. You are some of the best developers I've ever worked with, better than I am, I'll admit. There are some features I would like to see added to the next version, and I know that if we work together, we can pull it off. But we can save that for another meeting." Turning to Peter, he said, "Mr. Steele, I don't think it will be hard leading this team, because these are some good guys, every one of them."

Garth interrupted, "Ronja is not a guy. She is, in fact, a woman."

Ronja gazed at Garth as if he had just said the most romantic thing she had ever heard. "Oh Garth," she gushed, as if accepting a marriage proposal.

We looked to Garth to see how he would respond, but he just rolled his eyes. "I was merely promoting accuracy."

"Very well," Peter began, "Nigel is your new boss. Go to him with your questions and concerns. Have a wonderful day, everyone. We are dismissed."

"CKGD just put out a news story about what happened," Scott yelled out. "I'll send it to everyone."

We filed out of the board room, and on my way to my desk, I noticed Cheryl was watching the news clip from CKGD. I knelt beside her to watch. She smiled and gave me one of her ear buds. Girlfriends do that.

The reporter Donald Roberts stood at the driveway to Yash Nagi's house and said, "Several arrests were made ever the weekend, in the wake of two deaths that the police are calling homicides. One of the men, Victor Akulov, worked at Omniscient Technologies, a company that makes communications software.

He may have been involved in an attempt to take down Yash Nagi, a ring leader of a group of men accused of computer fraud. Also involved was Jeff Davis, the same man involved in the taking down of the criminal known as Jade, who is currently behind bars for corporate espionage. I talked with Jeff Davis about what happened."

The video changed to a shot of me outside the Johnston Terminal, with Donald beside me holding a mic. He said, "Jeff, what was it like working with Victor Akulov, who gave his life to take down a criminal and make the world a safer place for all of us?"

If I normally looked shy in real life, I was three times as shy on camera. I spoke quietly and said, "He was my boss... I worked for him... and then he... gave his life." Donald kept holding the microphone to me, and the camera stayed on me, so I had to think of something else to say. I said these words, "I guess I would be honored if I could give my life for something good too."

The camera moved back to Donald. "There you have it. Victor Akulov is an inspiration to us all."

I gave Cheryl back the ear bud. "That was hard," I said.

"I'm very proud of you for doing the interview."

"Thanks."

"So I guess the gold is really yours, huh?"

"Yeah, I can't give it back now."

My phone chirp-bonged and I saw that I got a message. "It's from my boss," I said.

"Who?"

"God."

She laughed. "Anything interesting? I mean, it's always interesting, but you know."

I read the message to her.

From: god@heaven
To: jeffdavis@omniscient.software

Subject: Assignment

Jeff, my son, my friend, my loved one. I'm so proud of you. You are doing so good. You have served me well. You have given yourself to me, your heart, your whole life. You are mine, and I am yours.

Before I give you your next assignment, there is something you must do. Take my email address, god@heaven, and go give it to Garth Fonte, Scott Stark, and Doug Grimm. I don't want just one server, I want a whole network.

CHERYL'S STORY

Do you want to read Cheryl's story?
Get this FREE short story and find out what happened with her.

timkoop.com/cheryl

THE AUTHOR NEEDS HELP

Hi there.

I noticed you read through this whole book.

I hope you enjoyed it. If you did, or if you just want to help a guy in need, it would be awesome if you could do this:

Could you please go to where you got this book from, or some other popular place, and leave a review? Reviews go a long way to to help sell books, and a minute of your time would do a lot.

Thank you very much!

ABOUT THE AUTHOR

Tim Koop lives and writes in Canada, eh?

He is married and they have four children. His background is in software development, and he enjoys it.

As of the time of this writing, he has never been to the east coast of Canada, nor has he seen any tuna factories there. For the record, he doesn't believe that tuna is actually seaweed, at least he wouldn't admit to that publicly, but you know, it's good stuff for a story.

One of the greatest gifts God has given man is the roasted peanut. I know, I know, there are a lot of other really nice things out there, but peanut butter is one of the good ones.

God bless the humble peanut.

I once heard that the only two flavors scientists couldn't synthetically reproduce are coffee and peanuts. This probably isn't true, but if it was, that means freshly roasted and ground peanut butter should be held in as much respect as freshly ground and brewed coffee.

I'm looking forward to the day when I can walk into a high-end specialty peanut butter shop and order a cup to my liking, with my choice of Valencia or Virginia nut, amount and type of sweetener, and sea salt or Himalayan pink salt to my liking.

Sigh. One day.

PROLOGUE FROM GOD'S NETWORK (BOOK 3)

To avoid suspicion, the two assassins held hands, pretending to be out on a date. But they weren't dating. She worked for him. And he wasn't an assassin for hire, either. He just killed people. And after what this target had done, he deserved to die.

Car bomb instructions are surprisingly hard to find on the surface web, but when you dig a little deeper into the dark web, everything is available to you. All you need is a wireless radio controller, a blasting cap, a battery to power it, and some explosive material. These materials were purchased locally, and for a reasonable price, even though the killer didn't need to be frugal. He already was a millionaire several times over.

Most of his wealth came from illegal activity, and a lot of that had dried up because of one man. That's why that one man had to die. Nothing personal. He was just bad for business. Most rich people would hire out a job like this, but this man wasn't normal.

Stopping next to a silver Mercedes-Benz C300 Coupe, the murdering millionaire dropped to a knee as if to tie his shoe which was already tied. When he did, his backpack fell off his back and onto the ground. He quickly pushed it underneath the car, directly under the driver's seat.

"I can see it," the woman whispered loudly while glancing around.

"What?"

"I can see it. He'll notice it."

The man scowled and pushed it farther in. "How's that?"

She glanced down. "Fine."

The man started unzipping the backpack to get at the switch that armed it when the woman said something again.

"You're mumbling," he said. "Talk louder."

"I said someone's coming!"

The man quickly armed the car bomb and got up. They held hands and started walking away when the person who was coming drew near. She had a dog.

The man, displaying absolutely no remorse for what he had just set in motion, beamed at the animal. "I love dogs!" he gushed and walked over. "What kind of dog is this?"

The lady smiled. "It's a Shiba Inu."

"Ha! He looks just like the Internet."

"That's why I got him."

The killer scratched the dog behind the ears. "Are you a good boy, good boy? Yes you are." Then he stood up. "Beautiful dog you have there."

"Thanks," she responded, and kept on walking.

They continued retreating when the assistant remarked, "You love dogs but kill people?"

He scowled again. "It's a weakness of mine."

She smirked. "Killing?"

"Dogs! Loving dogs!"

"Love isn't a weakness."

This made him stop in his tracks. Then he stared at her until she became flustered. "What?" she demanded.

He pointed in her face. "You have a lot to learn." He gestured around him. "Everyone has a lot to learn. Love is not just a weakness. It is the greatest weakness of all. When you love something or someone, it is a point of vulnerability. It's like a ring in the nose of a bull. He would otherwise be a strong animal, but with a little ring, a little love, he becomes weak. He can no longer do what he wants to do. He moves from being the master to the slave. All because of love. I'll show you what to do with love. I'll show everyone."

Even though his assistant had a seed of love in her, she had seen enough pain in her life related to love to believe that this just might be true. "Well, you won't show this guy."

"Why not?"

"Because he'll soon be dead."

He stared at the Mercedes for a long time. "You have the remote detonator?"

"Yes. Why?"
"Change of plan."

CHAPTER 1

Tuesday, 8:18 PM

Scott Stark jumped out from behind a bush, aimed his pistol at Garth, and fired five times. Two bullets missed, but three hit their mark, wounding his fellow programmer severely. "Ha! Gotcha!"

"Dastardly move, Stark!" spat Garth, as he fled as fast as he could. Scott chased him at a sprint over level terrain, up steep hills, and down into holes and caves in the earth.

But as Scott chased Garth from one direction, Doug hunted him from the other. As soon as Garth was in range, Doug lobbed a grenade at him. It missed, but took out Scott completely, killing him instantly.

"Doug, you're supposed to be on my side!" Scott moaned.

"Sorry, Scott. I missed."

"Where are you guys, even?" I mumbled out loud.

"Near the left!" replied Garth and Doug.

"Not me," said Scott. "I reappeared near the middle, I think. And I see you, and I'm coming to get you."

I spied Scott coming at me from the left, so I pressed my right arrow key as hard as I could. Unfortunately for me, Scott could run faster than I could, just because he was a better player than I was, and soon he had taken me out with a few grenades. My character died, and soon reappeared on another part of the map. I sighed. I hated dying. I was getting tired of dying so often. If I ever die again, it will be too soon.

A grenade exploded in front of me, taking half my life. Did I mention I was getting tired of explosions, too? Real life isn't nearly so interesting. There weren't any explosions when you're computer programming all day long.

"Jeff Davis," Garth said to me. "Are you guarding our flag, or are you going for their flag?"

"Um...," I replied. "I guess I'll try guarding." I ran my character out to where our flag was supposed to be.

"Then do that. They've captured it several times already."

"And we have it now, color too!" Scott beamed. "Yeah! And we just delivered it!" Our screens suddenly changed from the game to the scoreboard. It was pretty close. Garth was such a good gamer that he made up for my complete lack of talent, but we were still losing.

Garth took another swig of Dr. Pepper, then another bite of pizza. He didn't seem very happy. "What's it like to be losing, Garth?" Scott asked.

"Quit your bragging, Stark. We all know why we're losing."

Doug came to my rescue. "Jeff isn't doing that bad."

Garth guffawed. "This was his idea. He could at least have practiced first."

"That wouldn't have been fair," I replied.

"It would have made it more fair," he replied.

"Thanks for thinking of us, though," Scott beamed. "But why did you call this games night, anyway? Just to hang out?"

Yes, why did I? Instead of answering, my heart grew weak and I had to control my breathing. "Well..." I tried to say the words that I had practiced for weeks, but they wouldn't come out. It just took too much courage. "I..." I tried again, then gave up. "Just to hang out," I answered, then breathed a sigh of relief. "Maybe I'll get some more coffee." I stood.

"It's too late for coffee," Scott said. "You won't sleep."

"OK, some Pepsi then." I went to fill my cup with liquid sugar.

"As you enjoy your non-Dr. Pepper beverage, can we be done this exercise in frivolity?" Garth asked. "I have things that need doing."

I shrugged. "Sure."

"Thanks for the games night, Jeff," said Scott.

"Yes. Good games, everyone," followed Doug.

"Yeah," I said, as I started packing up pizza boxes, and empty pop cans, and crushing them into a garbage can. I had failed. I had organized this event for one purpose, and one purpose only, and I had failed at it. I didn't know what I was going to do. Maybe my girlfriend Cheryl has an idea. She always has good ideas for me.

We had been playing computer games in our office at Omniscient Technologies, where we worked as software developers. Omniscient occupied most of the third floor of a downtown building. We locked the main door and headed toward the elevator.

"I've got a date coming over this evening," said Scott. It seems he was always dating someone new. Not me. I had a girlfriend Cheryl, and she was a keeper.

Soon we were on the ground, then walking to the parking lot to get in our cars. Garth went out to the parking garage and the rest of us three continued on to the outdoor parking.

I just said "Good night" to Scott and Garth for the last time and made my way towards my car. Then it exploded.

9:01 PM

I was thrown to the ground and instinctively curled up in the fetal position with my head in my hands. I didn't know what was happening, but my reflexes told me to cower and hide.

When I recovered enough that I could look around, my car was smoking, and in ruins. There was a hole where the driver's seat was, and the vehicles on either side were damaged, too. I expected the anti-theft alarm to be sounding, but it wasn't. The blast must have taken out the battery.

Soon Scott was helping me up, and the other guys were there too, gawking. "Was that your car?"

"Yeah," I nodded, still trying to catch my breath.

"Jeff, someone just tried to kill you!"

"Yeah," I repeated, letting the thought sink in. It was still scary, even though it wasn't the first time. A few months ago I got entangled with some bad guys, but I was hoping we were done with that. I groaned. Not again.

Suddenly I glanced around in panic.

"What?" asked Doug.

"I just thought he might still be out there"

"Who?"

"The guy who did this."

I looked around frantically, but couldn't see anyone. Well, that wasn't true. I saw lots of people. People were starting to stare. There was even one man still on the ground. He must have been blown over by the blast, too. He hobbled out to us. "Dude, that wasn't your car, was it?"

"Yeah," I nodded.

He ran his hand through his blond hair. "Someone tried to kill you! Who would do that?"

I didn't answer.

He continued. "And what did you do to tick someone off that bad?"

"Nothing!" I replied, then added, "Well..." I started walking. I just needed to stretch my legs.

"Someone should call the police," said Doug, then he added, "I'll do it." He pulled out his phone, and started dialing.

Scott asked me, "How's your head?"

"Fine," I replied, as I turned around, and walked back. People were starting to gather.

A lady called out, "Was anybody hurt? Was somebody in there?"

"Nobody was hurt!" Scott announced.

"Oh thank God!" she said. "What happened?!"

"Probably a car bomb."

"In who's car?"

I turned and walked away again. I didn't want to be involved in this.

The man with the blond hair answered, "It was his car!" and pointed at me.

I said, "Scott, would you like to get your car so I can sit in it and not have to be part of this crowd?"

"You bet," he said, and ran off for his Mustang.

"The police are on their way," said Doug.

Soon Scott's car was near, and the three of us got in. As soon as I had buckled my belt, the blond man knocked on my window. I looked up at him. "Open the window!" he yelled.

I cranked it down a little.

He said, "In case you need a witness, I was a witness. I saw your car explode."

"Thanks," I said, then started rolling up the window again.

"My name's Larry."

"Hi."

"What's your name?"

I sighed. "Jeff."

"Jeff what?"

"Jeff Davis."

"I'll tell the police it was your car that exploded."

"OK"

I rolled up the window. I was already feeling bad for losing the games night, then failing to accomplish what I was trying to do with the whole party. And now my car exploded. I didn't feel like doing anything else. I said, "Here's an idea. Let's go home. Scott, will you take me home, please?"

"The police are on their way," Doug responded from the back seat.

"I'll come in tomorrow morning."

"I would stay," said Doug.

But Scott said, "Why not go home? What are they going to do? Arrest you?"

"Yeah. Ha, ha," I spoke, but I didn't feel very happy about it, because a few months ago I did get arrested. That wasn't very fun at all, and I didn't feel like talking to the police again.

"OK, done. We're going home," said Scott. He dropped Doug off near his car, and then we drove away. On the way out, a police car passed us coming in. Scott waved to them, like the goofball he is, but I hoped to myself we wouldn't get in trouble. I hated getting in trouble.

At home, I got out, and Scott's cherry red Mustang roared away.

I lived on the second floor of a three-story apartment. I walked up the steps in front of the building, then beeped myself in. As I got out the key to my door, the first door on the left, I heard my name.

"Jeff! Hey! Jeff!"

I looked up and groaned inwardly. It was the blond guy from the parking lot. He came and stuck out his hand. "It's me. Larry."

I shook his hand. "Hi, Larry."

"I had no idea you lived here! Imagine this. Wow."

"Yeah. You live here, too, huh?"

"Yup. Just moved in. I guess we're neighbors."

"I guess so."

"Hey, you're not hurt from the explosion, are you?"

"No, I'm fine."

"That's good to hear. I'm good, too. Hey, what do you do for work?"

"I'm a computer programmer."

"Really? I'm a computer security specialist. I'm a consultant for hire, so if you ever need a security consultant, let me know." He handed me a card that said, "Larry Trilbert, Systems Security Consultant."

I said, "Thanks."

"And you'll suggest me if it comes up?"

"Yeah, of course," I lied.

"Maybe your company needs a security specialist right now."

I thought about it. We could sure use a security specialist. We were dealing with lots of potentially sensitive information, and we did almost get hacked a while ago. I sure wasn't that great with security. Maybe Garth was, but that's it. Maybe I should suggest it to Nigel. But then again, that would mean working with this guy, not that I had anything against him, I suppose. I just don't like people in general.

"No, I don't think we do," I replied.

"OK, well, keep me in mind. Thanks, Jeff!!" He smacked me on the shoulder as if I were his good buddy. He was probably trying to be friendly, but I found it awkward. "Have a great night! I'll see you later."

He turned around and unlocked his way into number 203 down the hall. I sighed and opened up 201. It seems we were neighbors.

Before I got my shoes off, my phone rang.

"Hi, this is Jeff."

"Jeff, this is Mom." She sounded worried. "How are you?"

"Fine."

"I just heard that there was an explosion at The Forks. A car exploded, and I thought it was a kind of car you dove. It wasn't yours, was it? I wouldn't be able to sleep knowing it was your car. Jeff, tell me that wasn't your car."

I hesitated, but not very long. "Of course not, Mom. I'm fine."

"Oh, good. I was so worried. I just had to call and ask."

"That's OK. But I'm fine, Mom. You don't need to call."

"Of course not. I guess I worried for nothing. OK. Good." I heard her take a deep breath and let it out. "In that case, have a good night."

"Thanks. You, too."

"Bye."

"Bye."

For some reason, I had a bad feeling in my stomach. I suppose that happens when your car blows up, but it got really bad there when I was protecting my mom from worrying about me. Or was it Larry? I didn't understand it. Maybe if I ate something it would go away.

I wandered through the kitchen, looking for something to snack on, when I remembered that I was still full from pizza, so I didn't eat anything. But still, something didn't feel good inside of me. Maybe the feeling was left over from when I almost died. That must be it.

I got ready for bed, and then did what I did every night before going to sleep. I took out my wireless keyboard from beside my bed, and connected it to my phone. Then with the phone and keyboard in front of me, on my blanket, I started typing.

"Hello, God. It's me again, Jeff."

A while ago at work, a lady I didn't know handed me a piece of paper and she said it was God's email address. Then she said I could send God an email and he would respond. I immediately dismissed her as being crazy, because such a thought is, indeed, very crazy. But then I tried it, and I got a response. For a few days, this God and I talked. It rocked my life. A while later, I finally gave in, and surrendered to this God. His unconditional love for me did me in. Now I am his.

And in the meantime, I have learned the skill of communicating with him without an email address. After typing "Hello," I closed my eyes and pictured him next to me. When some thoughts popped into my head, I wrote them down.

"Hi, Jeff. It's always good to meet with you."

Then I wrote down words of my own. I didn't know how to be very spiritual, so I just made conversation.

"How are you?"

More words came to me, so I typed them in.

"Large and in charge. How are you, my friend, Jeff Davis?"

"I'm fine."

"Are you?"

"Maybe not. My car got bombed. I almost died. I might want to see you face to face one day, but maybe not quite yet."

"You'll see me soon enough, but you're not done down here yet."

"What would you like me to do?"

"I want you to open your heart to me. Let me love you, my son. Let me pour my love into your life. I love you, Jeffery. I love you my son, my friend."

I paused with my eyes closed. I sat there, swimming in the feelings of it all. I have been accused of not having feelings, but it's not true. There is something about spending time with this God of love that has a way of setting free the emotions of the heart.

And speaking of emotions of the heart, just then my phone rang. It was my girlfriend, Cheryl, the same person who gave me God's email address in the first place.

"Hey, Sweety!" I answered.

"Jeff, I just heard that a car exploded in the parking lot."

I sighed. I was feeling so good, now we're back to this. "You heard about that, huh?"

"Was it your car?"

"Yup. My car. It went boom."

"Jeff, don't joke about this. You could have been seriously injured."

"Or worse."

"You mean death? No, I don't think that's going to happen."

"It could. If I would have been in it…"

"Please don't even talk about that. But you could have been hurt."

"OK, I could have been hurt, or killed."

"I don't want you to get hurt. Have you talked to the police, yet?"

"I will tomorrow."

"Hey, how are you going to get to work?"

"You want to give me a ride?"

"Sure. We can talk more then. Good night, Jeff."

"Good night, Cheryl. I love you."

"I love you too. Bye."

"Bye."

I hung up the phone. I liked her.

I journaled a bit more, then went to sleep for real. As I was drifting off to sleep, I remembered the last time I was at a police station. I had been arrested for brandishing a weapon. Tomorrow, I'll have to go back there, and talk with the same people who arrested me, to report my car. I wasn't sure I wanted to do that.

Wednesday, 7:55 AM

My favorite part of arriving at work with Cheryl was taking the elevator to the third floor with just her, because I could give her a nice good morning kiss before the doors opened. That's a good way to start the day.

Through the front glass doors, and then through the lobby, I walked her to her cubicle, then continued to my room, which was a room in the corner of the building. The four of us developers sat there. Garth Fonte was the senior developer, and I admit he was pretty good. He was also a large man who enjoyed his Dr. Pepper. I suppose he also had a sense of humor, because he kept a joke-of-the-day posted on his little whiteboard. This morning it said, "Why do programmers prefer dark mode? Because light attracts bugs." I snickered. Yeah.

"Hello, Jeff Davis," Garth said.

"Hi."

"Hey, Jeff!" greeted Scott Stark, my best friend, if you don't count Cheryl. He was kind of my opposite. He seemed to actually enjoy people, and get along with everyone he met.

"Hi, Scott," I replied.

"Good morning, Jeff." That was Doug Grimm. He must have been at least twenty years older than me. I was twenty-eight, so he was pushing fifty. He was nice enough, I guess. He once gave me a gun to protect myself. I'm not sure that was a good idea, because I ended up shooting at my own dad, and intimidating other people with it. That was a dark period of time in my life, but I'm doing a lot better now. It's amazing how much better your life goes when you finally surrender your life to God. Anyway, I threw that gun in the Red River that day when the police were chasing me.

"Hi Doug." I sat down, and went right to my email.

Then, in the midst of our clatter of typing, Garth spat out, "Scott, for the sake of everything holy, you aren't going to type in those blues all day, are you?"

Scott grinned like he was guilty, and not ashamed of it. "I was thinking of it."

I looked around, wondering what "blues" he was referring to. Not his clothes. He had a different keyboard, but the keys were clearly black, not blue.

"There should be a law against it," Garth continued. "Or at least an office policy."

"I kinda like it. It feels like gaming at work. It lightens the mood."

"It does no such thing. You're annoying everyone around you."

I looked at Doug, and shrugged.

Doug said, "I believe Garth is referring to Scott's mechanical keyboard switches."

I looked at his keyboard again, but his keys were still black.

"His switches," said Garth, "connect his key caps to his mechanical keyboard, and dictate the feel and sound. Scott here is using blue switches, which are the loudest available on the market."

"They're great for gaming," Scott said.

"But not for working in a group setting. Use something else." Garth pointed. "There. That's your usual keyboard. Use that one."

"Fine," said Scott swapping keyboards, "but I won't like it as much. I won't be as happy."

"You can buy yourself some browns, and keep the rest of us happy."

Doug leaned toward me, and commented, "Brown switches are known to be quieter."

We worked in relative quiet for a while, before Garth again broke the silence. "Scott!" he said, leaning in to look closer at his screen. "Did you really name this variable 'first_name'?"

"Oh, probably," Scott replied. "I don't remember every single variable I've ever declared, but if it refers to someone's first name, that sounds like something I'd do. Why? What's wrong with it?"

"Shall I list all the problems with it?"

"Sure. Go for it, Garth. Knock yourself out."

"First of all, the case is wrong. It's in snake case, but should be in camel case."

"Fine. Change it."

"And second, the name of the variable should match the name of the database column, which is 'name_first', not 'first_name.' Therefore, your variable should be 'nameFirst', not 'firstName'."

"That sounds awfully silly," Scott rolled his eyes. "'firstName' is obviously the best name for the variable, since that's what it describes."

Both Garth and Scott swivelled their chairs around so they could face each other. Garth frowned, and began, "Must I explain to you the ways of the programmer?"

"You're free to share your opinion, but I might not take it."

"Yes, it is my opinion, but it is also the correct way to do things. You first establish the category, then you describe the details of that category. For example, consider these attributes: 'address_line_1', 'address_city', 'address_province', 'address_country'. Notice the category first, then the detail?"

Scott rolled his eyes again. "Yeah?"

"It's the same with name: 'name_first', 'name_last', 'name_middle', 'name_salutation', 'name_suffix'. Your variable should be called 'nameFirst', not 'firstName'."

"'firstName' sounds better."

"Programming is not about sound. It is about a systematic assemblage of characters."

"It flows off the tongue better."

"Programming is not spoken with the tongue. It is typed with the fingers."

"It's better English."

"This is not English!"

Just then our boss, Nigel, appeared at the doorway. "Speaking of an assemblage of characters, our morning meeting is about to begin in the board room."

I was looking forward to this meeting, because if all went well, we might roll out a new version of our software, Omniscient, that we have been working on for a while.

395 49 535 65

544 496 936 98 49 886 503 503 98 65 242 503 503 98 798 544 703 98 112 98 636 242 224 63 242 65 895

65 395 242 98 63 242 112 636 544 535 98 65 395 112 65 98 224 395 242 63 798 503 98 496 535 242 735 98 395 544 735 98 65 544 98 224 112 503 503 98 65 395 242 98 636 598 544 63 65 636 98 156 112 63 98 49 636 98 156 242 224 112 703 636 242 98 384 544 241 98 65 544 503 241 98 395 242 63 98 49 535 98 112 535 98 242 510 112 49 503 895 98 98 490 242 360 360 98 384 544 65 98 384 544 241 886 636 98 242 510 112 49 503 98 360 63 544 510 98 395 242 63 98 49 535 98 65 395 242 98 360 49 63 636 65 98 598 503 112 224 242 936 98 636 544 98 636 395 242 98 636 65 49 503 503 98 395 112 636 98 49 65 895

49 98 395 112 727 242 535 886 65 98 735 63 49 65 65 242 535 98 224 395 242 63 798 503 886 636 98 636 65 544 63 798 98 798 242 65 936 98 156 703 65 98 49 98 65 395 49 535 496 98 384 544 241 98 735 49 503 503 98 636 242 535 241 98 395 242 63 98 65 395 49 636 98 242 510 112 49 503 98 735 49 65 395 98 65 395 112 65 98 598 395 544 535 242 98 535 703 510 156 242 63 98 49 535 98 63 242 636 598 544 535 636 242 98 65 544 98 395 242 63 98 544 156 242 798 49 535 384 98 112 98 241 49 360 360 49 224 703 503 65 98 224 544 510 510 112 535 241 98 360 63 544 510 98 395 49 510 936 98 735 395 49 224 395 98 49 636 98 598 63 544 156 112 156 503 798 98 65 544 98 156 63 242 112 496 98 703 598 98 735 49 65 395 98 490 242 360 360 895

65 395 49 636 98 735 49 503 503 98 156 242 98 395 112 63 241 98 360 544 63 98 395 242 63 98 65 544 98 241 544 936 98 156 242 224 112 703 636 242 98 384 544 241 98 598 63 544 510 49 636 242 241 98 65 395 112 65 98 65 395 242 798 98 735 544

703 503 241 98 384 242 65 98 510 112 63 63 49 242 241 936 98 112 535 241 98 636 395 242 98 241 544 242 636 535 886 65 98 735 112 535 65 98 65 544 98 156 242 98 112 503 544 535 242 895 98 98 636 544 98 49 65 98 735 49 503 503 98 156 242 98 503 49 496 242 98 112 535 98 112 156 63 112 395 112 510 940 636 112 224 63 49 360 49 224 49 535 384 940 395 49 636 940 636 544 535 98 510 544 510 242 535 65 895 98 98 112 65 98 503 242 112 636 65 98 65 395 112 65 886 636 98 735 395 112 65 98 49 886 510 98 224 703 63 63 242 535 65 503 798 98 598 503 112 535 535 49 535 384 895

395 242 63 242 886 636 98 112 535 544 65 395 242 63 98 395 49 535 65 964 98 98 49 535 98 65 395 242 98 535 242 78 65 98 156 544 544 496 936 98 65 395 242 63 242 98 49 636 98 112 98 224 395 112 535 224 242 98 65 395 112 65 98 490 242 360 360 98 510 49 384 395 65 98 241 49 242 936 98 112 535 241 98 224 395 242 63 798 503 98 735 49 503 503 98 49 535 65 242 63 224 242 241 242 98 360 544 63 98 395 49 636 98 503 49 360 242 98 703 636 49 535 384 98 65 395 242 98 598 63 544 510 49 636 242 98 65 395 112 65 98 395 242 98 735 544 703 503 241 98 156 242 98 395 242 63 98 395 703 636 156 112 535 241 895